FIVE CORNERS

BOOK 1 OF THE MARKED ONES

BY Cathi Shaw

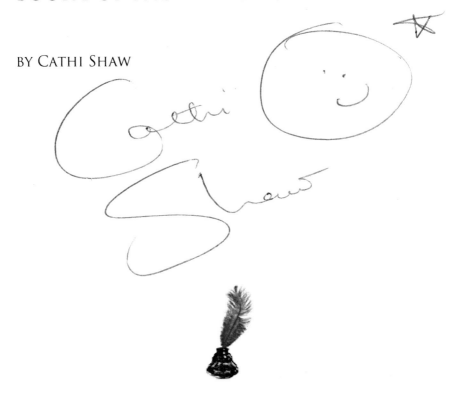

Ink Smith Publishing

www.ink-smith.com

ISBN: 978-1-939156-24-2

Ink Smith Publishing

P.O Box 1086

Glendora CA

Cover Art by Cover Design: Chris Arlidge of Cheeky Monkey Media

Map by Linda Bjarnason

Author Photo by Becca McNeil

http://www.beccamcneilphotography.com/

ACKNOWLEDGEMENTS

Very special thanks to my writing partner, first reader, and dear friend, Rochelle Dionne.

Thanks to all my reader/editors for their love of Five Corners and their exceptional feedback: Caitlin Shaw, Kassandra Planiden, Kate Fitzsimmons, Brina Coleman, Alannah Clark, Daniel Nixon, Mackenzie Bjarnason, Mason Bjarnason, and Matthew Shaw.

Special thanks to Linda Bjarnason and Caitlin Shaw for their artistic talent.

Thanks to Ashley Howie at Ink Smith Publishing for believing in my work and giving such excellent suggestions and feedback.

And thanks to my family for believing! I love you all!

DEDICATION

For my greatest cheerleader and muse, Caitlin.

I love you!

List of Names and Places

Characters

Minathrial (Min-ath-ree-al) called "Mina" (Meen-ah) – Sister to Thia and Kiara.

Elethia (E-leth-ee-ah) called "Thia" (Thee-ah) – Sister to Mina and Kiara

Kiara (Key-Ar-Ah)– Sister to Mina and Thia

Brijit (Bri-jeet)– Adopted mother of Mina, Thia and Kiara

Caedmon (C-ay-d-mon) – Brother to Teague

Teague (Tee-gue) – Brother to Caedmon

Weylon (Way-lon) – Adopted father of Caedmon and Teague

Arion (Air-ee-on) – Elder

Meldiron (Mel-dear-on)– Elder

Bellasiel (Bella-seel)– Elder and Healer

Saldur (Sale-dor) – Elder and Healer

Eöl Ar-Feiniel (Ay-owl Are-Fen-el) – Elder and Archivist

Celeste (Suh-leste) – Undergrounder

Delphine (Del-fee-nee) – Celeste's daughter

Manach (Men-ack) – Monks

Coimirceoirí (Coym-eer-see-oy-ri) – Guardians of the Elders

Draíodóir (Dray-Or-Door) – Druid/Magician

Places

Séreméla (Sar-A-Mell-A) – the Elders' home

Aranel Pallanén (Air-ran-ell Pall-an-een) – Legendary River in Séreméla

FIVE CORNERS

NORTHLANDS

PINE FREST MTS.

EAST SEA

GLACIER FIELD

AIRLEN LAKE

SILVERVALE

WESTERN REALM

REVJOVER

*BRINDLE

OAR HILLS MTS.

LSTER MTS.

★ REFUGE

SEREMELA

ARANI

FALLANUS

INN

LOWLANDS

BLACK PAW MTS.

OUTLANDS

EVENDEL

SOUTHLANDS

SEA OF ARCADIA

SAILSBURG

N

W   E

S

ISLAND OF NASSEET

FIVE CORNERS
THE MARKED ONES

CHAPTER ONE

Kiara stared at the small body laid out in the family's tiny kitchen. She didn't know the child but that didn't stop her heart from jerking in her chest as she looked at the perfect little girl lying in the wooden box. She was dressed in what were obviously her best clothes; her dark hair had been carefully combed and braided. She was only six years old.

Kiara felt her own mother watching her closely. She forced her gaze away from the small lifeless form. Brijit murmured softly to the parents and then moved to Kiara's side.

"Come away from here, Kiara," her mother said firmly.

But Kiara couldn't stop herself from looking back at the child, noting how someone had twined a pretty scarf around her neck, concealing the ugly slashes that she knew were hidden beneath the colorful material. The result of a blade taken to vulnerable flesh. This poor girl had had no chance against her assailant.

Brijit tugged on her arm insistently. "There is nothing more for us to do here," she whispered in a hushed undertone. "Let's go and give the family some peace."

Kiara shook her head, noticing for the first time the buzz of voices around her. The small room was filled with interested townsfolk, people who had never given a care for this family, suddenly drawn to the run down shack out of morbid curiosity. Kiara felt a sudden wave of shame wash over her. She suddenly wondered what she was doing here?

True, Brijit had come to wash and dress the child and had asked for Kiara's help in carrying the dead body, remarkably heavy for one so small. Death did not bother Kiara and she was strong enough to hoist weights around. Her little sister, Thia, while a healer like her mother, had not been large enough to help with this task.

But the heavy work had been completed hours ago. And still Kiara had stayed, transfixed by this tiny person who was no more.

Don't try to deny it, she told herself vehemently, *you know why you're here.*

She had seen the Mark on the child's shoulder. She resisted the urge to rub her own shoulder where an identical Mark was hidden beneath her tunic. It was something she'd believed she only shared with her sisters. But this child proved different.

And there was no question that this child had been assassinated.

Suddenly it was hard to breath and the walls were closing in around her. She had to get away from this place. Kiara pushed through the door of the shack while her mother was stopped by one of the family members.

She stood in the muddy yard, drawing in deep breaths of the frosty fall air, trying to calm down.

"Tell no one of what you have seen, Kiara."

She whipped around and saw Brijit behind her, calmly tying her bonnet before they started the journey home.

"Why?" Kiara asked, her voice rough with emotion.

Brijit did not answer for moment, instead she pushed past Kiara to where the horses were waiting and mounted her small mare.

Kiara watched her mother through narrowed eyes. She had begun to suspect that Brijit was hiding things from her. And she didn't like it.

When it was clear that Brijit intended to leave this place with or without her, Kiara mounted in silence and turned her horse toward home.

"I saw it, Brijit," she said quietly, refusing to let the matter rest.

Brijit looked up suddenly, worry lines on her forehead.

"You can tell me to be silent but until you share what you know, I'm not likely to be. What in Five Corners is happening? This isn't the first death like this ...?" She heard the question lingering in her voice, even though she knew the truth. She was sure, based on her mother's reaction when they'd arrived, that this was not the first innocent death Brijit had stumbled upon.

Brijit sighed. Then looked ahead on the path. "No. It's not," she admitted, confirming Kiara's suspicions. "Another child was found in the Lowlands. He was killed in the same way."

"Did he have the ..." Kiara hesitated. They never spoke of the Mark.

"Yes," Brijit said quickly, before Kiara could voice it. "And two more near the mountains to the North."

A rock of fear tightened in Kiara's stomach. She never would have guessed her mother would keep so many deaths a secret.

"Who is doing this?" Kiara asked quietly, trying to calm her mind. "And why?"

"Stop with the interrogation, Kiara!" Brijit's voice was high pitched and shrill and so unlike her mother that Kiara could only stare in shock.

Brijit closed her eyes for a moment. Then she opened them and forced a brittle smile to her lips. "I don't know who would do such a thing, Kiara. Sometimes there are people who are ... not right in their head. And they kill things they shouldn't."

Like Johnny Oldsfeld, Kiara thought. He killed small animals for the sport of it. He liked to watch them suffer and eventually die. But this was different. Johnny didn't chose only those animals that had white spots.

And Brijit was avoiding Kiara's eyes a little too much. She was focused on the road refusing to look at her. She looked almost guilty. But why would that be? Her mother was a healer not a killer. Surely Brijit had nothing to feel guilty for.

"Is there nothing we can do?" Kiara asked, anger tingeing her words.

Brijit shook her head. "Be on the lookout for strangers," she offered softly.

Kiara stared at the back of her mother's head as Brijit rode ahead of her. Suddenly Brijit turned back. "Oh, and Kiara ..."

"Yes?"

"Say nothing of this to your sisters."

Kiara's eyes narrowed as she considered her mother's words. Brijit knew more than she was letting Kiara believe. And Kiara was determined to uncover what her mother was hiding.

****

They were only a few miles from the Inn when a frantic looking farmer intercepted Kiara and Brijit.

"Mistress Carnesîr!" He called, his voice raw with emotion. "Thank the stars, I've found you."

4

Brijit smiled gently at the man, all traces of her earlier angst erased. "Hamish, calm yourself. What is it?"

"It's Shila. She's in a bad way. The baby started coming but then it just stopped and now Shila is so sick."

Brijit straightened. She was the only midwife for miles around. But Kiara knew that this was not Shila's first born. She had four children already, the last she'd birthed in the barn in the middle of milking. Brijit and Kiara exchanged a look. If Shila was having trouble birthing this child, then it didn't bode well.

"When did she go into labor, Hamish?"

The farmer looked at her blankly.

"When did the pains start?" Brijit asked a bit more firmly.

The rough farmer sniffed and rubbed his nose on his sleeve. "The day before yesterday. I don't know what to do. Please say you'll come."

Brijit nodded. "Of course, I will." She turned back to Kiara. "You go straight back to the Inn, Kiara. Let your sisters know that I've been called away." She paused and looked around the woods nervously. "And don't linger here today. I don't like the feel of it."

Annoyance pricked at Kiara. Brijit had been nothing but jumpy since they left the dead child. She's noticed how her mother kept pausing and peering left then right deep into the woods. Not that she would share her concerns with Kiara. Now she was telling her to be careful simply because of how she felt. Kiara shrugged and turned back to her horse.

Brijit suddenly gripped her upper arm. Kiara looked back at her mother in surprise. "Kiara promise me, you'll go straight back to the Inn."

Stunned by the urgency in her mother's voice, Kiara's mouth went dry. Unable to talk, she just nodded.

Brijit watched her for a moment longer, clearly fighting some inner emotion.

Exacerbated Kiara mounted and turned her horse toward the Inn. "I'm going, I'm going." She caught the farmer's anxious eye and felt a stab of guilt. "I hope Shila is well," she added before urging her mare to a jog in the direction of home.

The last few miles to the Inn passed uneventfully but Kiara couldn't help wondering what had set her mother on edge. She was clearly upset by the dead child but there had to be something more to it. Brijit's insistence that Kiara go straight home and watch for strangers was odd.

But as the gables of the Inn came into view, Kiara was no closer to figuring out what was on her mother's mind. She shrugged and gave up her analysis. Her sisters understood their mother better than she did. She decided to go over the matter with them and see what they could make of it.

Satisfied that her sisters would be able to find an answer to the puzzle, Kiara looked up with a small smile on her lips. But it fast faded as she rode into the stable yard. Her eyes snagged on a sight that had her worries returning thrice fold.

In front of her were three large and tough looking horses, the like of which she'd never seen in the Lowlands. And standing beside their mounts were three wild looking men. New arrivals to the Inn and they were definitely strangers!

CHAPTER TWO

Even without Brijit's warning Kiara would have been wary of this group of strangers. They were a rough looking threesome with horses that were built for both speed and endurance. Warhorses, Kiara suspected.

As she approached she could see that one of the men was significantly older than the other two. He had what should have been a warm and friendly face except for sternness around his mouth.

The younger men were opposites. One was a monster of a man. Kiara estimated him to be close to seven feet in height, his muscular arms laced with tattoos that marked him as a member of the army.

Kiara's unease doubled when she saw the tattoos. While they were aware of soldiers in the Lowlands, they rarely saw them. And the soldiers of the Five Corners were not the kind of men one wanted to find oneself mixed up with. They were a brutal band of ruthless killers who the governing heads insisted were necessary to protect the country from raiders beyond the sea to the South and the far mountains to the Northeast. But rumors abounded that the army spent more time harassing citizens of the country than they did defending it. A soldier at the Inn was not a good sign.

Swallowing, Kiara turned her attention to the last of the party. He was small in stature and had an easy, friendly manner. It wasn't until Kiara was a few feet away that she saw his eyes. They were silver with a strange metallic glint to them. They were almost mesmerizing. She forced her gaze away from them and focused instead on the older man.

"Can I help you?" she asked, her tone purposely cool.

She tried not to flinch under the weight of those three sets of eyes on her as she brought her mare to a halt in front of them.

"Do you live here?" the older man asked carefully.

Kiara nodded.

"Then you can. We are looking for lodging." He smiled but Kiara couldn't shake the coldness that seemed to emanate from him.

She forced a disappointed facade to her face. "Oh, I'm sorry but I believe we are all booked up for now. Pinefell has a nice Inn and it's not far from here."

The soldier's dark eyes narrowed. "Your stable is remarkably empty for a full Inn."

Kiara widened her eyes in what she hoped was an innocent expression. "It is, isn't it?"

Before she could say anymore, the side door to the Inn opened and Mina came hurrying out. Before Kiara could give Mina any kind of signal or warning, her sister was saying, "Welcome! Welcome to the Inn! Are you seeking lodgings? We have the best venison stew in the Five Corners."

The older man turned his attention to Mina. "We are looking for lodging but were given to believe that you were fully booked." He gestured casually toward Kiara.

8

Mina laughed. "Hardly! We are never fully booked at this time of year." Then she saw her sister. "Kiara! You're back. Did Mama go with Hamish?"

Kiara glared at her sister. Not only had she admitted that the Inn was empty, she'd effectively told them that their mother was away. Precisely the knowledge that strangers such as these should not have. Kiara watched in dismay as Mina led the men and their mounts toward the stable and shook her head. So much for staying away from strangers!

****

Kiara put her mare away in the stables and then went to find Thia. It wasn't difficult as her little sister was in the kitchen as she always was. Kiara stepped into the room and was immediately assaulted by the enticing aroma of freshly baked bread. Her stomach rumbled loudly, reminding her that she'd had nothing to eat since early morning.

Thia looked up in surprise before a wide grin lit up her face. "Kiara! You're home."

Kiara nodded and reached for one of the loaves of bread that were cooling on the counter. Thia smacked her hand away, "Don't you dare, you've not even washed up."

"C'mon, Thia, I'm starving."

Thia shook her head before slicing a thick piece of bread and putting it on a plate. As she handed it to Kiara, she looked up her brow furrowed in concern.

"Did Mama come home with you?"

Kiara shook her head as she took a huge bite of the still warm bread. She closed her eyes in delight as the warm hominess melted in her mouth. "Hamish met us on the road."

Thia sighed as she cut another slice of bread of put it on Kiara's plate. "Shila shouldn't be having trouble with birthing. This is her fifth child." Worry was thick in Thia's voice.

Kiara nodded in agreement. Then she remembered what her mother had said about avoiding strangers. And yet Mina was taking the newcomers on a tour of the Inn at this very moment. Kiara closed her eyes in frustration.

"What's wrong?" Thia asked softly. Kiara opened her eyes to see her little sister watching her with concern.

"I'm not sure," Kiara admitted trying to think of how she could share her worries with Thia without telling her sister too much about her trip with Brijit. She decided to focus on the travelers. Perhaps she could convince Thia that it was a bad idea to let them stay at the Inn. Then maybe they could talk to Mina together. "A group of three strangers arrived asking for lodging for the night just as I got home."

Thia shrugged as she added the chopped potatoes to the stew pot. "Well, we are the Village Inn, Kiara, so that's hardly surprising," she teased, wiping her hands on her apron. "There are four vacant rooms in the East wing."

Kiara waved her hand impatiently. "Yes, I know that, Thia, but there's something odd about these strangers."

Thia paused and frowned, her brow furrowed. "Odd in what way?" she asked seriously as she went back to dicing the vegetables.

"Their appearance for one," Kiara sighed in frustration, struggling to explain what she meant. "They look ..." she paused searching for the right word. "Menacing."

Thia stopped chopping and looked sharply at Kiara. "What do you mean?"

Kiara told Thia what she had seen when she rode into the stable yard and her initial impressions of the strangers.

Thia shivered. "Are you certain one is a soldier?"

Kiara shrugged. She couldn't be absolutely certain that he was currently a soldier. But the tattoos indicated that he had been one at some stage. And he didn't look old enough to have retired. Kiara wet her lips. "There's more."

Thia looked at her.

"They're Outlanders."

Thia paled. Kiara knew what her sister was thinking. Outlanders and one of them a soldier. "Mina is thrilled, isn't she?"

Kiara frowned and nodded. Their sister was obsessed with travelers from other parts of the Five Corners. She would see the strangers as sources of information rather than potential sources of danger.

Thia sighed and untied her apron. "Where are they?" she asked grimly.

****

In contrast to the warm, cheery atmosphere in the kitchen, the entrance of the Inn was dim at all hours of the day and prone to draughts. The Great Room, just off the entrance where they found Mina and the travelers, wasn't much better although the roaring fire at the one end provided a bit more heat. Thia preferred to spend most of her time in the kitchen and typically avoided the Great Room, which served as the only pub in town.

But right now, in the center of the room, her pretty blond sister was smiling at an older man. He must be one of the strangers Kiara had mentioned. Thia studied him as she approached. He was of average height and looked to be in his mid-forties. His shoulder-length wavy brown hair framed a weathered face and his brown eyes, which should have been warm, were hard edged. Thia could feel the coldness oozing from him. Instantly she was sure that Kiara was right to be concerned.

11

"Ah, my other sister, Elethia," Mina said as she turned to Thia with a smile, her clear green eyes sparking. Just as they'd feared Mina was clearly thrilled by the arrival of the visitors. "Thia, this is Weylon Forborrow. He's travelling with his sons and looking for lodging."

Thia nodded briefly in the man's direction.

Weylon bobbed his head at Thia and took one of her hands in his large rough ones. "How wonderful to make your acquaintance, Elethia. Your inn is just the fortress we were hoping to find on this leg of our journey." His voice had a pleasant lilting, musical quality to it but Thia fought the urge to pull her hand from his cool grasp. There was no apparent reason she should feel so uneasy about this man but her instincts told her to be wary.

From his accent she knew they were definitely Outlanders. Travelers from the Outlands always had interesting tales to tell of creatures and places foreign to the Lowlands where the girls lived.

Mina was clearly thrilled. Her sister was always intrigued with stories from foreign places. No wonder her eyes were sparkling with excitement.

Thia could understand her sister's fascination with foreigners. Even she could be tempted into the Great Room when they had storytelling Outlanders as guests. She studied Weylon's face and wondered if he was the storytelling kind, for some reason she rather doubted it. Or, a little voice in her head murmured, if he was a storyteller she was sure to not like the tales he told.

He gave her hand a hard final squeeze as if he could read her thoughts. Thia met his eyes in shock but he smoothly released her hand and gestured to the tall man standing behind him. Thia resisted the urge to rub her hand and turned her attention to the other visitor.

One could not imagine two more different men. Unlike Weylon, this man was, as Kiara had suggested, huge. A brooding look was on his handsome face. He had dark eyes and he towered over everyone in the foyer of the Inn, including Kiara. He was thick across the chest and his arms were heavily muscled and laced with the tattoos that marked him as a soldier. He had long dark hair that was pulled back and secured at his neck with a leather tie. And he was studying Kiara with an intensity that worried Thia.

While Kiara, to her continued dismay, seemed to attract suitors without trying, this man's fixation on her sister was disturbing. Thia frowned. Kiara usually fought any man who tried to court her. She wondered idly what kind of chance Kiara would have against the man in front of them. He had the appearance of a great warrior. As Thia was pondering this, Weylon captured her attention again.

"Elethia, this is my son, Caedmon," Weylon was saying. Caedmon glanced her briefly giving her a curt nod before turning his focus back onto Kiara. Thia was trying to process the fact that this mountain of a man was supposedly the son of Weylon when a crash captured the attention of the room.

The front door had unexpectedly burst opened with a bang and a blast of cold air and another figure was now stumbling into the Great Room. He was weighed down with an assortment of bags, including a small mandolin. Thia saw Mina's eyes light on the instrument - she knew her sister would be even more delighted if one of the travelers was a musician.

"Ah, Teague!" Weylon was shaking his head with a rueful smile. "Ladies, may I present my other son! Teague, this is Minathrial, Kiara and Elethia."

Thia's polite smile immediately froze on her lips. She felt a pang deep in her stomach as the new arrival approached.

Something seemed eerily familiar about him. He turned to her with an easy smile on his face. And Thia barely suppressed a gasp. This was a face that she knew only too well. Her heart began to pound as she took in the soft brown curls and unique silver colored eyes. Eyes that, despite his smile, reflected the same stunned surprise she was feeling. Thia's stomach dropped and her legs froze, her instinct rejecting what her brain was telling her was true.

It couldn't be him. It was impossible. Mina cleared her throat and hurried forward to welcome Teague. She raised her eyebrows at Thia, clearly concerned by her rude lack of response to his greeting. But Thia was incapable of uttering a sound.

Teague stepped forward and offered her his gloved hand. "Pleased to meet you, Elethia." She felt his fingers tighten around her own in an unspoken warning. Thia felt as though she would fall into those unmistakable pewter colored eyes.

Thia swallowed attempting to dislodge the sudden lump in her throat as he gave her fingers one more tight squeeze. So he *did* recognize her. Her heart began to pound even more erratically as panic set in. She had to get away. Instinctively she looked from side to side, attempting to locate a plausible escape route. Her eyes settled instead on her sisters, Caedmon and Weylon all watching her expectantly, their faces reflecting the identical expression of mild confusion.

Teague released her hand and she looked up at him trying to read the expression on his face. But he turned to Mina before she had a chance. Her sister immediately started to explain to the men that their rooms overlooked the stables.

"We have four other rooms there that are currently unoccupied," she was saying. "We could offer you rooms overlooking the forest but they wouldn't be ready until later this afternoon, as they are not currently made up."

Weylon assured her that the rooms she had chosen would be suitable for them and thanked her for her hospitality.

Thia half listened to Mina's friendly chatter as she tried to get her emotions under control. Her heart was still racing as she racked her brains for an explanation to this puzzle. She felt slightly sick to her stomach.

"Are you okay, Thia?" Kiara touched her arm. Thia looked up and saw her sister's dark blue eyes filled with concern.

She glanced sideways and caught Teague watching her, the warning in his eyes perfectly clear. Thia forced a weak smile in Kiara's direction.

"Actually, since Mina is speaking of meals, I'm feeling a bit worried that the stew might need my attention," she said loud enough for the visitors to hear her. "Nice to meet you, Teague," she murmured as she slipped past him, ignoring the knowing expression on his face. She didn't think she'd fooled him with her weak excuse for escape.

Thia all but ran to the kitchen. Once there she closed her eyes and leaned against the door as she tried to come up with a rational reason for why Teague had suddenly appeared in the waking world.

There had to be an explanation for why the boy who had been haunting her dreams for the last ten years had suddenly appeared in person.

Pulling away from the door, she crossed the kitchen to the stew pot and gave it a stir. It was possible that the boy in her dreams resembled a real person. Thia nodded. Someone she'd caught a glimpse of transformed into a dream. And besides, except for those strange silver colored eyes, Teague wasn't so unique looking that he didn't resemble any number of young men who'd stayed at the Inn. She began chopping more carrots and added them to the pot before adjusting the flame. Perhaps it was not so surprising, she reasoned, feeling a bit better already.

She frowned suddenly. What was surprising was that Teague had clearly recognized her. Thia paused, a chill running down her spine. The boy who had been in her dreams for most of her life seemed to know it and Thia knew there was no explanation for that!

CHAPTER THREE

Kiara whirled in the late morning sun, feeling the muscles in her arms contract as her sword clashed against Jake's heavy blade. Excitement coursed through her veins as she continued sparring with the heavyset blacksmith. She grinned as she backed him across the yard. Jake's face was furrowed in concentration as he went into defense mode, trying to hold her off but not succeeding.

A rush of exhilaration shot through Kiara. She loved beating her opponents, particularly big tough ones like Jake. She laughed suddenly as she sensed Tom closing in behind her and in a lightning quick movement blocked Jake's next blow and disarmed him, his heavy sword clanging to the ground. Without hesitation, Kiara swung around and began to parry with Tom. Tom had an expression of intense absorption on his sun burnt face but he wasn't as skilled as Jake. Kiara continued to easily force him backward until she'd cornered him and quickly disarmed him.

"You'll have to do better than that in the guard, Tom," she teased as he bent to pick up his sword. He retrieved his weapon, his face flushed red beneath his freckles. He refused to meet Kiara's eyes. Jake approached the two of them breathing heavily and chuckling.

"I don't reckon they'll have many border guards as gifted as you at swordplay, Kiara," Jake said good-naturedly, clearly trying to ease the sting of defeat for Tom. But Tom didn't look convinced.

Kiara forced herself to smile at the men but she feared Tom would not return for training, regardless of what kind of practice he might need for the guards. Although Jake and Tom both came to train with her often, they were about the only ones left in the Village who *would* train with her. And Kiara suspected their numbers were about to be reduced by half if Tom's sulky expression was any indication.

She should be used to the Village boys resenting her for her talent. There were enough of them making nasty comments whenever she went into the Village now.

She scowled for a moment as she thought of the insult Sandy Collins had thrown her way the last time she'd gone for supplies at the Village general store. "Still fighting the lads because you can't find any who'd marry a witch like you?" he'd taunted.

Kiara had been livid and tempted to make him eat those words but she knew Brijit would have been mortified to hear of her almost-grown daughter fighting with the Village boys. It was bad enough when she'd been a small girl but now that she was almost a woman, Brijit didn't understand her need to continue to fight. She tolerated the training but a brawl in the Village Square would not have pleased her mother.

Kiara knew part of Sandy's venom came from the fact that she'd rejected his advances when he'd decided he would be a good suitor for her. At one point she'd been good friends with him but now he couldn't stand seeing her without throwing a nasty remark her way. Why did boys always ruin things by deciding to complicate life with romance?

Pushing that thought aside, Kiara put her sword in its scabbard and crossed to the water barrel. She scooped up a cup of water and drank deeply. Two hours of training had taken some of the edge off of her restlessness but not much.

"Again?" she challenged hopefully.

"Enough already, Kiara!" Tom complained, "I've had it, I've got to get home for chores." He paused on the edge of the stable yard and looked back at her, a scowl darkening his boyish features. "And I don't know how much longer I'm going to be able to take time out to play with you. I have to prepare for the guards, you know, and pretending to train with a girl is hardly sufficient." Kiara stared at him in shock. She didn't know Tom had it in him to talk back to her. But before she could answer he hurried away.

Disgusted Kiara said to Jake, "He's never going to make it in the border guards."

Jake laughed and shook his head. "You might be right there." He started to pack up his gear. Seeing her disappointed look he added apologetically, "I've got to get down to the smithy. Don't listen to, Tom; his pride is bruised as the Village lads are jibing him about training with you. Regardless of what he says, you know this was a good training session. You always give me a good workout."

She smiled at her friend. Jake had a homely face that was open and honest. She truly loved training with him but she couldn't deny that she was glad he was leaving at the same time as Tom. Sometimes he would linger and things would start to become uncomfortable, as he had taken to making comments that were a bit too personal. She wondered just how uncomfortable training would be if he started to truly make romantic advances.

Mina had told her that he was clearly holding out in the hopes that she would consent to his courting her. But Kiara steadfastly told her sister that she refused to believe such a thing. They were merely training partners, she insisted. Sometimes though she wondered if her sister was right. It was a complication she certainly didn't need in her life.

She waved Jake off, feeling rather dejected as she watched him finish gathering his things and depart. She was standing alone in the stable yard when she suddenly became aware of another presence.

Kiara turned quickly, her hand on the hilt of her sword. She scanned the yard, seeking the source of her unease. She didn't have to look far. At the end of the stable, the large stranger, the one called Caedmon, was lounging against the side of the building.

He looked pointedly at her hand on her sword and then uncrossed his tattooed arms from his broad chest. For a moment, Kiara was distracted by the way the black serpentine tattoos encircled his muscular arms. She idly wondered how many years one had to be in the army before he accumulated so many tattoos. She knew the more senior a soldier's rank the more of the ink he acquired but this Caedmon didn't look that much older than she.

Before she could ponder the matter further, he lazily pushed himself from the side of the stable and began to saunter across the yard toward her, a look of disdain on his face.

"Tell me, do you always fight young men who are clearly so infatuated with you that they'll let you win every time?" he asked, his lilting accent at odds with the harshness of the words. He stopped within arm's length of her, his dark eyes questioning.

20

Kiara forced her hand from the hilt of her sword and resisted the urge to cross her own arms in a defensive stance. She studied his face, momentarily distracted by his handsome features.

Kiara felt heat rise to her cheeks as she realized he was waiting for her to reply to his words. "Don't be absurd," she said dismissively. "Jake is merely a good friend. And Tom is scared of me."

"Oh?" he scoffed, "You mean to tell me you think they were actually trying?" He shook his head, a tuft of dark hair falling into his eyes. He brushed it away impatiently. "Either they are completely inept or they were taking it easy on you."

Kiara straightened to her full height, a move that usually intimidated whomever she was speaking to but Caedmon merely raised his dark brows. She'd forgotten he was so much taller than she. She tried to estimate his height but couldn't even fathom a guess. But she did note with dismay that her own head barely reached his shoulders.

"Jake and Tom always work hard when they train with me," she defended, hating the way her voice rose in explanation.

"Mmm-hmmm." He didn't look convinced. "You're telling me that blacksmith couldn't have disarmed you when he had you in the corner?"

Kiara thought back to when Jake had backed her into a tight space between the water barrel and the stable wall. He had seemed to be fighting hard but then, when she was sure he would have disarmed her, he suddenly lost his footing. It was a coincidence perhaps. She'd never considered that he might have done it on purpose – at least not until now. Uncertainty crept into her mind. She quickly pushed the thought aside as absurd. Why would Jake do such a thing?

"He wouldn't do that," she insisted aloud as if saying the words would make it true.

"'You always give me a good workout,'" Caedmon mimicked Jake's deep voice cruelly.

Kiara felt her face flush even more. She turned her back to him and walked over to the corner of the yard where she began to gather up her training gear.

Once she had collected all her gear, she forced herself to turn and meet his eyes.

"If you doubt my skills, I'd be happy to spar with you next time I train," she said coldly.

"Oh, please." He laughed mockingly, causing her to flush more. "As if you would last even two minutes with me." He crossed the yard with a speed that momentarily distracted Kiara. A man as large as he shouldn't be able to move that fast her instincts shouted. It wasn't normal.

Before the thought was fully formed, he was leaning down towards her and for the first time in her life Kiara felt both small and weak.

He bent close and whispered sardonically, "I don't fight girls."

Then before Kiara could respond he strode off across the yard, walking at a normal pace for a man of his size and making her wonder if she'd imagined his earlier burst of unnatural speed.

Kiara watched Caedmon until he disappeared around the side of the Inn and only when he'd gone from view did she turn and finish gathering up her training gear.

She wasn't sure what had just happened but she felt like a gauntlet of sorts had been thrown down between them.

Kiara shook her head. Avoiding strangers was proving to be not as easy as her mother had hoped.

****

Mina was in the Great Room, polishing the already gleaming wooden bar when Kiara stormed in.

"Oh good, you're finished training. Kiara, do you have time to help with the mid-day meal?" Mina asked. "Sukey Greensleaves did not show up for work again."

Sukey was a Village girl that Brijit had hired to help with serving and other jobs around the Inn. Mina knew that Brijit had only offered the girl the work to help out her family. Her mother was a widow with seven other children to feed at home but Mina had been cursing the day Brijit had been so generous.

Sukey was completely unreliable and when she did report for work, she often fraternized with male guests. A well endowed girl who had taken to altering her gowns so her ample cleavage was very visible, Sukey was always a favorite with the traveling men who stopped at the Inn. And more than once Mina had caught the girl sneaking from a guest's room in the wee hours. She was going to have to speak to Brijit about letting her go.

Sukey was *not* a favorite with either of her sisters. Kiara stopped in her tracks and glared. "What? Again?" She lowered her dark brows over her eyes and scowled in a way that twisted her pretty features into something truly frightening. "Well, that just tops off my morning." She dropped her training gear behind the bar and reached for an apron that was stowed beneath the counter.

"Oh, Kiara, don't look so black! Did Jake finally better you at sparring?" Mina teased.

Kiara turned swiftly a look of outrage on her face. "Why would you say that, Mina?" she asked vehemently.

Mina was taken aback at her sister's response. Although Kiara tended towards bouts of temper, she was usually good-natured about jokes. Mina wondered what had happened to put her sister into such a foul humor.

"I was teasing you, Kee," she said gently. "What's got under your skin?"

Kiara reached for her tray on the end of the bar.

"Not a what but a who," she muttered under her breath.

Mina raised her eyebrows. Well, someone certainly had put Kiara in a cranky mood. She moved behind the bar and began polished the ale mugs that she would need when the travelers came down for their luncheon. Kiara took over setting out cutlery on the tables, the work seeming to ease her anger.

Mina watched her sister for a few minutes. Kiara was widely considered a beauty. The young men in the Village certainly had thought so at one time. But most of them had been on the losing end of a fight with Kiara and that tended to dampen the attraction. From an early age Kiara had been a fighter and she'd made a point of getting into battles with the Village boys and beating them. By the time she was in her early teens almost all of the boys were too scared of her to see her as a beauty. Or too resentful of her prowess as a fighter to appreciate it!

It was a shame Kiara was so prickly when it came to the opposite sex. She insisted on seeing them as opponents rather than potential suitors. Mina watched as her sister ran her fingers through her short dark hair impatiently.

Kiara was completely oblivious to her own beauty but strangers usually were not. In fact, at times she wondered if Kiara tried to make herself look less attractive by shearing her hair so short and wearing an almost constant costume of thigh length tunics and leggings. Of course, Kiara said she did such things because they were practical whereas the gowns and long locks Mina favored were not. Mina shook her head. Her sister didn't realize that it was all for nothing, as nothing her sister did dampened her stunning beauty.

24

"You don't have to tell me, if you don't want to," Mina called over to her. Then a thought suddenly popped into her mind. Caedmon, the large older brother, had barely been able to keep his eyes off Kiara. And he was so different than the Village lads or even other travelers who frequented the Inn. Kiara had never met a warrior before. Mina wondered if her sister might actually have found a man who interested her. "I wonder if it had to do with the large handsome stranger who was paying an extraordinary amount of attention to you when he arrived?"

Kiara straightened and glared at her. "He is not handsome!" she growled.

Bingo! Mina nodded with satisfaction. So it was the stranger's attention that had put Kiara in such a bad mood. This was something new. Typically Kiara would reject a potential suitor and that would be the end of it. She rarely got worked up over such things.

"You should be happy when a man pays attention to you, Kiara! You're a beautiful girl - despite the fact that you would wish to hide behind trousers and men's clothing. It shouldn't be surprising that you are noticed."

"He did *not* find me attractive," she glowered.

Mina raised her eyebrows as she began to line up the polished pint mugs on the bar, but decided to let the subject go for now. Kiara wasn't the only one who seemed to be stirred up by the arrival of these three visitors, she thought to herself. Thia's reaction to the other brother – the one called Teague – had been apparent even if her little sister had tried to hide it. Mina intended to get to the bottom of that mystery later today.

She didn't understand why her sisters were so negative about the new arrivals. She thought it was rather exciting to have strangers visiting the Inn at this time of year. And besides they seemed like good fellows to her. She was hoping they'd have a story or two to tell about life in the Outlands.

Mina had a longing to travel but the farthest she'd been from the Inn was to Silvervale, which was only two days journey from home. A place as far away as the Outlands sounded exotic and thrilling to her.

Her thoughts went back to Thia's reaction to the boy named Teague. It wasn't like her small sister to be so affected by strangers. As a healer, she dealt with more strangers than even Mina did as a barkeep. And Thia was usually professional and calm – certainly not shaken or flustered as she had been yesterday.

No something was definitely odd about the way her sisters were reacting to these travelers. Mina was determined to get to the bottom of this mystery.

No sooner had the thought formed in her mind than Teague entered the Great Room. He paused just inside the doorframe and looked around the room, his strange silver eyes glinting in the dim light. He seemed to note Kiara and then he saw Mina behind the bar and came towards her.

"Minathrial, right?" he asked cheerfully.

He had the type of face that was quick to smile and encouraged one to do likewise. Mina nodded, a smile coming easily to her lips. "My friends call me Mina," she told him.

"Mina, it is then!" He grinned and then looked around the Great Room. "Am I too early for luncheon?" he asked glumly as he gestured toward the empty room.

"Oh, not that much too early. I'm sure Thia will have the meal ready in less than a quarter hour," she assured him.

He looked relieved. "I'm starving," he confided with a wink. "I might be smaller than Caedmon but I swear some days I eat more than him!"

Mina laughed, liking this Teague boy more and more by the minute.

And he was a boy she realized. He couldn't be more than 18 years old. It was easy to see now that he was up close and conversing. When he'd first arrived, particularly when he'd seen Thia, he seemed older than his years but now he appeared to be a happy-go-lucky young man.

"Have you always competed for food with your older brother?" Mina asked with a grin.

Teague raised his eyebrows. "My lady!" he teased, "I'm the elder brother. I thought that would be obvious," he said with mock hurt. "I'm shocked that you would make such an error."

Mina laughed again. She couldn't help it; his expression was so earnest her giggles just kept bubbling over her lips. She made an attempt to sober herself and then looked at him through narrowed eyes. "Truly?"

He nodded solemnly. "I'm a full 18 months older than that brat," he grinned suddenly. "Of course he's always been larger than me."

"How old are you then?" she asked as she set a mug of ale down in front of him.

"I'm almost 19. Caedmon is only 17 years old - although I agree he looks and acts close to thirty." He nodded at her. "Are you the eldest of your sisters?"

Mina shook her head. "Oh, no. We are the same age within a few weeks."

Teague looked confused. "Are you saying you're triplets, then?"

She giggled again. "Did you honestly believe that?" she asked in surprise. Her sisters and her didn't bear the slightest resemblance to one another. Kiara with her short dark hair and flashing blue eyes was the precise opposite of her own long blond hair and green eyes. Then there was Thia, who was tiny compared to the two of them, her tumble of red curls and unique golden eyes marking her as something different again. No one from outside the Village ever assumed them to be related.

"We are adopted," Mina explained. "And we are all sixteen."

Understanding dawned on Teague's face as he sat on one of the high stools close to the bar, swinging his legs with an air of abandon. He examined the room more closely, his eyes suddenly halting on the harp at the far end of the room.

"Are you the musician?" he asked her with a smile.

Mina nodded in surprise. "How did you know?"

He shrugged. "Your laugh is quite musical and your voice is melodic. My ear just picked it out."

"Are you a musician as well?" she asked in delight. "I noticed the mandolin among your things."

He nodded eagerly. "Do you play for guests at all?"

"Yes, often in fact. But it's rare that I get the chance to play with other musicians. Do you think you'd like to play with me tonight?" she asked eagerly.

Teague nodded. "I would! Perhaps, if you have time after luncheon, we could go over a few melodies and see what we can come up with for some evening entertainment."

Mina clapped happily. "I would love that," she said with true pleasure. And maybe Teague would tell her about life in the Outlands as well. Or at the very least teach her a few songs from his homeland.

"Teague!" They both turned at the sound of Weylon's gruff voice. Teague's father was standing in the doorway, displeasure evident on his face as he watched them.

Teague gathered up his mug of ale and gave her an apologetic smile. "I'd best go find a table with my father and brother. But we'll meet later, yes?"

Mina nodded. "I'm looking forward to it!"

She smiled happily. She was even more convinced that her sisters were being overly sensitive now that she'd spoken to Teague. These strangers seemed to be just what they needed to bring some life to the wintertime at the Inn.

CHAPTER FOUR

After spending an enjoyable music-filled afternoon in Teague's company, Mina found Thia in the kitchen chopping vegetables for the evening meal.

"Don't you ever rest, little sister?" Mina asked teasingly.

Thia pushed her copper curls out of her face and added the onions to the large wooden bowl on the counter beside her. "We have guests to feed and if I don't get started now, there won't be any dinner ready," she replied. "Besides I'm making a batch of turkey pies for dinner – so the sooner I get the chopping and rolling finished, the sooner I can put my feet up and have a cup of tea while they bake in the oven."

Mina reached for an apron. "Well, I can help with the chopping if nothing else." She hummed pleasantly under her breath. She was always filled with a sense of satisfaction and contentment when she'd spent time with her music. Today that feeling was amplified thanks to the few hours she'd shared songs with Teague. He was truly gifted as a musician. And the stories he had shared of the Outlands were so inspiring.

Thia smiled. "You seem especially happy today," she noted as she placed a bunch of freshly washed carrots on the chopping board.

"Hmm." Mina nodded. "Luncheon finished relatively early and I've been practicing ever since."

Pleasure filled Thia's face, "Oh, are you playing tonight then?" she asked, happy anticipation clear in her voice.

Mina nodded but decided not to tell Thia about Teague's participation in the evening's entertainment. Something told her to tread carefully when it came to talking about Teague with her small sister. Instead she changed the subject.

"By the way, I think Kiara has finally found a man who is not attracted to her for once," Mina confided with a grin, before adding, "And it's driving her mad."

Thia looked up from her work, interest sparking in her golden eyes. "Whom?" she asked.

"Caedmon, the larger brother from the group that arrived yesterday," Mina said as she began to carefully dice the carrots. "I don't know what he said to Kiara but she was in a quite a state when she came in from training."

"Oh, dear." Thia shook her head looking worried. "I suppose Sukey's not showing up didn't help with her sour mood?"

Mina shrugged. "Ah, well, you know Kiara, it doesn't take much to set her off."

They worked in silence for a while, Thia rolling the pastry and lining the pie plates, while Mina finely chopped the ingredients her sister gave her. After the meat and vegetables had all been prepared and added to the bowl, Mina sat on the stool in the corner where she watched her small sister work.

There was no question that Thia took great pleasure from being in the kitchen. But this afternoon there were fine lines on her forehead as she concentrated on preparing the evening meal. Mina was willing to wage her sister's preoccupation had to do with Teague but she couldn't understand how he could have upset her sister. He really seemed to be a very sweet boy. She just couldn't imagine why Thia had reacted so strongly to him. Her sister was typically welcoming of all strangers.

"What about you, Thia? You seemed to be rather distracted by Teague. I thought I saw a flicker of recognition in your eyes," Mina paused, as she saw her sister's mouth tighten slightly.

A moment of silence passed.

"Was it a vision?" she nudged gently.

Thia shook her head quickly. Mina knew she had a hard time talking about her visions. Thia only saw the bad in those episodes because they were always accompanied by violent seizures, but over the years she'd been able to do much good with her visions.

Mina remembered when they were nine and Thia had foreseen an attack on Kiara. A large forest cat had come upon her unawares and Kiara very likely would have died from the gaping wound in her side had Thia not had one of her visions. She'd been able to tell them precisely where Kiara was in the vast woods and the time saved had no doubt spared her life.

Mina waited patiently as her sister crimped the crust on the last pie. Finally Thia looked up from her work. "Should I make us some tea?" she asked.

Mina nodded and watched as Thia took her time putting the kettle on the stove. She was clearly stalling and Mina wondered if she should let the whole topic of Teague drop. But her curiosity was piqued.

When the tea was brewing, Thia came and sat at the big oak table Mina had moved to.

"*Have* you seen Teague before?" she asked when it became apparent that Thia was not going to start the conversation.

Thia answered slowly, choosing her words carefully as she poured the tea. "Yes, I've seen Teague. But I don't know him ..." she trailed off. "It's hard to explain."

Mina considered her sister's odd choice of words. It didn't make sense. How could someone she recognize Teague but not know him? She added milk to her tea while she was waited for her sister to explain what she meant but Thia's golden eyes were focused on her cup.

Mina pushed her hair behind her ears. "But if he wasn't in a vision and you've never met him ... I don't understand. You're sure he wasn't one of your visions? You are sometimes confused a bit afterward."

Thia was focused on her hands, which were interlaced on the table. Mina understood that her sister didn't like speaking of her seizures. Whenever one came over her, they resulted in visions of a sort. Thia had told her once that even when they resulted in something good, like the time Kiara was hurt, she still found them extremely upsetting. She never knew what to do with the images and when she regained consciousness, often on the ground, bloodied and lying in her own urine, she felt shame and horror, unable to meet the eyes of those around her.

Mina knew that Thia had helped Brijit to treat patients with the same kinds of fits that Thia, herself, suffered from. Once she'd admitted to Mina that she was secretly horrified to think that she also looked like that when the visions hit; her eyes rolling up in her head, her body stiff and jerking. Mina had tried to reassure Thia that it wasn't as bad as she imagined but Mina suspected her sister didn't believe her.

Thia closed her eyes for a moment. As she watched her, Mina felt a flicker of worry. She was starting to fear that there was something more serious going on here but Mina couldn't imagine what it might be.

Thia opened her eyes and met Mina's gaze, her golden eyes were filled with torment and Mina suddenly felt guilty for pushing her sister.

"I'm not ready to speak about it," Thia said softly. Mina nodded in understanding and decided to let it be. She knew that her little sister would eventually tell her what was going on but right now she needed some time and space to sort out what she was going through. She had learned a long time ago that Thia was a deep thinker and sometimes needed to process her thoughts before sharing.

Mina lifted her cup and took a sip of the warm tea. Then she purposely changed the topic and began to discuss the challenges of working with Sukey. Soon the angst left Thia's face and for once Mina was thankful for her mother's poor choice in employees.

****

Mina had said that there would be music in the Great Room that night. So after Thia had finished the dinner and Sukey was in the kitchen cleaning up, she made her way out to the bar to take over Mina's duties and listen to the music. She never missed a chance to hear her sister's beautiful voice.

Despite her anticipation for Mina's performance, Thia couldn't stop thinking about Teague. In her mind's eye, she saw the strange silver eyes that belonged to him. She had decided that she was not yet ready to deal with whatever his sudden appearance might mean. Now that she was faced with the reality of him, she sensed he would be important in her life but she didn't know exactly what role he would play. Tonight she was hoping Mina's music

34

would weave its usual magic and take her thoughts away from the sudden appearance of Teague.

But no sooner had Thia moved behind the bar than she noticed Teague standing beside the harp, his mandolin in his hands. Her heart dropped as she realized that he would be performing with her sister. Clearly there would be no escaping her troubled thoughts tonight.

"Looks like our guests brought the entertainment with them."

Thia turned to see Kiara leaning against the bar, her pretty mouth turned down in disapproval.

"Is that why it's been so busy this evening?" Thia asked. She had sold out of the last of the dinner pies an hour earlier. Typically they would have leftovers at this time of year but the Great Room was teeming with Villagers. Somehow the news of evening entertainment at the Inn must have spread through the town.

Kiara nodded and grimaced as Sukey flounced up to the bar and ordered a round of ale for her table

"What do you think of the strangers, Thia?" Sukey asked, her voice rising in excitement. "That Caedmon is a handsome lad, isn't he? And the other one can play and sing. Oh! We hardly ever get this kind of excitement in the Village during the winter months!"

Kiara made a face behind Sukey's back. Thia hid her smile as she turned to fill the glasses. Kiara had always been vocal about her disapproval of Sukey but Thia was happy for her empty prattle tonight. It kept her mind off darker thoughts.

"Don't *you* think that Caedmon fellow is handsome, Kiara?" Sukey asked, oblivious to Kiara's black mood.

"Not in the least," Kiara responded coldly.

Sukey's mouth fell open. "Well, I'm going to bed him before he leaves, mark my words! A big lad like that!" She giggled and put the frothing mugs on her tray before sashaying across the room.

"I swear, if that girl doesn't stop throwing herself at the customers…" Kiara trailed off angrily. "Why did Brijit ever offer such a girl a job?"

Thia reached out and put her hand over Kiara's, which was gripping the bar so hard her knuckles were turning white as she watched Sukey flirt with Caedmon across the Great Room.

"Hush. You know why Brijit hired her," Thia said softly. "Her mother needs the money."

Kiara loosened her grip slightly. "But I don't need the aggravation," she said.

Before Kiara could say any more, music filled the room and all talk ceased.

Mina's voice and talent on the harp always drew a crowd but tonight with Teague harmonizing and playing his mandolin the atmosphere in the bar became almost magical.

They sang some lively songs together and Sukey was able to get Jake, the blacksmith, to dance a jig with her. Thia noticed that the girl first tried to get Caedmon to join her on the dance floor but he flatly refused her. She saw Kiara closely watching the exchange from the other end of the room. She didn't miss the satisfied smile on her sister's pretty face when it became clear that the big stranger would not consent to dance with Sukey. Perhaps Mina was right about Caedmon's effect on Kiara.

As the night wore on, Thia was kept busy filling mugs of ale. She found to her surprise that even with Teague singing and playing with her sister, the music was soothing to her nerves. She was actually starting to relax a bit when

Teague began to pluck a sad melody on the mandolin. His voice lifted in song and he seemed to be looking directly at Thia.

On a deserted river bank
In the sad summer sun
A wee lass sat and wept
As though her life were undone

I came across her accidentally
And asked her why she cried
In her loneliness and grief
She said her parents had died

Sadness and sorrow
Wash, wash away
Leave and don't follow
To the end of days

Thia froze as the bewitching notes wove the story he was singing through the Great Room. The entire room seemed to have paused, lost in haunting melody that Teague was playing.

As the last notes faded away, Thia looked down and wiped her eyes. The feelings swirling within her were conflicting. The song he sang told the story of how they had met. Her weak hope that Teague was merely a boy who just happened to look like someone in a dream was shattered. It was clear from his song that Teague was the boy who dreamwalked with her. The only question left was why was he here?

CHAPTER FIVE

Thia turned the dead bird in her hands and began to quickly remove its feathers. She absolutely despised cleaning and plucking the chickens but had decided the nasty task might take her mind off the haunting song that had been running through her head since the previous evening.

It hadn't helped that everyone seemed to be talking of Teague's musical talents today. Mina couldn't contain her joy at having a musician of her own caliber staying at the Inn indefinitely. Sukey had dreamily recounted the events of the night as she helped prepare lunch. Apparently after Caedmon had rejected her advances Jake, the blacksmith, had been more than happy to walk her home at the end of the evening. Sukey was certain it was the magical quality of the music that had turned Jake's eyes her way since he hadn't noticed her before. Thia thought it probably had more to do with the fact that Jake had finally accepted that Kiara was never going to be romantically interested in him. Jake was a practical man. He had moved on to a woman who would have him.

Kiara seemed to be in a blacker mood than normal and was only too happy to help when Thia asked her to do the dirty job of slaughtering the six birds.

Thia's fingers worked rapidly pulling the tough feathers from the bird's skin. Her mind was racing, she needed time to dissect was going on and she needed to do so away from Teague! She was still dwelling on the words from his song.

The dreamwalks were something she never spoke of. She knew the dreams she shared with Teague were different than her other dreams but she never considered that they might be real or that Teague might be anything more than a figment of her imagination. Thia turned the bird over and continued to viciously remove feathers, trying to push the disturbing thoughts aside. She'd lain awake most of the previous night trying to come up with an explanation for what was happening and the only reward she'd gained was a sleepless night.

This was no use. She would just have to find Teague and talk to him, whether she liked it or not. No sooner had the thought formed than a familiar voice suddenly filled her head.

It's time we talked, Thia. Teague's voice was so real that she stopped what she was doing and looked around the small yard behind her only confirming what she already knew. She was alone.

What was going on? Teague was not present and yet she could have sworn she heard him clear as a bell. Thia shook her head and wondered if she really was going crazy. She recognized Teague's voice perfectly. It was the voice she'd been hearing since she was six years old. A voice she thought only existed in her dreams.

Putting the bird aside, Thia moved towards the kitchen door. She was just reaching for it when it opened, and she found herself face to face with Teague.

For a moment they just stood and stared at each other. Thia took in his familiar features: the unruly brown curls on top of his head and the high cheekbones that seemed to be at odds with his boyish face. The faint beginnings of laugh lines that were forming at the corners of his eyes. And those eyes. She felt a shiver run down her spine as she held his gaze with her own. His eyes were closer to silver in color than grey and they currently had so many emotions shifting through them that she couldn't identify any of them, despite the fact that they clearly reflected what she was feeling inside.

"I thought it was probably best we talk in private, don't you agree?" he said aloud.

Thia nodded. He was right. Sukey would be arriving to start helping with dinner preparation soon and there was no telling whether Kiara might come to see if she needed more birds. Her sister had been in a killing mood earlier. It was probably best that she talk to Teague away from curious eyes until she figured out what was going on. She moved out of his path and Teague stepped out into the small, enclosed yard shutting the kitchen door firmly behind him.

"What are you doing?" Thia asked, trying to ignore the veiled panic in her voice as she watched him move to the table where the dead birds lay. Grimacing slightly he removed his gloves and reached for one of the birds.

"It's more probable that I saw you doing work and offered to help than that I sought out a supposed stranger for a private talk, don't you think?" he asked reasonably.

Thia nodded and moved wordlessly behind the opposite end of the table to resume work on her abandoned bird. She watched Teague's hands as he

40

skillfully removed feathers from the bird he was holding. Clearly he'd plucked chickens before despite the look of distaste on his face.

"Who are you?" she demanded. "And how do you do that?"

Do what? he asked without speaking aloud, the boyish grin on his face.

Thia felt a pang in her gut. That grin was so familiar. She'd seen it so many times in her dreams. Even as his features had shifted, the round youthful face lengthening into that of a young man, two things had stayed the same in her dreams: Teague's eyes and his smile.

She swallowed, sudden fear curling in the pit of her stomach. Teague paused in his work and looked across at her.

"Please stop doing that!" Thia said, flinching when she heard the desperation in own voice. "It's bad enough that you're here, in person. I don't need to be hearing you in my head, too!"

"Okay," he said guiltily. Thia fought to suppress dream memories. His eyes, an even more amazing silver grey in person, glimmered in the late afternoon light.

She looked down, taking solace in the sudden silence between them.

"It's not a dream this time, Thia."

"I know," she admitted in a whisper. "But how is this happening?"

Teague shook his head at her, his hair falling forward over his forehead. "I know you're shocked. I was, too, when I first saw you. Then I realized that what we thought were only dreams, were just forays into a different reality." Excitement lit up his features. "A reality that, at times, feels more real than this one, don't you agree?"

Thia opened her mouth to deny what he was saying, even as a dozen memories burst to life in her head. Her mind focused on her first dream memory of him.

Teague had been a boy, only a few years her senior. He'd found her scared and alone along a small river, just as his song had depicted. It must have been some time after Brijit had told her the truth about her birth parents - that they had both been killed in a horrible accident. In the dream, she'd been looking for her parents and found herself suddenly alone.

She remembered the feeling of utter loneliness and despair that had flooded her. She'd wandered lost and afraid, sobbing her heart out. And then suddenly the boy – Teague - had been there. He had led her along a path and back to where Brijit and her sisters had been waiting for her. When she woke she'd felt safe and overwhelmed by the sense that everything was going to be all right.

Thia stared at the boy in front of her, studying his face for any sign that he was joking. But Teague was serious, his eyes willing her to understand but Thia refused to admit that what he was saying could be true.

"It's not possible, is it? After all, there are no such things as different realities," she insisted vehemently. "There has to be some other explanation. If I dreamwalk, why don't I do it with my sisters? My mother? My friends?" She gestured helplessly. "The only person I've ever shared a dreamwalk with is you. Why is that?"

Teague was silent.

The silence seemed to stretch between them, heavy with shared knowledge. Thia blinked. She finished her last bird and saw that he had also finished and put his gloves back on. The early winter afternoon sun was low on the horizon.

She reached for the tray of birds to carry them into the kitchen. Teague hurried around the table and took the heavy tray from her before she could protest. For the first time Thia noticed he was taller than in her dreams. Not as tall as her sisters but certainly taller than she.

42

He looked down at her, his eyes unreadable in the fading afternoon light.

And yet the essence of him was so familiar. Before she could stop herself Thia instinctively reached out to touch his forearm, wanted to feel the warm muscles above his gloves, to reassure herself that he was real.

Teague jerked away before she could reach him and Thia felt an inexplicable sense of hurt flood through her.

"I'm real, Thia," he whispered aloud, his breath stirring the hair on her forehead. "But you can't touch me. I can't explain right now but please don't try."

Suddenly needing to put some space between them, Thia whirled and opened the kitchen door. The room beyond was empty.

As they entered the warmth of the kitchen, the inner door opened and Sukey came rushing in, babbling an apology and instantly breaking the tension. "I'm so sorry I'm late, Miss Elethia. Miss Minathrial asked me to help Miss Kiara clear the dining tables." She stopped short when she saw Teague standing in the kitchen, his arms full of the plucked chickens. She smiled winningly. "Oh, sir, I hope you don't mind me saying but your music last night was amazing." She fluttered her eyelashes in a flirtatious manner.

Irritation filled Thia and she found her voice. "That's fine, Sukey. Why don't you get started on dressing the birds?" The sharpness in her tone making Sukey flinch in surprise.

Teague put the tray on the large wooden counter. Thia smiled politely at him, very aware that Sukey's curious eyes were on them both. "Thank you for your assistance with birds. It was very kind of you."

Teague's mouth twitched as he suppressed a grin. "My pleasure," he answered politely as he backed out of the kitchen but his eyes glinted in a way that suggested their conversation was far from over.

CHAPTER SIX

Moments after Teague departed, Kiara ran into the kitchen.

"Brijit is back," she announced breathlessly.

Leaving Sukey to follow her instructions for dinner, Thia went with Kiara in search of her mother. They found Brijit with Mina in her small private sitting room.

Brijit had removed her travelling cloak but her face was creased with exhaustion, her grey curls starting to slip from the braid at her neck and her shoulders drooping in fatigue. Nevertheless, she smiled when she saw the girls arrive.

"We didn't expect you to be gone so long," Mina told her.

Brijit nodded. "Neither did I. It was a long, hard delivery for the mother. Sadly the child was stillborn." She paused for a moment, blinking back tears. "There was nothing I could do except save the life of the mother."

Thia felt her mother's grief. Brijit rarely lost a patient. Her healing ability was almost legendary in the Village. But when she did lose someone, regardless of age, she felt it keenly.

Brijit shuddered once and then looked up, tears in her pale blue eyes. "But tell me what has been happening around here since I left?" she asked, sniffling and changing the subject. "Nothing too exciting, I trust?"

It was Kiara who spoke up. "A group of strangers arrived the day you left."

Brijit and Kiara exchanged a dark look that Thia couldn't decipher. Then Brijit smiled so quickly Thia wondered if she'd imagined it.

"Strangers? Well, Kiara don't look so glum. Business at this time of year must be seen as a blessing," she said then gave a knowing laugh. "Tell me, my dear, is one of them handsome and paying you an inordinate amount of attention?"

Mina piped up. "Well, there is a handsome young man in the party but Kiara insists that he's rejected her rather than giving her attention!"

Kiara glared at her sister. "I did not say he rejected me. I said he insulted me."

Brijit raised her eyebrows as laughter filled the room. "Well, how long are these strangers staying?" she asked after the laughter died down.

Mina wrinkled her brow. "There was something strange in that. They weren't sure how long they would stay." She paused and seemed to be thinking over her words. "They are an interesting group. At first we were quite nervous about their rough appearance but it turns out that they are a very nice family."

"You weren't nervous at all," Kiara corrected her sister. "All you could think of was how exciting it was to have a group of Outlanders staying at the Inn."

"Outlanders?" Brijit asked, faintly.

"Yes. A father and his two sons."

Brijit looked up, suddenly sober. "What are their names?" she asked sharply.

Thia looked at her mother in surprise. Brijit rarely spoke in that shrill tone of voice.

Kiara answered her question. "The father's name is Weylon and the sons are Caedmon and Teague."

A cry of alarm slipped from Brijit's lips and she leapt to her feet.

"I must see them immediately," she said as she hurried to the door.

"But Brijit, we don't know if they are in their rooms and you are tired from your journey. Can't you see them at dinner?" Mina asked, clearly surprised by her mother's haste.

Brijit shook her head so violently that rest of her grey hair slipped from its braid. "No. I must see them now," she insisted and rushed into the hallway.

They found Weylon, Teague and Caedmon in the Great Room.

"Weylon!" Brijit exclaimed and flew across the room into the older man's arms. Thia noticed that he took a step back and then seemed to hesitate before his arms closed around her mother. But Brijit wasn't hesitating at all!

Thia stared at her mother in shock. She looked at her sisters and saw they were just as stunned by Brijit's reception of Weylon. Their adoptive mother, who had never courted any man as far as the girls could remember, had thrown herself into the arms of a stranger. As they watched Weylon lowered his lips to hers and it became clear that, to Brijit at least, he was no stranger.

****

A few hours later they found Brijit alone in the kitchen. There was no sign of Weylon or his sons.

Mina and Thia followed Kiara into the kitchen. Kiara stopped just inside the door when she saw her mother and stood there menacingly. Brijit, who had raised her since babyhood, continued dressing the last chicken without a sideways glance at her adopted daughter even though Kiara was clearly worked up.

Mina smiled to herself.

"I started the bread, Thia," Brijit said, ignoring Kiara's attempt to intimidate her. "I don't know where Sukey disappeared to," she said vaguely. Mina looked around the kitchen, seeing the half dressed chickens abandoned.

Thia let out a small cry of dismay and then set to work placing the birds on the spit to roast, muttering under her breath.

Mina silently moved to the counter and began to knead the bread that had been rising on the top of the great stove. She sunk her fingers into the soft, warm dough waiting patiently for what would happen next.

Kiara, as usual, ignored the kitchen duties but put her hands on her hips and began to tap her foot impatiently. "Where have our guests disappeared to, Brijit?"

Brijit smiled at her tall daughter, as if Kiara had asked her the question in the most conversational of voices rather than in that surly tone.

"The men decided to go into town," she answered slowly.

Mina watched as Kiara glowered at their mother. "Are you going to make us ask how you know that man well enough to ..." she paused searching for words. "To throw yourself at him?" she finished lamely. Mina hid a smile.

But Brijit sighed. "There is much to tell you but to be frank, I'm dreading doing so," she paused then looked at them. A shadow of regret passed over her face. "There has been so much I've had to keep from you, hoping to protect you but now ..." Her words trailed off. Then she straightened her back. "Now I need to tell you the truth."

She put the final chicken in the great oven and moved to Mina's side and began kneading a second pile of dough.

"You know that none of you are my true daughters," she began softly. "At least not by blood. But there is more you don't know ..."

Mina watched as Brijit's strong hands worked the dough on the wooden counter.

Kiara made a derisive noise. "Apparently - given how you greeted that stranger."

Mina stifled a giggle. She had no idea her sister was such a prude. Brijit stopped kneading for a moment and stared out the window into the fading light. Although dusk was settling she seemed to be gazing at something in the distance. Mina wondered what she was thinking.

"His name is Weylon, as you already know," she said the corners of her mouth lifting in a small smile. "But what you don't know is that he is my husband."

Mina stopped her work and stared at Brijit. Kiara's mouth fell open. Even Thia stopped chopping vegetables in stunned surprise.

"How?" Kiara asked at the same moment as Thia said "When?"

Brijit sighed. "Weylon and I were married 23 years ago. In Evendel, which was our home."

Mina gasped. Evendel was far west in the Outlands of the Five Corners. She never imagined that her mother had lived so far away. Despite the current circumstances, she was suddenly overcome with a great desire to ask Brijit about her homeland. Surely her mother must have stories about the Outlands. And yet she'd never once said anything that suggested her roots. Then as the reality of her mother's words sunk in Mina felt a jab of betrayal. Brijit knew how Mina longed for information of the lands outside their small village and yet she'd kept her past a secret. Why would she do that?

Brijit deftly shaped round loaves and placed them in the oven with the roasting birds. Dusting off her hands she turned around and looked at each of the girls in turn. "This was long before any of you were born and I came to this tiny corner of the woods."

"Then why have we never met him before, Brijit?" Mina couldn't help asking. How could one be married for so many years and stay apart, never mind keep it a secret from her daughters? What else had Brijit hidden from them?

"Weylon and I are what the folks of the Western realm call *coimirceoiri*."

"Guardians ..." Kiara whispered as she sank into a chair, shock on her face. Mina swallowed. The Guardians were legendary. It didn't seem possible that their mother could be one of them.

Brijit nodded. "Yes. The story is long and complicated but I'll tell you what I can," she paused, then turn back to the oven and set the kettle on to boil.

"I have told you the truth, as much as I could over the years, you know. I don't like keeping secrets and telling falsehoods but some of it could not be avoided," she gestured to the table. "Sit, girls, this will take a while to unravel."

They were silent for a few moments and then Thia spoke hesitantly. "I know this might be painful for you, Brijit, but did your marriage fail?"

Brijit looked shocked. "No!" she answered as she brought the teapot to the table and began pouring them each a mug of the mint tea.

"Weylon and I were, and still are, very much in love. But we were also bound by duty." She lowered herself into her chair. "Had we been at all practical we would never have married knowing what each of us was."

"*Coimirceoirí*," Kiara whispered again, completely transfixed by the idea.

Brijit nodded. "It was only a matter of time before we would have been separated one way or another but we loved each other so much. And we were young. We reasoned that even some time together was better than being apart." She paused and looked out the window at the gathering dusk. "We should have known that the Elders would never have allowed us be together in the first place if they hadn't had larger plans for us."

She took a sip of her tea and then began to tell her story.

Weylon and her had been married no more than two years when they had their first visitors. And not your typical guests but three members of the senior council of the Western realm.

The visitors told the couple of their visions. The time of something they called 'The Prophecy' was drawing near. And to their surprise Weylon and Brijit were told they would both play a role in it.

After that first visit, it was so long before anything more happened that they almost forgot what the visiting Elders had told them. Except Brijit began having visions of her own. Her visions were of three girls, all so different from the other and yet somehow linked. Weylon didn't have the gift of sight but he began to grow more and more uneasy. Five years after the first visit, the Elders returned.

This time they told Brijit and Weylon that they must be separated. It was time that they fulfilled their separate destinies.

Weylon was to go to a small village two days journey from where he and Brijit had been living. It was far from where Brijit would find herself running an Inn and raising three girls in a few years' time. Weylon had two young charges that he would take with him. He was not overly excited about having two boys under the age of five years put into his care, especially without his wife present. But the Elders were non-negotiable. They did not give explanations, all they told Weylon was that these two must be kept safe and raised to be strong.

Brijit meanwhile was sent to a cottage in the woods. She wasn't given any explanation but two days after she arrived the first baby came. She knew immediately the girl was a child from the Elders' realm. She was only a few days old but her eyes were always on the forest, reflecting back the multiple hues of green. Brijit smiled at Mina. "You were a beautiful sweet tempered child. Even though I missed Weylon terribly, having you to care for lightened the weight on my heart."

Brijit had longed for children of her own but Weylon and her refrained from starting a family after the Elders' first visit. It just didn't seem right when their loyalties were to the greater good.

Mina was not alone in Brijit's home for long. Two weeks after she arrived, Kiara was delivered to the cottage by a group of Elders. With dark hair and deep blue eyes, she was the utter opposite of Mina.

Brijit laughed. "I'd lie you beside one another on your blankets and marvel at how completely different the two of you were." She smiled at the memory. "And I'm not just speaking of looks but of your temperament as well."

Kiara was a cankerous and angry baby, her wails echoing loudly through the forest where their small cottage was located. And then four weeks later, Thia was delivered, a tiny bundle with copper hair and golden eyes the like of which Brijit had never seen before. She couldn't even fathom a guess as to Thia's origins; she just knew that it was her duty to care for yet another child.

"And we all had the Mark?" Kiara asked suddenly.

Brijit met her eyes, her expression serious.

"Yes," she whispered.

Mina saw anger flash across Kiara's face. "And you never thought to ask what it meant?" Her tone was disbelieving.

"The *Coimirceoirí* do not question the Elders," Brijit said firmly. "It is not done."

There was a moment of silence before Brijit continued.

She had gone from longing for a baby to suddenly having three little ones thrust upon her.

Then two weeks after she arrived, Thia began having queer spells. The Elders sent their healers but they soon concluded that the child was not ill. They could not explain the seizures that would envelop Thia's small frame, causing her little eyes to roll back in their sockets and her limbs to go rigid, but they could say that the fits did her no harm

Brijit, on the other hand, was dealing with a colicky, fussy Kiara, a quiet and gentle Mina and Thia with her strange seizures. It was obvious to everyone that she needed help.

"That's when Ana came to live with us."

"Granny Ana!" Mina exclaimed with pleasure, remembering the wide grey haired woman who dominated her childhood memories. Ana had always been in the kitchen with a warm lap and comforting arms. And stories, so many stories of her homeland in the North. "Oh how I miss her."

Thia nodded in agreement.

"Yes, Ana was absolutely a gift. I don't think I would have lasted that first year with you three if it weren't for her." Brijit smiled.

"Why did she leave us?" Kiara asked suspicion heavy in her tone. Mina tried to remember the reason but she found that she could not. It just seemed that one day Ana was with them and the next she was gone.

Brijit became serious. "While we were comfortable and safe in our forest cottage for the first few years, as you girls aged it became clear that we couldn't stay there. We were far too vulnerable alone in a forest. The Elders wanted us to be in a place where they could keep a close eye on you girls and check in on a regular basis. Just after your sixth birthdays, we were told that we would be moving to the Inn." Brijit sighed. "When the Elders gave us orders, there was no question as to whether we would follow them. Ana was old and decided that she was not up to life in an Inn, even one as quiet the Elders promised this one would be. She reasoned that I would be perfectly fine raising you on my own now that you'd matured into fine young girls. She was sad to say goodbye to you – you know she loved you all - but in the end she decided to return to her homeland in the North and resume her life with her own children and grandchildren."

Kiara's lips thinned. "And the Elders just let her go?"

Brijit was silent.

"Funny how dear Granny Ana didn't take the time to write to us even once," Kiara continued coldly.

Mina wondered what her sister was suggesting. Didn't Kiara believe their mother? And why was Brijit looking so guilty. Mina had the sudden feeling that Granny Ana's leaving had resulted in a more sinister ending than Brijit was admitting.

To her surprise Kiara suddenly let the topic drop. Mina wondered if her sister didn't want to know the truth. Kiara abruptly changed the direction of her questioning.

"Do you mean to say that all these years the Inn has been a ruse so the Elders could watch us?" Kiara asked, a sharp edge in her voice.

Brijit nodded. "Yes, through the years the Elders have come to check on you often. You didn't even know when they were here."

"And now?" Thia asked, a serious light coming into her golden eyes. "What has changed that has brought Weylon and the boys here?"

Brijit shook her head. "I wish I knew. The Elders don't tell us what is happening. Our job is to keep you safe but we are not permitted to question why." She looked at them, worry reflected on her face. "Weylon received the message to come to the Inn a fortnight ago. He believes the Elders will make their way here soon. Within a few days even. You'll have to be patient for a little bit longer. When they arrive, perhaps they will have some answers to the rest of your questions."

Mina nodded and finished her tea in silence. But deep down she had the feeling that Brijit was still keeping secrets. And she wondered if they would ever uncover what those secrets might be.

CHAPTER SEVEN

Patience was not one of Kiara's strong suits. And when she was forced to wait for things she often became confrontational. She was keenly aware of this flaw in her personality and in times of stress tried to remove herself as much as possible from situations that might set her off. That's what she was doing in the yard, shooting at targets, when Caedmon and Teague suddenly appeared. Thia had joined her about five minutes before the boys did, trying to talk Kiara into accompanying her into town.

Kiara swore that she was going to start training in the forest if she couldn't get some peace and quiet. Here she was trying to avoid confrontations and everyone around her seemed hell-bent on starting one.

To be fair she had to admit that her sister wasn't trying to start a confrontation but Thia should know by now that a walk into the Village would certainly provoke one. Kiara was bound to run into one of the Village boys in town. And she could do without that! She'd rather stay in the yard and train.

But it was difficult to focus when she had an audience. Kiara tried to ignore the fact that Caedmon was watching her shoot her targets. But after a quarter of an hour had passed, she turned to where he and his brother were standing and raised her eyebrows questioningly.

"Do you want something?" she asked, struggling to keep the annoyance out of her voice. While she was proud that their presence hadn't reduced her shooting accuracy, it *had* distracted her.

Caedmon waited a long moment before he spoke. "You playact at being a soldier, girl," he said quietly, not even looking up from sharpening the small dagger in his hand.

"What would you know about it?" Kiara demanded angrily. A part of her was actually happy that he was also feeling confrontational. What she needed right now was a good fight to take the edge off her tension. Caedmon looked like a worthy opponent.

Thia put her hand on her sister's arm, glancing nervously at Caedmon's bent head. "Kiara, don't."

She ignored her sister's worried face. What was Thia so concerned about? "Oh, I will, Thia! Who does he think he is telling me who I am or what I do?"

Caedmon was on his feet so quickly Kiara instinctively took a step backward and then silently cursed herself for showing weakness. His face was implacable.

"I've been watching you, girl. You are happy to fight your suitors; that's true. A group of farmers and Village boys but look at you - " His brown eyes seemed to grow darker as he purposely examined Kiara, his gaze sweeping from the tips of her feet to the top of her head before he shook his head dismissively. Kiara felt a stab of pain in her chest at his easy dismissal of her but then she pushed it away. "You wouldn't hold yourself for more than two minutes with a real soldier."

Kiara felt her face heat with anger. "You judge me too quickly, Outlander," she said coldly.

Kiara felt Thia's fingers grasping her arm. "Kiara, stop, this is not helpful."

Caedmon nodded. "Listen to your little sister, girl. She at least speaks sense."

Kiara shook Thia off. "What do you know of it?" she demanded as she took three steps closer until she was within arm's length of Caedmon. She forced herself to ignore the fact that her head barely reached his shoulders. Showing Caedmon how his physical size affected her would not help matters.

"Hey, I was thinking of going into the Village to see what we could find. How about it?" Teague broke in with a grin and a nod toward the street. "C'mon Caedmon, you know a pint of ale and a pretty new face might lighten your mood."

Caedmon ignored his brother and took a step closer to Kiara, erasing the little space that had remained between them. Kiara fought the sudden urge to step away again. Instead she smiled dismissively.

"Yes, why don't you listen to your brother, Caedmon, and go find a sweet Village lass to dally with. Stars knows, our serving maids have had their fill of you."

Caedmon's dark eyes were devoid of emotion. "How many men have you killed, Kiara?" he asked, his deep voice taking on a menacing tone as it radiated through her.

She tossed her head. "I've had plenty of kills."

He shook his head. "Animals, perhaps." He leaned closer using his size and physical proximity in an attempt to intimidate her.

Realizing what he was doing, Kiara forced her lips to tilt up in a shadow of a smile. Then she leaned even closer and whispered, "Same thing."

His eyes hardened. "That statement shows how naïve and unprepared you are." He turned away in disgust and said to Teague, "They really thought she would help? Are we to babysit?"

Teague's teasing manner disappeared swiftly. "Caedmon, you know why we're here."

"Why are you here?" Thia asked suddenly. "I, for one, would like an answer to that question."

Her sister had a point. What was the reason for their sudden appearance at the Inn?

Teague immediately became absorbed in something at his feet.

Caedmon ignored Thia altogether. And his next words made Kiara forget her sister's question. "You would do best to stop thinking of yourself as some kind of she-warrior and focus on what your real skills are." His voice dripped ice.

"And, pray tell, what are my real skills?" Kiara asked with a snarl.

"Hunting. You're a decent tracker and you've show you can shoot that." He nodded at her bow. "And you're adept at skinning and cleaning your game." Kiara was surprised – obviously he had been observing her over the last few days. But the warmth from his compliment faded as he glanced at his brother and said, "Perhaps that is her use."

She felt her anger crest. "Put your actions where your words are."

Caedmon raised his dark brows. "How do you propose I do that?"

"Fight me." The words were out before she realized what she was saying.

"Kiara no!" Thia cried in dismay.

Caedmon watched her for a moment as if judging the earnestness of her words. Then he tipped his head back and laughed. The sound was rich and

CATHI SHAW

warm and so completely at odds with the man she'd seen to date that she was momentarily stunned.

But as he continued to laugh, Kiara felt her face flushing and her anger growing. He had no right to laugh at her as if she were a mere child.

"I'm serious. Fight me." She took two strides to where he stood guffawing and shoved him hard enough that he lost his balance and stepped back. Kiara felt an irrational sense of satisfaction at that small step. "You think I'm so inept, then fight me."

His laughter stopped as abruptly as it started. "I don't think so."

"Are you scared?" Caedmon turned his back to her, ignoring her taunts.

Kiara's anger surged. "I've heard them say that about the large ones," she said loudly so their siblings could hear. "They talk big but when it comes to putting those words in action, they flee."

Caedmon stopped in his tracks. Once again he moved so fast Kiara was taken by surprise. In one move he turned her around, trapping her arm between their bodies. "Don't do this," he hissed into her ear as he held her fast

"Too late," she spat back and twisted herself loose. She stepped away and threw her bow and sheath of arrows on the ground.

Caedmon shook his head at her but dropped his sword with a clang, his dark eyes never leaving her face.

Kiara smiled. Finally here was something that was going to challenge her. She felt anticipation growing as her senses came to life with the promise of a fight.

Thia twisted her hands in dismay. "Kiara no!" she moaned softly under her breath. But Kiara focused her attention on her opponent and Thia's words faded to the background.

****

Teague moved to stand by Thia's side and for once his trademark grin was missing. "This is not good," he murmured in concern.

Thia watched as Caedmon reluctantly turned to Kiara, preparing to fight her.

"I've never seen anyone beat Kiara before."

Teague looked grim. "And I've never seen Caedmon lose to anyone." He paused and grimaced. "But I've never seen him fight a woman before. He's always been dead set against that."

Thia looked at her sister and Caedmon and saw how Teague's brother was delaying the sparring by continuing to circle her. She could tell from her body language that Kiara was starting to get annoyed. Perhaps Kiara had finally met her match. She let herself relax a bit.

Thia turned to Teague. "There's something that's been bothering me." She paused waiting for him to look at her.

He turned, a look of foreboding clear in his silver eyes. "Don't ask me something I can't answer, Thia," he pleaded.

Thia hated to push him but she needed to know the truth.

"Can't you tell me why you're here?"

Teague looked at her, remorse on his face. "Thia, I would tell you if I could," he said earnestly. Then he shook his head. "But I can't."

Frustration swept over her. "That's not fair and you know it. Teague, we're not strangers. We know each other. Keeping what you know from me is cruel. "

"I'm sorry, Thia," he said quietly, "I really am."

Thia looked at him closely. He did look sorry but she couldn't help being angry. It wasn't fair that the boys knew more about what was happening than she did. It seemed that everyone was keeping secrets.

60

"Are you really sorry?" she couldn't help saying, hurt making her words come out more harshly than she intended.

Teague looked miserable. "The most I can do is try to convince them to tell you."

Thia shook her head. "Who are they – can you at least tell me that?"

He turned back to their siblings. Thia also turned in that direction and saw they were still circling one another. Kiara was fuming. Suddenly she lunged at Caedmon but he sidestepped her with what seemed like superhuman speed. Thia blinked not believing her eyes. How could anyone move that fast? She turned to Teague but he seemed to be mesmerized by the dance Kiara and Caedmon were doing.

"Teague!" Thia reached out and grasped his forearm.

"Thia no!" Teague jerked away but it was too late. A hot prickly sensation began snaking up Thia's arm from where her fingertips had connected with his bare skin. She saw Teague's worried face as the electric shivers claimed her and then she was falling into a vision.

Fourteen strangers riding magnificent horses travelling through the forest. The hooves thundering into the earth. Then blackness filled the air and a vision of Mina surfaced. She was unconscious and limp in Caedmon's arms while Teague was at her side bleeding. Then the scene shifted again. The five of them were together and then fractured into separate pieces surrounded by falling rocks and dust. Then all faded to black.

****

"I told you I don't fight girls," Caedmon was saying patiently as he placed his hand on her forehead and proceeded to hold Kiara at arm's length.

Kiara growled. She was beyond frustrated. She'd never had a man refuse to fight her before. But Caedmon was just circling her and refusing to engage. And he was so fast and so strong that he had no trouble doing so.

Kiara pulled back and held up her hands. "Fine," she said. "You win. I'll back off."

He narrowed his eyes at her but then his attention was suddenly diverted. Kiara saw her opening and lunged at him. He quickly sidestepped her, then in one smooth movement pinned her to the ground. Kiara struggled to free one of her limbs but even though his attention was not focused on her, he refused to let her rise.

"Your sister," he said urgently and then pulled her to her feet in another one of those strange lightning quick motions that seemed to defy what should have been true about him.

It took Kiara a moment to compute what he'd said before her gaze flew to where Thia had been watching them duel. She saw her sister crumpled to the ground, her eyes rolled back and her limbs jerking.

Kiara was at her side in a moment pushing Teague away.

"She touched me," Teague said insensibly to Caedmon. It meant nothing to Kiara but Caedmon looked concerned. Kiara quickly moved Thia onto her side and gently cradled her head.

"It's okay," Kiara explained to them quickly. "She has episodes like this. It means she's having one of her visions." Teague looked horrified. Kiara added, "She will be fine."

Teague shook his head. "You don't understand," he moaned.

The jerky movements Thia was making slowly stopped, her eyelids fluttering. "See, she's fine," Kiara assured them. "We just need to move her inside to her bed now."

Caedmon reached for Thia.

"No," Kiara said firmly. "I will carry her."

Caedmon pushed her aside and scooped Thia up. She looked like a small rag doll in his arms. He looked at Kiara, his dark eyes softening for the first time. "I don't doubt your ability to carry her," he said, "but I will be faster."

Based on what she'd just experienced, Kiara couldn't argue with that. She led them through the Inn to their living quarters where Brijit was working.

Brijit looked up and when she saw Thia unconscious, dropped the mending in her hands and rushed forward. "A vision?" she asked Kiara.

Kiara nodded.

"How long did it last?"

Kiara shook her head. Truthfully she'd been sparring with Caedmon so she wasn't sure how long Thia had been having her spell before she noticed.

Teague stepped forward. "It lasted almost two minutes," he said, distress on his face. "This is my fault."

Brijit shook her head as Caedmon lay Thia down on the settee. "Nonsense," she said. "Thia's has had these spells since she was a baby. It's almost normal for her."

Kiara watched Teague, as he seemed to be struggling for words. "But this time it was my fault. You see she touched me." He gestured toward his bare arm. "Then ..."

To Kiara's surprise Brijit did not try to reassure Teague. Instead her mouth thinned and she asked Kiara to get a blanket for Thia. As she was leaving the room Mina arrived.

"Is everything okay?" Mina asked, her expression worried. "I saw Caedmon carrying Thia."

"She had another vision," Kiara explained. "She's still unconscious but maybe you should go in. I'm just grabbing a blanket."

Mina nodded and entered the room. Kiara smiled to herself. Now if her mother did say anything to the boys, at least Mina would be present. She was tired of secrets being kept.

****

Thia slowly became aware of the usual sensations. The iron taste of blood in her mouth, her wet skirts and undergarments. Her head aching. She moaned softly, hoping that Teague was no longer present. That somehow he'd not witnessed her fit.

She opened her eyes to see Brijit's face hovering over her.

"You're alright, Thia."

"Mina," she whispered.

Her beautiful blond sister stepped close to her side. "I'm here, love," she said reassuringly.

Thia closed her eyes.

Then she heard Teague's voice.

"This is my fault," he was telling Brijit.

"Nonsense, Teague. This happens to Thia. She has visions fairly regularly. There was nothing you could have done to stop it."

"You don't understand," he said miserably.

He was right, thought Thia, Brijit did not understand but for some reason Thia did not want him to try to explain it to her mother just yet either.

"Teague," she whispered, opening her eyes.

He leaned close to her, his silver eyes filled with concern. "I'm sorry, Thia," he said softly. "I tried to warn you …"

"I'm okay. It's not you." She closed her eyes feeling fatigue weighing her down. "I'm fine." She forced her heavy eyelids open and met his gaze. *Don't tell her.*

She watched as understanding dawned on his face. Then she slept.

CHAPTER EIGHT

When ten days had passed and the Elders still hadn't arrived, everyone was on edge and anxious. Kiara was practically climbing the walls. She paced the kitchen, her unrest almost overpowering.

"Why don't you go hunting?" Brijit asked her gently. Her mother was sitting at the big oak table in the kitchen sharing a pot of tea with Weylon.

Kiara looked at the wall clock and suddenly realized she had been pacing the kitchen floor restlessly for a quarter of an hour. She forced herself to stop and consider her mother's suggestion. She hadn't been out hunting in a few days. The thought of escaping into the woods was tempting.

"It would help you to burn off some energy," Brijit coaxed. "And we would be happy for a venison stew."

Kiara thought about it. Running through the forest for a few hours, tracking down prey sounded so appealing. She nodded in agreement.

"Why don't you take Caedmon with you?" Weylon suggested mildly.

Kiara physically recoiled. "I don't think so," she said immediately. The last thing she wanted to do was to spend time with Caedmon and open herself up to more of his insults. Since their aborted fight he'd refrained from speaking to her completely. And he'd been fairly easy to avoid as he'd taken to training at regimented times. All Kiara had to do was keep clear of the stable yard when he was training.

"Kiara, if you're this restless, imagine what he's feeling. He's used to training with an army and he's been cooped up in the Inn for days now," Brijit reminded her softly.

Kiara wanted to say that she didn't really care how he was feeling but she was aware of Weylon watching her closely. Weylon still gave Kiara an uneasy feeling but he was her mother's husband. And Brijit's unspoken message was to not disappoint her. Even if Brijit had been keeping secrets, she was still the only mother Kiara had known and one who had cared for and loved her through thick and thin. She owed it to her to be kind to their visitors.

"Alright," she finally agreed. "I'll find him and see if he wants to accompany me but I'm not talking him into it if he declines." And she intended to make the invitation so unappealing that he wouldn't be likely to accompany her.

"Of course not, dear," Brijit said with a warm smile and Kiara felt a stab of guilt. She pushed it aside, reasoning that she'd only promised to invite him not to encourage him.

Caedmon was easy to find. He was in the stable yard sharpening his dagger, which he seemed to spend a lot of time doing. Kiara wondered what he possibly could be dulling the knife on for it to need such regular sharpening. Perhaps it was just a habit he had. She smiled slightly, liking the thought of him having an irrational habit. Caedmon seemed far too collected and controlled, it was nice to imagine him having human quirks.

As she approached where he was standing, her heart sank because she saw that Teague was lounging nearby. And the fact was that she liked Teague. In fact she'd come to the conclusion that Teague was impossible not to like. He always had a ready smile for everyone. And he'd been very worried about Thia since her seizure, which automatically put him into Kiara's good books.

Kiara sighed. Both Teague and Caedmon looked beyond bored. And as much as she'd planned on being rude to Caedmon, she couldn't help feeling a bit of sympathy for them. The Inn in the winter was deathly boring. It must be more so for young men used to the more exciting places they saw on their travels.

"I'm going hunting," Kiara said off-handedly as she strode up to them. "Do you want to come?" She didn't put much enthusiasm into her voice.

Caedmon looked at her with suspicion. "Why are you inviting us?" he asked bluntly, his dark eyes narrowing as he studied her.

"My mother suggested I ask you," she admitted reluctantly.

Caedmon's face darkened and he opened his mouth with what Kiara was sure would be a refusal but before he could say a word his brother beat him to it.

"That sounds fine!" Teague said with excitement. "I could use a bit of a hunt. Just the thing, don't you think, Caedmon? I'll collect our bows."

Caedmon glowered at his smaller sibling as Teague hurried into the Inn. Kiara felt a spark of humor at his expense. Her heart lightened. This might actually be fun!

"I hope you know how to keep your soldier's feet quiet in the forest," she couldn't help quipping as she went to gather her hunting gear.

****

Mina and Thia were in the storeroom behind the Inn taking an inventory of the various medicines. Mina was noting what was running low. She planned to spend some time in the forest in the afternoon, replenishing what she could while Thia restocked other items, such as bandages and salves.

They worked silently for a while neither of them speaking of the unease that had fallen over the Inn.

"Kiara's gone hunting with Teague and Caedmon," Mina finally said to Thia with a grin. "I wonder how that's working out for her."

Thia looked up in surprise. Kiara had been avoiding Caedmon religiously for the past few days. Thia tried to imagine her hunting with him in the forest she considered her own private grounds. She couldn't help smiling at Mina. "It's probably a good thing. Kiara was going mad waiting for the Elders. This will burn off some of her frustration – provided Caedmon and her don't end up quarreling again."

"Well, Teague went with them," Mina grimaced, screwing her pretty nose up. "And aren't we all going mad? It feels like we're stuck in a holding pattern until the Elders arrive. I wonder why they are coming anyway? It's driving me nuts. That's why I'm going gathering this afternoon. Something to get my mind off the waiting." She paused. "Are you sure you don't want to come, Thia?"

Thia hesitated. She knew her sister was asking more than just if she wanted to come gathering herbs. She was really asking her if she was okay. Ever since her last seizure, Thia had stayed at the Inn, mostly in the kitchen and her rooms. She knew her sisters were both worried about her but she also knew that until the Elders came and explained what was going on there was going to be little peace in their house.

And she was sure the vision of the fourteen riders was somehow related to the Elders. She just didn't know how.

She looked up and saw that Mina was watching her closely, her green eyes filled with concern.

For her sister's sake, Thia forced a smile to her lips. "I'm fine, Mina." She reached over and squeezed her sister's hand. "Really I am. I'm just a bit tired this time."

Mina looked concerned. "It was different this time, wasn't it, Thia?"

Thia remembered the sensations that had overcome her before she lost consciousness. Touching Teague somehow induced the episode. She'd never had that happen before. And, although they hadn't spoken of it, Teague knew he'd sparked her latest spell.

But she didn't want her sisters or mother suspecting such a thing. Not until she'd had time to talk to Teague herself and tried to make sense of what had happened that day.

She forced what she hoped was a reassuring smile to her face. "Really I'm fine. I just would like a bit of quiet time this afternoon."

"Okay, if you're sure," Mina said and gave Thia a quick hug then gathered up her basket and gloves and disappeared through the back door.

It wasn't until Mina had been gone for a few minutes that Thia remembered the other part of her vision. Mina lying limp and broken in Caedmon's arms. Fear suddenly gripped her heart and she ran out the door, across the yard to where the gate was swinging in the wind.

"Mina!" Thia called.

She listened but all the she could hear was the wind stirring the leaves in the trees overhead. Mina was gone. And Thia couldn't shake the feeling that she might not be coming back.

****

Kiara had to admit she was surprised at how quietly Caedmon moved. Although she'd made the jibe about his soldier's feet just to rattle him, she'd truly expected him to be loud enough to scare the game away. But both he and Teague were almost eerily silent as they followed her.

Kiara was not only happy to be in the forest but confident she could show the brothers some of her favorite hunting spots. Although she told herself that she wasn't trying to show off her skills to them, she was proud of her prowess as a hunter. But they hadn't been in the woods for long when Kiara realized that something was amiss.

After they'd been hunting for almost two hours and there'd been no sign of game, Kiara knew something was seriously unnatural in her favorite domain. There were some days when she went hunting and returned home empty handed but this was different. On those days she would be sure to stumble across the odd rabbit or squirrel, she didn't hunt those because when you were providing game for an entire inn, small animals were of little use. And Kiara didn't kill for the fun of it. But today there was a strange absence of living things.

Kiara paused and looked at the boys. Teague smiled at her winningly. "Your woods are beautiful, Kiara," he said politely, but she saw the uneasy expression in his silver eyes.

Kiara automatically smiled back at him but then Caedmon intoned, "Where is the game?"

She frowned. Although she didn't really believe he meant it as an insult, part of her felt that Caedmon was blaming the poor hunting on her.

Kiara lifted her chin. "Usually the woods are teeming with animals." The feeling of unnaturalness swept over her again. She shook her head and looked around. "I don't understand it."

Teague's smile slipped and he looked troubled.

Caedmon spoke. "This forest feels wrong." His eyes shifted from left to right as if he were searching for an enemy that couldn't be seen.

Kiara suddenly felt a shiver run down her spine. Caedmon clearly felt it, too, which only confirmed what she'd been sensing. There was definitely something off today. The woods were deserted and there was almost a sinister feeling in the air.

Teague paused and seemed to be listening. "There's something here," he said suddenly.

That's when they heard the scream.

****

As Mina stepped into the forest she paused and took a deep breath filling her lungs with the fresh scents that always raised her spirits. Despite it being the early part of winter, the land was still green and there hadn't been any snow yet.

Mina realized that she hadn't taken the time for her usual wanderings since Brijit had broken the news to them about their origins. She'd missed this place so much. Usually this was her refuge.

Mina let her feet lead her, finding her favorite corners of the forest, places she'd been visiting since she was a little girl. As she began to fill her basket with herbs, roots and bark, she wondered about the Elders. Although no one had come out and said anymore about them, she hadn't forgotten that Brijit had suggested that Mina's birth parents were Elders. She wasn't sure how she felt about that.

Even though she'd longed to travel since she was a little girl, she'd always assumed that the Village was her home and that she'd came from, if not Village stock, then somewhere close by in the Lowlands.

She knew that she didn't resemble the Village folk – most of them were stocky dark featured people. In fact, she and her sisters really did stand out from the locally born children. But they hadn't moved to the Village until they were six or so. She'd assumed that at the very least they were Lowlanders. To discover that she was neither was unsettling.

As she wandered, Mina remembered a time when she was a young girl, shortly after they had moved to the Inn, and she'd caught a group of three or four Village children staring at her. When she'd smiled and tried to play with them, one of them had asked her what was wrong with her hair and eyes. She remembered the hurt she'd felt at being rejected by the children based on her appearance. When she'd arrived home and told Brijit about what had happened, her mother had sighed and taken Mina to the small looking glass in her bedchamber.

As Brijit stood behind her, they had studied her reflection together in the mirror.

"What do you see, Mina?" her mother had prompted.

Mina had stared at her reflection. She'd seen her long blond hair hanging in gentle waves framing her face. Her eyes were the same as they'd always been; a shade of green that she was told reminded people of the trees. But as her six-year old self had studied the reflection in the mirror, she hadn't seen anything too special.

She'd sniffled and said, "I see me."

Brijit had smiled at her then and hugged her. "Yes, you see you. My beautiful, unique girl. You *are* different than the other children, Mina, and people sometimes fear things that are different. You will make friends here. It will just take time."

But Brijit had been wrong. Making friends hadn't been easy for herself or either of her sisters. If the Village children thought her blond locks were strange, they found poor little Thia completely disturbing. With her copper curls that seemed to catch fire in the sun and her odd gold colored eyes, the children were often cruel to her. And Kiara, who might have had a chance of fitting in with her dark hair, couldn't help her naturally protective nature. She'd stood up for both her sisters when they were teased. Before any of the Village children could try to make friends with them Kiara had threatened the girls and challenged the boys to fights. It wasn't conducive to making a lot of friends.

But even without an abundance of friends, the sisters had one another and that had been enough when they were small children. But now that they were almost grown, Mina couldn't shake her growing desire to leave the Inn and explore the greater world. To maybe discover other people like her. She wondered if Séreméla, where the Elders came from, might be the place for her to start her travels.

Lost in her thoughts, Mina wandered deeper into the forest. She hardly noticed where she was going, as she was so familiar with this part of the wood. But a few minutes later when she knelt to gather some White Pine needles, she suddenly sensed she wasn't alone.

You're being silly, she told herself as she looked around the empty copse of trees she was kneeling in. There was no one else here. Still as she started to think it might be time to head back to the Inn, she couldn't resist the urge to turn every few feet and survey the area around her. Each time she stopped she saw nothing and felt foolish for doing so. Shaking her head she tried to lose the sensation that she was being stalked.

For some reason Mina found herself wandering forward instead of turning back toward the Inn. Soon her herbal collection was forgotten. Vaguely she realized that she was almost being herded toward the centre of the woods where there was a clearing but she couldn't stop herself. She began walking faster. Eventually she broke into a run and that's when the shadow made itself seen.

It swooped at her and she screamed.

Its hands were outstretched as it lunged at her and grabbed her arms. Then she was overcome by light and pain before darkness enveloped her.

CHAPTER NINE

Kiara starting running before she'd even consciously registered that the scream had come from Mina. An inner protective instinct set her feet in the direction of the scream and it took a few seconds before her mind registered what she'd heard.

Vaguely she was aware of Caedmon cursing under his breath as he followed her through the trees but Kiara ignored him focusing only on the overwhelming sense that she had to reach her sister; that Mina was in terrible danger.

The forest shifted, opening before her into a clearing and Kiara came to a sudden halt, horrified by the sight before her. In the centre of the clearing was Mina, suspended in a black shadow's embrace. Her sister was limp, her arms hanging uselessly by her sides, her head lolling back and, most horrifying of all, her feet not touching the ground. Kiara reached for her dagger but before she could pull it from her belt Caedmon had grabbed her arms and held fast.

"Let Teague deal with this," he whispered in her ear.

Kiara began to struggle. He was crazy if he thought she was going sit back and just let his little brother help her sister. But as Kiara fruitlessly fought against him as she saw Teague remove his gloves and slowly advance on the creature.

Before Kiara's stunned eyes silver light flashed from Teague hands as he stretched his fingers toward the creature. It let out an unnatural screech and dropped Mina's limp body then turned toward Teague.

Kiara stopped struggling against Caedmon and stared at the thing in horror. Its body was cloaked in black robes but as it turned to Teague, the hood fell back revealing a man-like head.

The creature's hairless head was covered with translucent skin, through which fine blue veins were visible. Its eyes were a deep red and were trained on Teague but he held his ground, the silver light growing stronger. The creature advanced toward Teague reaching out its own hands, an inky blackness flying from the tips of them and blending with Teague's silver light. For a moment Teague seemed to be held by the creature, his face leaching of all color and the creature let out a hissing laugh and turned toward Mina again.

"No!" Kiara cried, once again struggling against Caedmon's grasp but his arms were like two bands of steel holding her fast. "Let me go!" she begged.

"Trust him," he said softly into her ear. "Teague can do this!" His voice was filled with utter confidence and conviction.

Teague took a deep breath and a sudden flash of the silver light flew from his fingers toward the creature. It howled in anger and pain, then in a blue white flash of light dissolved into black smoke and was gone.

Kiara broke from Caedmon's arms and rushed to her sister's side.

"Mina," she sobbed. Her sister's beautiful green eyes were open but they were staring into nothingness. Fear suddenly gripped Kiara's heart. "Is she …" she trailed off, unable to finish the sentence.

Teague was kneeling beside her, his ungloved hands running over her body as he whispered something in a foreign tongue. Small sparks of silver were leaving his hands and entering Mina's lifeless form.

"She's alive," Caedmon said calmly. "Stay back and let Teague do his work."

Kiara nodding feeling hot tears well up in her eyes. If she should lose Mina... She pushed the thought away and continued to watch her sister's still lifeless face, willing her to respond to whatever Teague was doing.

Suddenly Mina took a deep breath and closed her eyes.

"Mina?" Kiara whispered. Her sister was breathing but unconscious.

Teague seemed exhausted from all he'd been through but he gestured to Caedmon, who scooped Mina up in his arms.

"We must get her back to the Inn as quickly as possible. Others will be near and will have seen the light," Teague said weakly as he gathered up his gloves and slipped them back onto his hands.

A million questions were racing through Kiara's mind but she suppressed them. She focused instead on leading them directly home. There would be time for questions later.

****

Weylon was waiting for them when they arrived at the Inn. He was heavily armed. The fleeting question of how he knew something was amiss flashed through Kiara's mind.

"What happened?" he asked Caedmon.

78

"They've found us," Caedmon replied grimly.

Who? Kiara wondered.

"The wards will keep them away from the Inn," Weylon said.

Caedmon nodded grimly, carrying Mina through the Great Room toward their private chambers.

Kiara heard their words as if from a great distance. She was too concerned about Mina, who still lay limp in Caedmon's arms, to really process what they were saying.

Brijit came running to greet them with Thia on her heels. Clearly Weylon was not the only one who had known something was amiss.

"No!" Brijit cried when she saw Mina.

"She lives," Teague said softly.

Thia looked at her sister, her golden eyes filling with tears. Kiara knew her little sister was as shocked as she had been but Thia immediately stepped into healer mode.

Hurriedly, Brijit led Caedmon through the kitchen to their private rooms. Kiara followed numbly. Brijit directed them to her own bedchamber. Caedmon lay Mina gently down on the bed. Kiara stood in the corner, biting her lip as she watched her sister for any sign of consciousness.

Kiara shook her head, as she looked at her sister, pale and unconscious on the bed. Mina's long platinum locks spilled over the pillow in soft waves, making her look younger and more vulnerable. Kiara clenched her fingers. *What* had happened to her?

****

Thia moved to Mina's side and was running her hands over her sister's body in rhythmic motions. She concentrated on attempting to soothe Mina's energy fields. She had been successful using such techniques in the past but something was wrong here. Mina's energy felt ... disturbed. It was as though waves were pulsing through it at irregular intervals. Trying to smooth it was not working. Suddenly Thia stopped the rhythmic movements and touched Mina's forehead. "She is burning with a fever but I don't know what's causing it," she told Brijit. "And her energy feels ... wrong." Thia looked over at Teague who was standing in the far corner of the room. He was pale with a faint sheen of sweat on his face.

"Teague, are you well?" Thia asked.

Caedmon stood beside his brother protectively. "He will be. He needs rest. I'll take him to our rooms and then I must speak with my father. Kiara can tell you what happened."

Teague, Thia called out silently.

He looked at her, his silver eyes filled with utter exhaustion. *I'll be fine, Thia.*

And with that they were gone.

****

Kiara stayed with her sisters and mother for most of the afternoon. Although Brijit and Thia were doing their best to treat Mina, Kiara could tell they weren't making any progress. And she still had no idea what had happened to her sister.

As she looked at Mina's limp body, she felt a wave a despair wash over her. She had to get out of this room, to do something, anything, rather than just stand here uselessly.

With Brijit and Thia completely occupied with Mina, she slipped unnoticed out of the room and began to wander through the Inn. The last thing she wanted was to run into Sukey so she slipped into her mother's private study, thinking that she might find something useful in one of the many books Brijit kept there. Kiara was wishing she'd paid better attention to the tedious lessons her mother had forced upon the girls as they were growing up. If she had she might have a better idea now as to what had happened to Mina.

She was trying to remember which of Brijit's old books discussed magiks. She was sure there were a few on such topics. She pulled the door open and found Weylon behind her mother's desk, clearly sifting through Brijit's personal papers. She froze.

"Weylon, what are you doing in here?"

He looked up with guilty surprise on his face. Then his features cleared. "Your mother asked me to look over a few documents for her," he said quickly. "What are you doing here, Kiara?"

She watched as he straightened the papers on Brijit's desk then looked at her expectantly.

"I was looking for a book. To see if I could find anything that might be of use in treating Mina."

"Ah," he nodded in understanding and looked at the bookshelves, teeming with volumes. "I'll leave you to it then," he said smoothly and quickly slipped by her into the hall.

Kiara stood for a moment after he left trying to pinpoint why she felt so uneasy about their exchange. Weylon was her mother's husband; it shouldn't be surprising that Brijit might ask for his advice. Still Kiara couldn't help looking at her mother's desk. The papers that he'd been going through were all neatly stacked. Kiara looked at the door and then moved behind the desk, her foot striking against something.

"Ow." Kiara bent down and rubbed her foot and then saw what it was she'd stubbed her toe on. It was an intricately carved narrow wooden box.

Kiara picked it up and placed it on the desk before opening the lid. It swung open to reveal a paper scroll.

Puzzled Kiara lifted the scroll out and spread it on the desk. It was very old if the faded ink was any indication. She studied the words on the page in front of her. If she had to guess, she would say it was an ancient dialect from the Western Realm.

Kiara had always had a gift for languages and Brijit had spent the long winters teaching the girls a variety of dialects used in the Five Corners. While Kiara generally despised books and complained when they were confined to studying in the house, she actually enjoyed their language lessons.

Now Kiara squinted at the words in front of her, trying to decipher this puzzle but she could only make out a few of the words. Suddenly she swept the scroll in her arms. While she might only understand a bit, it was clear that her mother was hiding more than just her secret marriage from them. Clearly Brijit knew the meaning of the Mark.

****

Thia sat exhausted by Mina's side. She'd done everything she could think of to try to help her sister, but Mina was unresponsive. Brijit was sitting in the rocker in the corner, her eyes closed. Thia knew just how worried her mother was. She sighed wishing there was something she could do.

Suddenly the door burst open and Kiara stormed into the room, a scroll tucked under her arm. Brijit's eyes flew open and she stared at her daughter.

"You have some explaining to do." Kiara's tone was acid.

"Kiara!" Thia protested but Brijit held up her hand and looked at Kiara.

"So you've found it," she noted, her voice quiet.

What was she talking about? What had Kiara found?

Kiara dropped the scroll she'd been carrying onto the table at the side of the room and then unrolled the parchment. Brijit moved to the table. Curious, Thia followed them.

"This was entrusted to me sixteen years ago. It is not the only copy but one of a handful," her mother told them.

Thia leaned forward and looked at the scroll then felt a pang of disappointment. "Oh," she murmured. "It's written in ..."

"... the language of the Western realm," Kiara finished for her.

Thia watched as Kiara squinted at the words in front of her. "It appears to be an ancient dialect, I can only make out a few of the phrases."

Brijit was watching her closely. "It's over two thousand years old. A fragment of a prophecy."

Kiara looked up, surprise and accusation on her face.

Brijit smiled gently. "As you've discovered, Kiara, each of you three girls is mentioned." She traced the ancient writing on the parchment with her index finger. Then she sighed.

"It speaks here of an Elder child, a fierce dark haired warrior-girl and a golden eyed ... hmm, I've never understood that part ..." Brijit trailed off.

"A golden eyed what, Brijit?" Thia asked before she could stop herself.

"Well, it seems to be the word for Halfling. But I don't know what is meant by that."

Kiara was still bent over the words. She looked up at Brijit with accusation in her eyes. "What else does it say?" she asked, her tone almost threatening. Thia was shocked.

But Kiara's mouth thinned, her eyes were cold. "Thia, Brijit is keeping more from us." She gestured at the writing. "I may not be able to perfectly translate this but it says a lot more than just mentioning us." She jabbed the parchment suddenly. "Here it makes reference to a child."

Brijit's eyes were filled with sadness. "I'm sorry," she whispered, wilting under Kiara's anger.

"Don't be sorry," Kiara said coldly. "Just tell us what it says."

Brijit shook her head. "I don't know precisely what it says. I only know what I was told and the pieces I can decipher."

Kiara didn't look convinced.

Thia laid her hand on her mother's arm. "Well, what were you told?" she asked gently. "It might help if you told us what you do know, Brijit."

Brijit nodded and looked at the parchment again. "This parchment outlines an ancient prophecy in the Five Corners. It speaks of the Marked Ones."

Thia gasped, her hand automatically going to her shoulder where she bore the strange birthmark she shared with her sisters.

Brijit looked at Kiara. "And this part, that you can almost translate but not quite, Kiara, it says 'From their number will be born a child who will end the current age of the living.'"

Thia stared at Brijit and shook her head. "You mean one of us is destined to give birth to ..."

"A savior or a destructor. Which the child will be, we do not know. But the Prophecy does indicate that this child will change the world as we know it."

Kiara made an angry noise. "The child will end the age as we know it, you mean."

Brijit rolled the scroll up and looked at the girls. "There are many in the Elder kingdom who believe this child will be a savior. That is why they took such pains to hide all of you here with me. The three Marked girls."

Thia unconsciously touched her shoulder again. She wondered how Kiara was resisting doing the same.

CATHI SHAW

Suddenly Brijit looked older than her years. "Please understand. I thought I'd done well with you three; I pushed the Prophecy to the back of my mind and concentrated on being your real mother. For you see, I fell in love with each of my girls. And over time I refused to believe that the Prophecy had any truth to it. Instead I looked at myself as blessed with the chance to be a real mother to you."

She stood and walked to the tiny window. "When you carried Mina in today," she closed her eyes to the memory. "Well, my duty was brought back to me in force," she whispered, "I thought I'd failed you."

"And you may well have at that," Kiara said savagely, anger making her voice raw. "Mina lives but doesn't she wake. Why is that, Brigit?"

Brijit shook her head. "I don't know what kind of magik was used on her. Teague has a better idea of what we are dealing with but he is too exhausted to speak now."

Thia started. "Why? What happened to Teague?" she asked, not bothering to hide the fear in her voice.

Kiara told them what had happened in the clearing. "I can't explain what I saw," she concluded, "But Teague brought Mina back to consciousness if not back from the brink of death."

Thia looked at her mother. "Could he be permanently harmed by what he has done?" she asked hearing the waver in her voice.

Brijit clasped her hands. "Thia, he is merely exhausted. What he did ..." she paused. "It is an ancient art, one that is almost lost and Teague is an infant in learning how to control his powers."

"His powers?" Thia whispered, not understanding what her mother was telling her.

Brijit spoke gently. "Teague is a *Draíodóir*, Thia."

85

And suddenly reality shifted and everything Thia had believed to be true wasn't.

CHAPTER TEN

Thia sat down suddenly, her heart beating unevenly. She fought to control the conflicting emotions that were racing through her mind. Teague was a *Draíodóir*. It didn't seem real.

"Who has been training him?" she asked softly.

Brijit came to stand behind her and stroked her hair gently. "He's been working with many different members of the Council over the last few years. His particular skill set is unique and he's not achieved mastery over it yet, hence the gloves. But what he did today was a miracle. He saved Mina's life."

Thia nodded, blinking back sudden tears. Teague had saved her sister's life. She tried to focus on that rather than on what it meant that he was *Draíodóir*. But it was useless.

The *Draíodóir* were an ancient brotherhood trained in the mystical and magical arts. They were generally feared in the Five Corners but at times they were also respected. The *Draíodóir* kept to themselves, often living solitary lives and as a result very little was known about them. There were many rumors that circulated about the *Draíodóir* and none of them were good.

"Are you certain he's saved her?" Kiara asked suddenly. "She is alive right now but just barely. The healing you've tried has done nothing to improve her condition. Perhaps he has only prolonged her dying."

"Kiara!" Thia protested, a sob escaping from her lips.

Brijit sat down behind her desk and put her head in her hands. When she finally looked up, her face was grey with grief. "I know she is alive now. That is something, Kiara. That is what I will hold on to."

"What do we do now?" Thia asked, as she fought to control the sinking sensations within her. "There must be something we can do, Brijit. If we use a healing rune together perhaps ..."

But Brijit was shaking her head before Thia could even finish. "I'm sorry, Thia, there is nothing more you and I can do. Whatever spell that thing threw at Mina was not of human design. I've sent word to the Elders but I think it's likely they are already on their way here. Weylon came here after a summoning. I am hopeful that their healers can help bring Mina back. I sense she is there, but unable to break from the spell. Until they arrive, we can only hope to keep her comfortable."

****

Thia escaped to the kitchen after the meeting with Brijit. As was her practice when she was upset, she took refuge in cooking. The order of preparing meals was a salve to her in times of great pain.

To say that this was one of those times was an understatement. Mina lay unconscious, how much damage she'd suffered was impossible to guess. Brijit had told them that they were at the centre of an ancient prophecy. And to top matters off, Teague was a *Draíodóir*.

The last bit of information felt almost like a betrayal. In her heart, Thia felt that she had known Teague for years. They had shared dreams and within those dreams she'd told him her deepest secrets and hopes. He was the closest thing to a friend that she had, even if their friendship was unconventional. As a child, due to her strange looks and unpredictable seizures, the Village children had rejected her. Teague had never judged her.

Thia could remember a myriad of occasions when she'd sought Teague out in her dreams to gain his advice and comfort. She thought Teague had done the same with her but now doubt crept into her mind and she wasn't so sure.

As she reviewed her memories of the time they'd spent together in the dreamscapes, she was starting to see a very different picture from the one she thought she knew. If Teague truly were a *Draíodóir*, he would have started his training very young, even before they'd started sharing dreams. And yet he'd never even hinted as to what he was.

Thia tried to remember what he had told her about himself and she realized that Teague had shared very little about the particulars of his life. She felt close to him that was true. She even felt as if she knew him and yet now she had to ask if she ever really *had* known him.

She supposed part of it could be explained by the fact that Teague claimed that he didn't realize she was a real girl until arriving in at the Inn. Why would one tell particulars of their life to a dream girl? One usually assumed that in dreams things were transparent.

This Thia could reason out but it didn't ease the keen pain she felt when she thought of what the future might hold. What did it mean to be friends with a *Draíodóir*? Did that even happen? She'd never heard of it.

FIVE CORNERS: THE MARKED ONES

CHAPTER ELEVEN

Kiara watched as the Elder party rode through the early winter sun. She'd been outside training again – she couldn't stand to be inside with Thia and Brijit hovering over Mina. Mina was still teetering on the brink of death, a fact they all knew but none of them would voice.

Kiara felt useless and inept. In an effort to get her mind off her sister's fate, she'd tried to recruit Jake and Tom to spar with her. Tom had flat out rejected her invitation and while Jake had accepted it, he'd done so reluctantly.

For Kiara's part she couldn't help feeling that he was just going through the motions with her. Caedmon's words haunted her training and finally she was the one to call an end to the sparring. Jake seemed relieved and made an excuse to go into the Inn for a drink. A few minutes later, Kiara caught a glimpse of him laughing with Sukey inside and she wondered if an interest in seeing the serving girl hadn't been behind his agreement to train today. Disgusted she returned outside to pack up her things.

She was gathering up the last of her training equipment when the sound of the hoofs from the Elder horses rang through the air.

Kiara stood where she was, wiping the sweat from her brow and squinting against the sun as she watched the party approach. She raised her eyebrows in surprise. There were more in the party than they'd expected. She counted fourteen riders. Brijit had said that never more than three Elders travelled to check on them at any one time. This looked like a small army.

The lead rider was clearly of the Western realm. He was tall and lean and, although it was hard to tell with Elders, Kiara would put him at a just a few years older than herself. He had blond hair and green eyes that were eerily similar to Mina's. He was clearly the leader of the party. He dismounted in a smooth fluid motion and the others followed his lead.

"Kiara Carnesîr?"

Kiara nodded; surprised that he knew her name.

"I am Meldiron Lossëhelin, of the Western Realm. We are here for Minathrial."

Kiara stiffened at his choice of words. He made it sound as if he were here to claim Mina. She reminded herself that the ways of the West were different than those of the Lowlands.

"We have been expecting you," she told him.

Meldiron gave Kiara a hard look. Then he turned to the rest of the party. Two Elders, a man and a woman, stepped forward. Although she could not say how she knew, Kiara could tell they were older than Meldiron. Elders did not age like humans. There were no lines on their faces and their heads were free from grey hairs and yet, they had the sense of wisdom and experience about them. But at the same time it was clear that they respected Meldiron.

"This is Saldur and Bellasiel. They are two of our most respected healers."

So they did know of Mina's condition. Kiara didn't even try to guess how they had come by that information. Elders had skills that normal mortals did not possess.

Bellasiel stepped forward and grasped Kiara's hand. Her eyes were such a pale blue they were almost without color entirely. "We are here to help your sister," she said, her voice soothing. "Will you take us to her?"

Kiara nodded and led them into the Inn.

"Brijit!" she called. Her mother emerged from her bedchamber, looking tired and old.

"Thank the spirits!" Brijit exclaimed when she saw the Elders. She stepped forward and clasped hands with Bellasiel, murmuring in the language of the Western realm.

Clearly her mother and Bellasiel were no strangers. Kiara felt a prick of annoyance. While Brijit claimed to know only what the Elders told her, it was becoming more and more obvious that her mother had been keeping secrets for a long time. Kiara wondered if Brijit even recognized when she was hiding information from them anymore?

Saldur stepped around the women and made his way into the sick room. Brijit followed with Bellasiel and the door closed firmly to everyone else. Kiara stood staring at the closed door for a moment, wondering what was happening on the other side.

A throat clearing reminded her that she was not alone. Kiara turned to find Meldiron immediately behind her with a tall Elder. She looked at them, questioningly.

"This is my kinsman, Arion." Meldiron gestured to the tall dark-haired Elder beside him. Kiara immediately did not like him. He had a haughty aura about him and gave her only the briefest of nods.

"Weylon Forborrow is here?" Meldiron asked Kiara.

Kiara nodded.

"We would have counsel with him. Bring him to us," Meldiron told her as if he expected her to do his bidding.

Fighting back her irritation, Kiara showed the Elders into the Great Room and then went to Weylon's room. He answered her knock immediately.

"They are here?" he asked before she could speak.

Kiara nodded silently wondering how he knew they had arrived.

"I will bring Teague and Caedmon."

"Fine," Kiara muttered under breath as she found herself now staring at Weylon's closed door. She wasn't impressed at the way she was having doors closed in her face this afternoon.

When the men had gathered in the Great Room, Kiara stood to the side of the room refusing to leave. They were in her home and she had some questions that she intended to get answers to. She wasn't going anywhere.

After preliminary greetings, the party sat at a long table. Kiara moved forward and took a seat at the end beside Caedmon. She looked around the table, silently daring them to ask her to leave. But no one questioned her presence and she felt a flicker of disappointment that there wasn't any opposition. She ignored Caedmon pretending that she hadn't seen the small twitch of his lips when she took her seat. He could read her mind far too easily.

"Where in the forest did the Hunter find her?" Meldiron asked Teague seriously.

Teague wrinkled his brow. "I'm not sure, we'd been hunting for a while. I don't know this area well ..." he looked helplessly at Kiara.

"We found them in Nell's Clearing," Kiara said in response. "It's the approximate centre point of the forest."

Meldiron nodded thoughtfully, his expression troubled. "*Draíodóir*, you say the Hunter disappeared without a trace."

Teague nodded. "There was no body."

Arion looked annoyed. "If there was no body, then you did not kill it," he said flatly. "It teleported. You know what this means."

A concerned murmur drifted around the table. The Elders were clearly upset.

"Your presence is known," Meldiron stated flatly.

Weylon nodded in agreement, his brown eyes serious.

"We will wait to consult with Bellasiel but time is now of the essence," Meldiron noted. "Weylon, I suggest you start making preparations."

Again Weylon nodded. Kiara was annoyed. They seemed to be talking in code even with her present. The next moment everyone rose. Apparently the meeting was adjourned and she still had no idea as to what was going on. Perhaps if she could talk to Meldiron alone she would get some answers.

"Shall we prepare rooms for your company?" Kiara asked Meldiron.

He smiled at her. "Thank you for your hospitality," he said politely. "But we will find our own lodging."

Teague appeared at her side. "Elders only sleep under the stars," he told her quietly as they watched the large party leave.

"In winter?" Kiara asked in confusion.

"In all seasons," Teague said with a wry shrug. Then he gave Kiara a small smile. She noticed that he looked especially strained and she wondered if he's recovered from his encounter in the forest.

"Thank you for what you did for Mina," she found herself voicing the words before she had fully formed her thoughts.

He looked surprised. Then shook his head. "Thanks are not necessary. She is essential to the future."

With that he left the room. Kiara watched him go, her brow wrinkled as she wondered what he knew that she did not.

****

On the second day after the Elders' arrival, Kiara and the others were told they were not permitted to leave the grounds of the Inn. Arion determined this rule when he caught Kiara trying to sneak off into the forest with her bow.

After being turned back and told that under no circumstances was she to leave the shelter of the Inn, Kiara stormed into the stable yard, her anger and unrest barely containable. She began training hoping to work off some of her energy but with no one to spar with she was stuck practicing her forms, which hardly burned off the energy she desired.

"Try lifting your elbow slightly in that move," a deep voice called from the other end of the yard.

Kiara whipped around to see Caedmon silently watching her from what she was coming to think of as his customary position against the stable. She felt a spark of irritation but pushed it down. He was the last person she felt like socializing with at the moment. But, she reminded herself, he was offering her training tips, perhaps it would be best to hear him out.

Lift her elbow. She tried his suggestion and executed the move again.

He was at her side before she knew it. Once again exhibiting that extreme speed she'd seen on occasion.

"How do you do that?" she asked him before she could stop herself.

"What?" he asked, his dark eyes puzzled.

"Move so fast," Kiara said irritably. "It's annoying."

The corners of Caedmon's mouth twitched.

"And it's not funny," she added angrily. "What did you mean about my elbow?"

"Like this." He reached around her and lifted her arm into position. Kiara tried the move again with her arm in the different position.

"Oh!" she gasped involuntarily as she saw what he was trying to show her. Suddenly she had more power behind her jab. She turned to him, excited. "Show me more."

Caedmon laughed. And Kiara stared at him for a moment. He'd not so much as cracked a real smile since he'd arrived but this was a real smile not a sarcastic smirk that he'd donned at her expense in the past. And suddenly his face was transformed into ... something attractive. She felt a jolt of awareness.

"What's wrong?" he asked suddenly, a suspicious scowl quickly replacing the smile on his lips. Well, that's more like it, Kiara thought as he glared at her.

"Nothing. Everything seems to be just fine," she assured him. "Will you show me more? I'm going mad inside the Inn. Just ... waiting."

He nodded as if he understood how she felt.

"Alright."

What followed were two of the most intense training hours Kiara had ever experienced in her life. Caedmon was a surprisingly patient teacher. He even acknowledged that she had more skill than he'd first given her credit for. Kiara accepted the praise graciously, resisting the urge to rub it in his face.

Finally they stopped and Kiara took a long drink from the rain barrel while Caedmon removed his shirt and then dumped the rainwater over his head. Kiara laughed; he looked like a giant drowned rat.

He cocked his head at her, then suddenly grabbed her and dumped a bucketful of water over her head.

"Hey!" she protested, looking down at her saturated tunic and trying not to stare at Caedmon's muscular chest glistening in the sunlight. "Not fair. Now my clothes are soaked."

He shrugged, "You deserved it for laughing for at me!"

Kiara looked at him, a smile on her face. This was a side of Caedmon she never guessed existed. A teasing, playful side – a Caedmon she could almost like. Since arriving at the Inn he'd been sullen and moody but beneath that rough exterior he actually had a fun-loving streak. He seemed so much younger when he was like this. Kiara shook her head wondering how old he really was.

"What?" he asked, a scowl marring his handsome face as he suddenly became aware of her scrutiny.

"I just didn't realize you had a playful side to you."

He raised his dark brows, "I am not playful."

"I like it," she added with a light punch to his shoulder. He rubbed it in mock pain and then turned to collect his gear. Kiara's gaze was drawn to the mark on his shoulder. She gasped and he looked back at her, questioningly.

"You have it too," she explained.

Caedmon looked confused for a moment.

Kiara loosened the laces on her tunic and pulled it down over her shoulder, turned her back toward him while pointing to the Mark on her own shoulder.

"The Mark of the Chosen Ones."

Caedmon looked at her, an unreadable expression in his dark eyes. "Where did you hear it called that?"

Kiara felt her cheeks heat. She turned and quickly pulled her tunic back into place. "My sisters and I are all Marked," she said lamely, for some reason not willing to give away Brijit's secrets. "We thought we were the only ones," she finished avoiding his eyes and trying not to think about the dead children she'd seen.

"Teague also has it," Caedmon offered.

"Do you know what it means?" she asked, trying to elevate the sudden tension in the air.

"No more than I suspect you do," he said as he pulled his own shirt over his head, all sign of teasing now erased from his features. Either Caedmon didn't know what the Mark meant or he wasn't permitted to talk to her about it.

"Have you always had it?" she asked suddenly

Caedmon nodded. "As long as I can remember."

Kiara paused thoughtfully. "Brijit said we also each arrived with the Mark already on us. And we were only days old when we came to be with her," she stopped then added musingly, "It makes one wonder, doesn't it?"

Caedmon looked at her sharply, "About what?"

"Well, whether we were born with the Mark or if it was put on us."

He paused in collecting his training gear and straightened. He looked stunned.

"What are you saying?" he asked suddenly.

"Just have you ever wondered if we were born with the Mark or if for some reason we were chosen and given the Mark?"

He stared off into the distance, a considering look on his face. "I hadn't much considered it," he admitted. "Does it make a difference?"

Kiara shrugged. "I suppose the end result might very well be the same for us. But if we were marked rather than born with it, then someone, somewhere is using us as pieces in a game."

"And if we were born with it ..." Caedmon trailed off.

Kiara thought about the dead girl. A shiver ran down her spine. She looked up at Caedmon. "If we were born with it, we have to ask are we really the Chosen Ones? I mean how do we know we are the only ones? There could others, couldn't there?" She held her breath. It was the closest she'd come to telling someone about the dead children she'd seen with Brijit.

But before Caedmon could reply Thia called to them from where she was standing at the door of the Inn.

Kiara turned to her sister.

"The Elders have called a council."

CHAPTER TWELVE

Kiara joined Thia and Brijit in the Great Room. All members of the Elders' party were present including the healers. She looked at Brijit, hoping that perhaps the reason for this gathering was that Mina had shown improvement. Her heart sank when Brijit gave a small shake of her head, indicating that nothing had changed with her sister.

Bellasiel was presiding over the gathering. "We need to take the girl to Séreméla. There is no hope of us doing more for her here. I can't seem to break through the magik that was used on her." She turned suddenly to Teague. "Can you describe what kind of magik it was, *Draíodóir*?"

Teague shook his head miserably. "I'm not yet knowledgeable enough to be able to easily name the different magiks," he admitted looking at his hands, failure on his face.

The dark haired Elder made an impatient sound. "He should be training in Séreméla," Arion said darkly.

Bellasiel waved away Arion's comments. "Yes, yes, in time but for now," she turned to Teague. "Tell me, can you describe what you felt?"

Teague cocked his head and seemed to be considering. "It was a darkness," he said slowly. "It seemed to be, this sounds odd but, feeding on her life force."

"*Deamhan*," Bellasiel murmured and the Elders around the table shifted uncomfortably.

Suddenly Arion was watching Teague keenly. "How did you stop its feeding, *Draíodóir*?"

Teague looked uncomfortable. "I'm not sure. I was acting out of desperation and used Brí to throw up a kind of wall. If that makes sense."

Bellasiel looked concerned. "What happened when you did that?" she asked urgently.

Teague paused and seemed to be struggling for words. "It was odd. At first nothing seemed to be happening, the creature was so intent on feeding from Minathrial that it was able to ignore me. So I pushed harder." Teague stopped.

"And?" Bellasiel urged her expression intent.

"It turned its full attention on me," Teague admitted quietly his eyes dropping to the table again.

"Did it feed from you?" Arion demanded.

Teague slowly nodded.

Arion said something in Elder language that suggested a curse.

Bellasiel's eyes narrowed. "But you are here, fully functioning and I don't believe anyone said you lost consciousness." She looked at both Kiara and Caedmon. Kiara shook her head. Teague had been exhausted after the encounter but he didn't lose consciousness.

"What did you do, *Draíodóir*?" Arion demanded.

Teague took a deep breath. "I don't know. I felt myself being sucked from my body and I pushed back. I don't know how else to explain it. Then it stopped and was gone in a puff of black smoke."

Bellasiel looked thoughtful. "Interesting," she murmured.

"It might be interesting," Arion said angrily, "But it also means that it will be tracking him."

Bellasiel nodded and turned to Meldiron. "It's clear that we can't stay here. They have been found and the enemy probably suspects that all the Chosen Ones are together. It would be too coincidental that the Hunter had fed on two of them in the same place." She paused. "And we can't give Minathrial the care she needs here."

"But we can't risk having them travel together," Arion interjected. "I recommend breaking them in to three groups at the least."

Meldiron nodded thoughtfully. "I agree." He looked at the faces around the table. "The Elders must accompany Minathrial back to Séreméla. Brijit and Weylon should come with us as well so we can gain a full understanding of what has happened in recent times." He looked at the remaining four. "And Teague must not travel with Minathrial. If they send the creature hunting then it will track both Teague and Minathrial - sending them on separate routes will keep it confused."

He paused, considering. "Instead of three groups, I think four would be best." He looked at Arion. "It would be too risky to send Teague without Caedmon and it makes more sense for the girls to accompany them. And two decoy groups would increase our chances of making it to Séreméla safely." He turned to Bellasiel. "Is it possible to create decoys?"

Bellasiel seemed to consider the question for a few moments. "In theory, yes. It was done in ancient times but not in at least a hundred years. I've never attempted it myself."

"I think we should at least attempt to do so. Arion will take one decoy group South and Saldur can take the other East."

"We will take the direct route West to Séreméla. With so many Elders in one group, the enemy is unlikely to attack while we are together, even if Minathrial is with us." He looked down the table at Caedmon. "Your group will take the Northern mountain passes. There are fewer of you."

"Mountain passes in the midst of winter?" Kiara protested, wondering if the Elders wanted them dead.

"Caedmon has trained for this kind of travel." Meldiron looked at Caedmon. "You've been through these mountain passes before?"

Caedmon looked uncomfortable. "Yes," was all he said.

"Good." Meldiron nodded satisfied. "He will get your party through."

Kiara did not like this plan at all. She did not trust the Elders to fully protect her mother and sister. And she certainly didn't like the idea of taking mountain passes in the dead of winter even if Caedmon did have experience traveling through them.

"Kiara, this is the best plan," Brijit assured her. "We must think of what is best for all."

Kiara looked down at her mother's steady eyes. At her side, Caedmon did not look happy but was not protesting the decision. Teague had not raised his eyes from the table since he'd shared his story. And Thia looked stunned by the sudden arrangements.

Kiara decided she had no choice but to follow through with the proposed plan. She pressed her lips together and tried to suppress the feeling that they were stepping into a trap.

****

Thia was in their common quarters, going through the cupboard where Brijit kept most of their medical supplies. She was putting together a small package of things that she thought they might need on the journey while trying to process the decisions that had just been made.

She didn't want to be separated from Mina and Brijit but the Elder's advice was logical. She was also still reeling from the information that had been revealed at the meeting about Teague. But she was trying not to think about that at the moment.

She reached for a roll of clean bandages and looked up as Brijit came into the room.

"I was wondering if you'd be here," she said with a smile as she crossed over and gave Thia a small hug. "How are you feeling?" she asked softly.

"Scared," Thia admitted. "Confused. Worried."

Brijit smiled. "All normal reactions and I'm feeling the same way, if that helps at all."

Brijit began to pack her own small medical bag.

"Caedmon and Kiara will take good care of you," Brijit continued assuredly and Thia wondered if her mother was trying to reassure Thia or herself. Brijit stopped pulling salves down and turned to her daughter. She sighed. "Logically I know that but at the same time I also have an irrational mother's instinct that I am the only one who can truly take care of you."

Thia gave her a small smile. "I haven't had as many seizures since the Elders arrived," she noted.

Brijit nodded, "It's always been that way. Your seizures tend to be less when they are present." She paused and seemed to be choosing her words carefully. "But you will be under an extreme amount of stress on this journey, Thia, and the seizures will come in abundance, I fear."

Thia nodded. She knew her mother was probably right. "I know," she whispered.

"I've spoken to both Meldiron and Bellasiel about including you in our party but they are both adamant that you belong with Teague, Kiara and Caedmon. They will not change their minds."

Thia looked at her mother, there were deep worry lines marring her pretty face. "I will be alright, Brijit," she said softly.

Brijit gave a tight smile. "I have to believe that is true, my daughter, but it is a mother's prerogative to worry."

She reached over and kissed Thia on the temple. "I will see you in Séreméla."

Thia nodded and hugged her mother, wishing she could cling to her like she used to when she was a small child. As they broke their embrace Bellasiel entered the room.

"You are both needed so we can ready the decoys," the tall Elder told them sternly.

Thia looked at her mother in confusion. While she had heard Meldiron mention decoy groups she did not understand how they would be formed.

"You will tend to Minathrial's wound and she can tend to that of the Draíodóir," Bellasiel told Brijit. Brijit nodded solemnly.

Hold it. Had she just said wounds? Why were Teague and Mina both needing wounds treated? She'd thought they were both starting to feel better. Thia shook her head. "What does she mean?" she asked her mother as Brijit collected bandaging supplies.

"In order to create a decoy party they must take a small amount of both Mina's and Teague's blood with them, Thia. Since the creature fed from them both, it is possible that it will sense the blood and think it is following them."

She focused on Thia's face, her eyes worried. "Are you comfortable treating Teague? I can do it if you'd rather."

Thia shook her head. "I'll be fine," she said hoping it was true. If she hesitated she feared Brijit would question her relationship with Teague and she didn't want to reveal too much about that until she'd had a chance to have a serious talk with him.

This would be the first time she'd been alone with Teague since she learned he was a Draíodóir. She still wasn't sure how she felt about that. While logically she could understand why he might have avoided telling her the truth, deep down she was still hurt.

She pushed such thoughts to the back of her mind as she followed her mother and Bellasiel into the hallway leading to Mina's chambers. There was no point worrying about such things now. This whole idea of harvesting blood worried her.

"The creature didn't drink their blood," she protested, trying to understand the Elder's reasoning.

Bellasiel smiled over her shoulder. "You ask very good questions, child," she said, but her voice was cold and the expression in her eyes was not pleasant. Thia sensed that she did not like being questioned. The Elder studied her for a moment and then explained how the blood contained the same markers as the energy force the Hunter had tasted. They were hoping that the Hunter would mistake the blood for the energy source itself. At least for a while.

Brijit squeezed Thia's arm reassuringly. "It will be okay."

Thia nodded but said nothing. She felt that Brijit was sending her a silent message not to question Bellasiel.

Teague was already waiting in Mina's room with Saldur. He stood when they entered, straightening when he saw Thia.

"We will start with Minathrial since she is already unconscious," Bellasiel told them.

Thia looked at her sister, so pale and unresponsive on her sheets and felt her heart twinge.

Saldur produced a curved blade and Bellasiel held Mina's arm, a silver dish poised beneath it waiting to catch the blood. There was something almost ritualistic about the way they were extracting the blood from her sister. Thia felt increasingly uneasy.

Brijit stood to the side with her bandaging supplies ready.

Quickly Saldur pressed the blade to Mina's fair skin. A small line of red appeared on her arm as blood rose quickly to the surface. Bellasiel put the silver dish under her arm and caught the blood.

Teague made a small noise and Thia turned to look at him and was alarmed at how pale he'd become.

"Are you alright?" she asked.

He nodded unconvincingly. He was so white he looked like he was going to collapse.

"Brijit?" Thia said softly.

Her mother looked up and saw Teague's white face. "Bellasiel," she said, and then spoke rapidly in the language they had used when they first met.

Bellasiel looked at Teague, her expression annoyed. She carefully covered the silver dish with Mina's blood in it and then motioned for Thia and Teague to follow her.

"This won't take more than a moment," she said as she led them to the room next door.

Bellasiel told Teague to lie down on the bed. She produced a blade and a silver container identical to the one she'd used to collect Mina's blood. She gave Thia the container.

"Hold it to catch the blood," she instructed coolly. "Do not touch his skin."

Thia positioned the container beneath Teague's arm and watched as Bellasiel put on a pair of leather gloves before steadily grasping his forearm and making the small incision on it. He turned an alarming shade of grey.

Thia caught the trickle of red liquid in the dish but her eyes were on Teague who looked exceedingly ill. Bellasiel took the container from her and then left Thia to bandage the arm.

"Are you sure you're all right?" she asked quietly after the Elder had left.

Teague opened his eyes and smiled weakly. "Yes," he said after a moment. "I'm fine." He tried for a smile. "I guess you discovered my weakness for blood."

Thia shook her head and smiled at him, forgetting for a moment how conflicted she was feeling about the *Draíodóir* business. He grinned back and she felt a pang in her heart. She looked down and readied the bandage, preparing to start wrapping his wound, which was still oozing blood.

"Don't touch my skin," he said as she reached for him, panic raw in his voice.

"I know," she said softly, remembering what had happened last time she had inadvertently grasped his forearm. She swallowed and gave him a reassuring smile.

You didn't hurt me, you know.

He looked at her, his silver eyes intense. Thia was suddenly aware of his blood dripping onto the floor.

"If you hold the one end of the bandage, I should be able to wrap it without making contact," she said quietly.

"Thia," Teague said softly as he held the end of the bandage in place. She knew he was watching her face but she kept her eyes on the task at hand and refused to meet his gaze.

"I'm sorry," he whispered miserably. "I should have told you."

Thia pressed her lips together and continued quickly bandaging the arm. She didn't want to have this conversation right now. When she was done she fastened the end of the bandage with a pin and only then met his gaze.

"A *Draíodóir*, Teague?" She couldn't keep the hurt out of her voice. "You never thought to tell me that?" She couldn't help it; the feeling of betrayal was keen.

He looked miserable but she refused to let it soften her resolve. She was devastated that he had kept such a thing from her.

"I didn't know *how* to tell you. Remember I wasn't sure you were a real person. And then when we did meet." He paused and then sat up slowly, his color faded fast but Thia pushed away her natural instinct to care for him. "How does one broach that topic? Oh by the way I'm a *Draíodóir*, I thought you should know."

"Yes!" Thia responded. "That's exactly how you could have told me. Why did you keep it a secret? Especially after what happened in the stable yard." She turned away blinking back tears. "You knew my secrets. It wasn't fair, Teague."

"I admit I played it wrong -"

She cut him off, anger bubbling over. "Played it? This isn't a game, Teague. I thought you were my friend. I thought we were close and that I knew you," she shook her head, suddenly furious with herself for the wetness she felt on her cheeks. "I've realized that I just don't know you at all," she whispered and then backed out of the room before he could say anything more. Before she lost control and said something she would truly regret.

CHAPTER THIRTEEN

The next morning the Inn was a hive of activity. The Elders were leaving two of their kinsmen to run the Inn while Brijit and the girls were gone. They wanted to keep an eye on things in the Village in case any more Hunters passed through this part of the Five Corners.

That morning before they left, Weylon called the four of them to a meeting. He had a detailed map for them that laid out their route including all the lodgings where they would stop between the Inn and the mountains.

"Once you enter the mountains you'll have to find your own places to make camp. Until then there are plenty of inns in the villages that will provide hot food and shelter."

Caedmon and Kiara studied the map side by side. Thia watched her sister leaning over the table beside Caedmon and was struck by how well they looked together. Almost as though they were made for one another. She suppressed a smile as she imagined Kiara's outrage if she knew Thia's thoughts. She would want her sister to pay more attention to the plans but, really, what was the point?

Thia didn't bother looking too closely at the map herself. She figured they'd have long days ahead of them and intended to follow Kiara's lead. She knew they would be expecting her to be the one holding back the group and tiring fastest. She actually expected that herself.

"There's one small problem we need to address before you leave," Weylon said after folding the map and giving it to Caedmon for safekeeping. He looked at them closely, his eyes very serious. "Under no circumstances must you draw attention to yourselves."

Caedmon nodded.

Kiara looked impatient. Thia knew how her sister hated being told the obvious.

"A group travelling to the mountains at this time of year is bound to draw some attention anyway. A group such as yourselves is bound to draw even more." Weylon paused.

"What do you mean such as ourselves?" Kiara asked irritably.

"Two young women in the company of two men. It isn't what one would expect in travelling companions at this time of year and in this part of the country." Weylon looked at them all. "The Elders and I have come up with a believable story."

Thia sensed that none of them was going to like this plan, based on Weylon's lengthy introduction of it.

"You," he pointed to Thia, "Will be travelling to see your grandmother in the foothills of the mountains. She's been ill and is a stubborn old woman who won't consent to leaving her home. To ensure her safety, you've decided that you will spend the winter with her."

That made good sense. Thia nodded, but had a feeling there was more to this story than just a sick grandmother.

"You are travelling with your sister and your husbands."

At the word husbands the entire group started protesting.

Weylon let them rant for a few minutes before he raised his hand for silence.

"Listen, there is no other plausible reason that you would be travelling with two foreigners." He looked at the men pointedly. "You are both easily recognized as Outlanders by your accents and don't even attempt to adopt a local accent, Teague, you failed miserably the last time you tried to do so."

Teague looked at the rest of them guiltily. "I still think that with enough practice I could manage it."

Weylon's face was stony.

Despite their alternate suggestions and protests, Weylon would not budge. Thia suspected that the plan had been confirmed with the Elders. When Weylon held out rings for each of them to wear, she realized that not only had it been confirmed but that it must have been planned even before the arrival of the group at the Inn. How else could the rings have been forged? There was no one with skill to make rings such as these in the Village.

It was an Outland tradition that married couples adopt the wearing of rings. The wives wore gold rings and the husbands wore silver.

"They have been made to the correct size," Weylon noted. When the four of them just continued to stare at the rings he added, "I would suggest you wear them to make the illusion more real."

Reluctantly they each took a ring and slipped it on the third finger of the right hand.

The meeting broke up soon after that. Weylon seemed satisfied with the results but as Thia returned to her chamber to finish her preparations for the trip, she couldn't help wondering how long this plan of action had been in place. And she wondered if Mina's attack had anything to do with it. But the Elders had not known of Mina's illness before they left Séreméla. Why had this ruse been preplanned unless the Elders had always intended to separate them from Mina? She couldn't help wondering if there wasn't a deeper purpose to this trip.

****

Shortly before noon, all the parties were assembled. The Elders had a special covered cart which Mina, Bellasiel and Brijit were settled into. Weylon was riding with Meldiron and two other Elders.

Each of the decoy parties had four Elders riding with them. The blood from Teague and Mina was carefully stowed in their saddlebags. Thia hoped it worked as Bellasiel had suggested.

Kiara, Caedmon, Teague and Thia were travelling to the North on four mounts. Thia approached the horses nervously, her stomach churning at the thought of riding. Even though Weylon had chosen a small gentle mare as her mount, she couldn't help feeling sick at the thought of riding for days on end. She rarely rode and when she did the horses were always nervous of her.

When she was a young girl, she'd tried to learn to ride as her sisters had done. But each time she approached a mount it would become frightened of her, shying and rearing. On one of the few times she'd managed to climb into the saddle, she'd been thrown so hard she ended up in bed for a week. After that Brijit had eliminated the riding lessons from Thia's daily activities.

The one bit of brighter news was from Caedmon. He had informed her that they would not be able to use the horses once they reached the mountain passes. But that meant the first part of the journey, which Kiara had estimated would take almost a month, would be spent in the saddle.

As they started out along the road, Thia caught herself looking at the gold ring that glinted on her hand. It had script in Outland language but she couldn't read it. She wondered what it said.

It reads together in this life and beyond.

Thia ignored the urge to turn her head to where Teague was riding behind her. Even though she knew it wasn't really fair, Thia couldn't shake the sharp feeling of disappointment in Teague. She was still upset by the fact that he'd hidden so much from her.

They rode for eight hours the first day. They only stopped once for a late afternoon meal of bread and cheese with some cold tea Brijit had packed into a jar. Because they had had such a late start, they planned to travel only as far as the inn at Brindle for their first night.

When they stopped for their small meal, Kiara outlined a potential problem. Both Thia and Kiara had been to the inn several times and they were well known in these parts. Tomorrow they would leave the areas of the Lowlands where they were known but with one sister a healer and both of them the daughters of a fellow innkeeper, people tended to recognize them close to home.

And this particular innkeeper, Mr. Grindel, was a sociable, kind man. He had two teenaged daughters and was always trading stories of raising troublesome girls with Brijit when they stopped at his inn. Brijit would always smile and listen sympathetically but she never shared stories of her own girls. If Mr. Grindel found that odd, he never said so. Thia believed that he was too distracted by the troubles his own daughters were constantly causing to really pay much heed to anyone else's. His wife was a quiet mousy woman who stayed in the kitchen. Thia had only seen her once and that was from a distance.

"Listen," Kiara said as she slowly chewed her bread. "We are well known in Brindle and I don't think anyone there is going to believe that both Thia and I suddenly married a pair of Outlanders." She paused and looked at the boys. "No offense or anything."

Caedmon grinned. "None taken." He looked rather amused by Kiara's unintentional jibe. "But what do you suggest as an explanation for being in our company?"

Kiara smiled. She'd obviously been giving this some thought. "I think we can tell the innkeeper that your father is an old friend of Brijit's. That much is true and Mr. Grindel is old enough to remember that Brijit is not originally from these parts. He'll not be suspicious to hear she had friends from the Outlands," Kiara reasoned.

Thia nodded in agreement. She liked Mr. Grindel and she suspected he would be more interested in hearing what was new in the Village than wondering why the girls were travelling with Caedmon and Teague.

"I'll tell him that we offered to take you on a tour of the Lowlands so we could prove how superior it is to the Outlands." Kiara laughed. "Mr. Grindel will like that, won't he, Thia?"

Thia smiled. Mr. Grindel was often complaining about the Midland travelers taking on airs when they passed through Brindle.

"What's more he'll think it's completely in character with what he knows of Kiara!" Thia couldn't help adding drily.

Caedmon considered. "Alright. But tomorrow we'll have to go back to the story concocted for us."

Kiara nodded. "That's fine but the other advantage to using this story now is that there won't be a clear trail of the married couples going to visit poor old granny."

Caedmon nodded. "By the time we get to Silver Vale tomorrow, we could have come from any of three directions?" he asked, his eyes indicating that he was following Kiara's line of reasoning.

Silver Vale acted as a kind of crossroads at the edge of the Lowlands where three main roads met. Provided no one saw them enter the town, they could have come from either the South, East or West roads.

Kiara nodded.

"Good thinking," Caedmon said with a satisfied smile.

By the time they arrived at Brindle it was well after dark and Thia was exhausted. She tried to keep her distress to herself but when she dismounted from her horse, she almost fell as she tried to walk into the entrance of the Inn. Teague caught her arm.

"Are you alright?" he asked, concern reflected in his silver eyes.

"Thanks," she said breathlessly, "I'm just a bit sore from riding. I'm not used to being on horseback for so long," she paused. "Can you keep a secret?"

"Of course."

Thia glanced over at Kiara but she was occupied collecting their bags and joking with Caedmon.

"I hate riding," she blurted out, surprised when she felt sudden tears pricking her eyes. "I'm sorry." She wiped hastily at her eyes. "I'm just tired."

Teague just nodded but he looked worried and kept his gloved hand on her arm as they walked the last few steps to the entrance of the inn. Thia didn't argue. To be honest she feared that without his support she would collapse on the inn's front steps.

Mr. Grindel greeted the girls as if they were long lost family. When they introduced the boys to him and Kiara gave her story, he responded with warmth and hearty laughter. His two daughters also greeted them with warmth although Thia noted it was directed at Teague and Caedmon more than Kiara and herself.

"You're a musician!" Annie Grindel squealed in delight when she saw Teague's mandolin.

"I like to play," Teague admitted modestly.

"Play for us tonight?!" Rachel begged, her glossy chestnut curls bouncing on her head, reflecting the light from the large fire. Annie clasped her hands in her excitement.

Thia resisted the urge to roll her eyes.

"Girls, the lad's had a long day of travel. Leave him be, there's no need for him to play his music," Mr. Grindel roared at his daughters as he set heaping bowls of lamb stew in front of them with chunks of fresh crusty bread.

As much as Thia didn't care for his daughters, she genuinely liked Mr. Grindel and his quiet wife was an amazing cook. She tucked into her dinner with more enthusiasm than usual, her appetite stimulated by the long ride.

They didn't linger in the great room, but used the long journey as an excuse to retire early. Weylon had warned them before they left that keeping a low profile would be especially important. Staying and visiting with Mr. Grindel and his family would have secured in the Innkeeper's mind that he'd seen them. And Teague playing his mandolin was out of the question because that would be a red flag to those forces that sought them out.

"You're going to have to lose the mandolin," Caedmon noted as the four of them made their way to their rooms.

Thia saw the pain in Teague's eyes. "Is that really necessary?" she asked.

"You saw the attention it drew, Thia," Kiara pointed out.

Teague nodded sadly. "Caedmon is right. We want to be invisible travelers and a musician is always in high demand at this time of the year," he sighed, his hands running over the body of the small instrument. "I'll sell it tomorrow morning."

Thia was especially grateful for the warm bed and her sister as her bedmate. She was not sure how she felt about sharing a room with Teague the next night.

She said as much to Kiara.

Kiara straightened. "I think Caedmon and Teague will behave in a reasonable manner," she said confidently. "I don't think either of them would want us to be ill at ease."

Thia studied her sister for a few moments, noting a softening around Kiara's mouth when she spoke of Caedmon.

"What happened between you and Caedmon, Kee?" Thia asked. "You were at each other's throats two weeks ago but now you seem to be almost ... friends."

Kiara laughed. "Not quite friends," she admitted. "But we have certainly called a truce."

Thia looked at her questioningly.

"He helped me with training," Kiara explained.

"He did? When?"

"Just after the Elders arrived." Kiara smiled ruefully. "You remember how I was going crazy stuck in the Inn with Mina so ill. The Elders refused to let me hunt after what had happened in the woods. Then I ran into Caedmon in the stable yard and he felt the same way, so we started training."

Thia raised her eyebrows.

"Turns out he knows a lot of strategic moves," Kiara admitted.

Thia watched the way her sister's face was lighting up as she spoke of Caedmon.

Kiara nodded. "You know he trained in the military?"

"Did he?" Thia said then mused aloud. "Are you sure that's right? Mina said he's only 17. If he's already trained in the army, how young do you think was he when he started?"

Kiara stared at her. "Are you sure he's that young?"

Thia nodded. "Yes, Teague told Mina. I know he seems older but I guess he's just one of those people who looks more mature than his age."

Kiara looked troubled.

"What is it?" Thia asked.

Kiara shook her head. "He told me he'd been training with the army for ten years." She paused. "Who sends a seven year old boy to train in the military? And how old was he when he received those tattoos?"

Thia was shocked. She tried to imagine a small boy in the barracks with soldiers. Kiara looked upset and Thia couldn't say she felt any better about it.

"There's something else, Thia," Kiara said slowly.

"What?"

"He's Marked."

Thia stared at her sister in stunned silence. How could that be? "Are you certain?"

Kiara nodded. "I saw the Mark myself when we were training." Her sister reddened. "He removed his shirt as it was hot. And there's more. He told me Teague is Marked as well."

Thia bit her lip as disbelief flooded her. Brijit had always told them they were the only Marked Ones.

"What does it mean?"

Kiara shook her head. "I don't know. And neither did Caedmon." She paused, seemed to be considering her next words. "Thia, what if there are others?"

"What do you mean?"

"Other Marked Ones?"

Thia noticed that Kiara was gripping the blanket a little too hard.

"What do you mean, Kee?"

Her sister seemed to be struggling with something. Then she forced a smile. "Never mind. I'm just tired. We should get some sleep."

Kiara then turned down the lamp and pulled the covers up. Thia lay in bed turning her sister's words over in her mind. What did it mean that Caedmon and Teague also were Marked? And what had her sister meant about others?

****

The next day as they prepared to set off from the inn, Teague was missing.

"Where is he?" Kiara asked.

Caedmon shook his head. "He was here this morning," he said, "he needed to take care of something. I assume he's selling his instrument."

They soon discovered that in addition to the missing brother, his horse and Thia's were also missing.

"Why would he take the horses?" Kiara asked impatiently.

Ten minutes later she had her answer as Teague came down the dusty dirt road driving a cart pulled by a sturdy pony.

"What is this?" Caedmon asked as Teague brought the cart to a halt.

122

"A cart," Teague said with a self-satisfied smile on his face. He jumped down from the seat and began piling their things in the back.

"I can see that," Caedmon muttered darkly. "What are you doing with it and where are your horses?"

"I've traded the horses and my mandolin for the cart," Teague informed him. "You and Kiara can ride your horses but Thia and I will travel this way from now on."

Caedmon looked about to argue. But Teague shook his head.

"Thia is uncomfortable riding, Caedmon. She is never going to make it to the mountain passes if we keep trying to make her ride at our pace."

"Teague," Thia protested, her face heating with embarrassment. What he said was true but she didn't want them altering the trip to accommodate her.

"No, Thia, you were exhausted last night and I'm willing to bet that you are feeling the effects of a full day in the saddle more than the rest of us." Teague looked at them. "What I suggest is you go ahead, do some tracking and hunting and then we'll meet at mid day break."

Kiara tilted her head considering for a moment. "It's not a bad idea. We may not be able to procure mid-day meals from all the lodgings we stay in and if we are keeping a low profile we may not even want to do so. If I hunt, Caedmon and I can prepare the meal so it's ready when you two catch up."

Teague nodded in agreement. "And having a cart makes the grandmother story more believable. After all most families going to visit Granny won't be riding the quality of horses we had."

Caedmon didn't look happy but he agreed. Teague helped Thia up into the seat beside him and they set off.

After they had been travelling for a few minutes Thia turned to him. "Thank you," she said softly.

Teague smiled. "You're welcome."

Thia licked her lips and swallowed. "Teague?" she began hesitantly.

He looked at her, "Yes?"

"I'm sorry I've been so hard on you for not telling me about being a *Draíodóir.*"

He looked at her in surprise. "It's alright, Thia. I know it must have been an additional surprise on top of finding out I was actually a real person. I do understand why you were upset."

Thia shook her head. "It wasn't alright," she argued. "It's just that we have been hearing stories about the *Draíodóir* our whole lives. Not many of them are good."

Teague nodded grimly. "I know. How do you think I responded when they told me I was a *Draíodóir*?" he asked. "I wasn't too impressed."

"How old were you?" Thia asked curious as to when he was given such news.

"Six," Teague said grimly.

Thia gasped. Even at six years of age she'd known what being a *Draíodóir* meant. She could only imagine how difficult that would have been for Teague.

She was silent for a few minutes, thinking about the upbringing the boys had received with Weylon. Both of them had been sent off to train in their respective professions, if that's what you called them, at an early age. It hardly seemed that they'd had childhoods at all. She was suddenly extremely grateful for the life she'd had with Brijit.

"You know, Thia, one of the nice things about you was that you didn't know I was a *Draíodóir*," Teague said after they driven a while in silence. "Mind you, I didn't know you were a real person but it was still nice to have someone, even in my dreams, who just liked who I was without the *Draíodóir* label attached."

Thia studied him for a moment. She could see how lonely he must have been growing up with the title of *Draíodóir* hanging over his head.

"I do like you, Teague," she said softly. "I'm sorry for how I reacted. I was being foolish. We have been friends, of a sort, for a very long time. It was silly of me to react the way I did."

Teague shrugged. "I didn't blame you."

"Well, it was wrong. I like you for who you are and that's something that will not change no matter what."

****

Even though they'd travelled for about 8 hours on the second day, Thia was much more comfortable in the cart. Teague and her had a companionable day, sharing stories and laughter. But they fell into silence as they approached Silver Vale. They were in strange territory now and there was almost a sinister feel about the land surrounding the town.

When they arrived at the Black Sparrow Inn in Silver Vale, they were all wearing their rings. Once again it was after nightfall when they arrived and Silver Vale was dark and unwelcoming. Unlike the previous night when it felt like they were visiting a friendly neighborhood, Silver Vale seemed to be locked up for the day and unwelcoming to strangers.

The Black Sparrow was located in the centre of the town and Thia was dismayed to see it filled with rough looking men. From their clothing she guessed they were miners on leave from the mines that were deep in the mountains to the northeast of the town. Their route did not take them through the mining mountains – Silver Vale was the closest they would come to that range, which was heavily mined for coal and precious metals.

Thia followed closely behind Teague and tried to ignore how the men were looking at her and Kiara. She made sure her hand with her "wedding" ring was visible.

"We are in need of lodging for the night, my good man," Teague said with a winning smile to the innkeeper. He was a thin, sour-faced man who had an air of bone deep fatigue about him. He didn't reply to Teague for a moment, just looked them up and down and Thia wondered if he was going to refuse their request. This was one of the lodgings that Weylon had specifically printed on their map.

"What brings you our way, Outlander, at such a time of the year?" he asked warily, his eyes shifting nervously to where Caedmon was towering.

"A woman, of course!" Teague said with a laugh, attempting to warm up the man. Thia wondered if it was even possible to warm this man up.

"My wife," Teague gestured to Thia. "Well not Thia, herself, mind you but her grandmother. She lives at the foot of Blackpaw Mountain and refuses to leave for the winter months," he said with a grimace. "Stubborn old dear," he added affectionately.

Thia hid the surprise from her face. The story Weylon had given them was to say the grandmother lived at the foot of Pinefrest Mountain, much further to the north. Blackpaw Mountain was at the eastern end of the Dark Hills range of mountains, where the mining took place. She wondered why Teague was changing the story but didn't question it. She would ask him when they were in their room.

The Innkeeper still looked suspicious but seemed to soften slightly.

Thia forced what she hoped was an apologetic smile to her face. "Granny is a dear but she is just so set in her ways. She doesn't like to leave her home."

The Innkeeper looked at her, then nodded as if he knew the type of woman.

"Anyway," Teague said, "My wife is close to her granny. We'd planned on visiting her on our way back to the Outlands but Thia here, I don't know how she did it, she talked me into spending the winter with Granny before we head for home." He lowered his voice. "We're newly married, you know."

The Innkeeper seemed to be believing their story.

"And my good friend here, Caedmon and his bonny wife agreed to accompany us to the old lady's home. " He leaned closer to the Innkeeper. "I'm hoping to talk them into staying for the winter as well. It's an isolated place, I understand."

The Innkeeper nodded. "It is that."

"Well I thought at least having another man present would save me from being snowed in with a houseful of women!" Teague said in a tone of male conspiracy.

"That's it would." The Innkeeper cracked a smile. "A bit of winter hunting to keep you sane, eh?"

Teague nodded.

"So you'll be needing two rooms then?" The Innkeeper asked, finally getting down to business. Relief washed over Thia. She hadn't been sure he would give them rooms and then where would they have gone in this dark town? She didn't want to think about it.

Teague nodded again. "We will. Just for the night – I want to try to beat the weather to Granny's house."

"I'd recommend a private dining room since the ladies are with you, sir." The Innkeeper suggested before lowering his voice. "There's a bit of a rough element here tonight with the mine shutting down. Some of them are determined to drink their last pay away, the fools!"

"The mine has closed?" Caedmon asked, speaking for the first time, surprise in his voice.

"Aye." The Innkeeper nodded, his expression grim. "It generally runs even through the winter but the owners have shut it down without a word of explanation. There are rumors that it won't be reopening even when spring rolls around. It's put some of the lads in foul humors."

Teague met Caedmon's eyes and the brothers seemed to be exchanging a silence communication. After a moment Teague turned his attention back to the Innkeeper. "We'd be very grateful for that private dining room. Thank you for suggesting it, sir."

The Innkeeper nodded and directed them to their rooms, which were adjoined by a small dining room.

Thia went into her room and looked around. It was a typical bedchamber; very similar to the ones they had in their own inn. Thia eyed the big double bed nervously wondering what Teague's thoughts were for sleeping arrangements. While they'd got on well during the journey, she wasn't keen to share a bed with him.

But her worries proved unfounded. Teague followed her into the room, opened his bag, and pulled out his sleeping roll.

"I'll sleep close to the door," he told her quietly as he rolled it out. "I don't like the look of those ruffians in the dining room. The sooner this night passes the better." He glanced up, his expression grim.

Thia nodded. She should have known Teague wouldn't presume to share the bed with her. He was her friend but she still felt a sense of relief go through her. She couldn't help feeling a bit guilty that Teague would be on the ground.

"I feel bad that you are taking the floor though."

"Don't worry. I'm used to it on our travels. Sharing beds can lead to unique problems for me," he said seriously.

Thia remembered what had happened when she'd touched him.

"Unfortunately, Caedmon learned that at an early age." Teague grinned, his voice taking on a playful tone. "Weylon wasn't too happy about having to purchase beds for two wee lads but he got tired of finding Caedmon on the floor in the middle of the night."

"Oh!" Thia could imagine poor Caedmon and Teague sharing a bed and Teague kicking out his bare foot in his sleep.

"Ah, don't worry about Caedmon. He was happy to have his own bed anyway once he started to grow!"

They laughed together.

Straightening from his bedding, he patted his stomach. "Let's go find dinner."

Thia nodded and turned to the inner door that led to the dining area. As she opened the door, a pleasant odor teased her nostrils.

The table had been set for four and the dinner of some kind of root vegetable and mutton stew was already served. There was a loaf of crusty bread and some cheese on the table as well.

Both Caedmon and Kiara were sitting at the table, clearly waiting for them.

"Come on, you two," Kiara grumbled. "I'm starving and Caedmon made me wait for you. The sooner we eat and get to sleep, the sooner we can leave this place behind. It has a unsettling feel to it."

Thia nodded in agreement. It seemed that all of them sensed the strange aura of the place. The sooner this night passed and they were back on the road, the better.

****

Kiara raised her eyebrows at Caedmon as they entered their bedchamber. There was one bed, as was to be expected for a married couple. But this bed did not look nearly big enough for her and Caedmon, both of them oversized to begin with.

They had merely dropped their bags on the floor before dinner, both of them hungry and eager to get some food in their bellies. Now they would have to discuss sleeping arrangements. And as eager as she was to sleep in the cozy looking bed, Kiara was not going to let Caedmon think she was soft. She planned on taking the floor in her bedroll tonight. But before she could say anything he spoke.

"I'll sleep on the floor," Caedmon said matter-of-factly as he began to pull his sleeping roll from his bag.

Kiara raised her eyebrows. "You just assumed that you'd take the floor?" she said testily. "I'm not soft, you know, I can easily take the floor myself."

Caedmon straightened up and looked at her. "You can take it tomorrow night," he told her. When she looked like she would argue, he added, "Humor me and don't argue for once, Kiara."

Taken aback, Kiara sat down on the edge of the bed.

"I'll happily let you sleep on the floor tomorrow," he assured her. "Tonight I'd feel better if I was in front of the door. I don't trust anything about this place." He paused and looked at her, his dark eyes troubled. "My gut tells me that you were right at dinner. The sooner we get on the road tomorrow the better."

Kiara climbed into the bed with her clothing still on. She couldn't shake the feeling that they might need to make a fast escape.

"If something does happen," Caedmon added, "Just remember that we are not supposed to be drawing attention to ourselves.

Kiara nodded.

Caedmon rolled into his makeshift bed on the floor.

Kiara turned down the oil lantern that was on the bedside table.

"Good night," he said a few minutes later.

"Good night," Kiara whispered and then closed her eyes and was surprised when sleep overcame her.

****

It was still dark when Kiara felt a large hand covering her mouth in the darkness. She began to struggle reaching for the dagger that was under her pillow.

"Shh, it's me." Caedmon's voice in her ear reassured her for a moment. "There's someone breaking into the room. Lie still and pretend to sleep."

Kiara nodded, listening carefully but all was silent. A moment later she heard the sound of the lock being picked on their chamber door. There was a click and then silence again. The door slowly opened inward.

Kiara strained her eyes to see who the intruder was but it was too dark to see more than a shadow figure.

The intruder moved silently through the room and glided toward their bed where it paused and studied them. Kiara forced herself to relax in Caedmon's arms, hoping she looked like a wife sleeping with her husband.

The intruder spent a long while watching them. Then it sniffed deeply, almost as an animal would if it were sensing prey. Caedmon stiffened. Then the intruder turned to the door leading to the dining room and glided silently toward it. *Thia and Teague*! Kiara's heart began to pound in alarm. Caedmon held her tight in a warning grip.

The intruder glided through the door. Caedmon was on his feet with that remarkable speed and across the room. Silently he followed the intruder through the door. Kiara reached for the lantern and lit it. There was a screech from the other room. Kiara hurried into the dining room.

Caedmon had the intruder in his grasp. It was wearing a long black robe with a hood that made it impossible to see its features. As Caedmon pulled back the hood to reveal a white hairless head, Teague and Thia burst into the room, clearly awakened by the noise.

Kiara stared at the thing in Caedmon's arms. It didn't struggle but stared at her with its blood red eyes. Kiara felt a shiver of cold run down her spine. This was a Hunter like the one who had attacked Mina in the forest that day.

It turned its head to Teague and Thia and hissed at Teague baring its pointed teeth. "*Draíodóir*." The voice was a scratching whisper. It started to raise its hands toward Teague and in a split second Caedmon violently twisted its head, breaking its neck with a loud cracking sound. He dropped the body to the ground, disgust on his face.

For a moment Kiara was frozen in horrified fascination as she stared at the body at Caedmon's feet. It was unlike any man she had seen before and yet she was almost certain it was a man of some kind.

Its head was bald and its skin was so pale and translucent that the blue veins under the skin were visible. Its red eyes were staring unseeingly at the ceiling and its mouth was open revealing the sharp points of its white teeth.

"Hunter," Teague said softly. "They know where we are."

Caedmon nodded grimly. "Perhaps this was a lone one," he said, the corners of his mouth turned down. "But we need to dispose of it and leave here at first light."

Kiara couldn't stop staring at the body. Even though she knew the Hunter had been there to kill Teague and perhaps all of them, she felt almost empty at seeing life so quickly removed from a man. And Caedmon seemed unconcerned about it.

132

She looked up at Caedmon, not sure what she felt. He had so easily taken a life. As she stared at the remains of the man in front of her, she suddenly realized how juvenile her comments about hunting must have seemed to him. She swallowed quickly, suddenly feeling sick.

Caedmon stepped toward her and she flinched away. She heard him speaking to her sister. "Thia, take Kiara to your room and stay there until morning. We leave at first light."

****

The next few days were uneventful. They spent their days travelling from village to village and there was no sign of more Hunters or any indication that they were being followed. Teague had come to the conclusion that the Hunter who found them must have been scouting on his own. Kiara shared Caedmon's bedchamber, taking turns sleeping in the bed but they did not discuss what had happened at the inn in Silver Vale. Kiara tried not to think about the side of Caedmon that had been revealed in that night.

The great mountains remained far in the distance and Kiara began to wonder if they would ever reach them.

Despite the distance of the mountains, the weather had decided to change. It had been bitterly cold all day and when they stopped for their mid-day meal, it was a miserable, freezing experience. As they were packing up Thia exclaimed over snowflakes starting to fall.

Kiara met Caedmon's eyes. They both knew that once they reached the mountains there would be snow on the ground but if snow was falling here on the Lowlands, then the mountains would be worse.

That night when they arrived at the hamlet of Green Lake, they were cold, wet and ready for warm beds.

The Innkeeper and his wife were kind and happy to see them. They didn't have many travelers at this time of the year, they admitted, so were pleased for both the business and the company.

It was when they were leaving their rooms to go down for dinner in the Great Room that Thia suddenly cried out.

Kiara felt a chill run down her spine. She knew from the sound her sister made exactly what was happening, and quickly looked up and down the hallway to see if anyone had seen her sister as she fell to the ground.

Stars, she thought to herself as she saw the chambermaid standing horrified in the hallway.

"She's fine," Kiara called reassuringly to the girl as Caedmon stepped forward, effectively blocking the girl's view of Thia. Teague was at Thia's side, her head cradled in his lap, his attention focused only on her.

When Thia opened her eyes she murmured. "No, no, no." Which was her typical response when she realized that she'd had a seizure.

"It's alright," Kiara said, in a reassuring tone. "You're okay, Thia."

But as often happened after one of her seizures, Thia seemed to be listening inward. This time it seemed to be more pronounced than was the norm after such a spell. And Teague did not seem to be aware of Kiara or Caedmon. Kiara couldn't help wondering if he was doing something to her sister.

"Thia," she said more sternly and Thia's golden eyes focused past Teague on Kiara.

"What did you see?" she asked.

Thia shook her head, tears filling her eyes. "Snow and falling rock and blood." She shuddered as Teague helped her sit up. "Something horrible is going to happen in the mountains," she whispered.

Kiara felt a shiver of foreboding snake down her spine. She looked at Caedmon. He looked back at her, concerned written on his face.

"We need to get you downstairs," Kiara said quickly. "That serving girl saw you and I'm sure she's shared what she saw with her employers. We are supposed to be keeping a low profile but word that a girl who is prone to seizures such as yours would not be the kind of news that could aid in our hiding."

To her dismay, Kiara discovered she was right. When they arrived downstairs the maid was speaking animatedly to the innkeeper and his wife. They both turned toward them as they arrived in the great room.

"I hope your servant wasn't scared," Teague said before Kiara could think of a plausible story. "My wife has taken to fainting spells." A look of concern passed over his face and Kiara was amazed at his acting abilities. "I can't help worrying but her mother has assured me that it's quite common for women in her, um" Teague reddened bashfully, "condition."

Teague could not have come up with a better explanation. The innkeeper's wife was all sympathy. She shook her head, putting her arm around Thia. "Come sit down, my dear," she said leading Thia to the table that had been set for them "A little bit of food will help. And don't you worry, young man, it is very common especially with first babies." She turned to her husband. "Why remember, Haros, I had such spells when I was expecting Jaerem to arrive?"

Her husband laughed and nodded. "That I do." He clamped Teague on the arm. "Nothing to worry about," he added with a grin. "But you look like you could do with a mug of ale!"

Teague, looking relieved, nodded at the man.

Kiara saw the servant girl watching them, suspicion on her face. The Innkeeper and his wife might have been convinced by that story but she sure wasn't.

"I told you she was fine. Just a faint, now you know why," Kiara called out to the girl, making sure she held her eye. While she didn't argue, Kiara felt the girl wasn't entirely convinced. If a Hunter passed through these parts she didn't think he'd have trouble getting this girl to talk to him.

Kiara swallowed her concern as the Innkeeper's wife brought them large bowls of steaming soup and crusty biscuits to dunk in it. There was nothing they could do about a suspicious servant except to move on quickly. Despite the discomfort they were sure to encounter, Kiara would be happy when they'd left the inns behind and were in the mountains. Her second sense told her they wouldn't be safe until that happened.

CHAPTER FOURTEEN

Seven more days found them in the mountains. Thia didn't speak of her vision again but they were all on edge. As they left the last inn, they had to abandon the pony and cart, as the snow was too deep for it to pass through. Teague sold the cart to the blacksmith in that town, while Caedmon sold his and Kiara's mounts to the innkeeper, who was hopeful to turn a profit on them the next time the army came through from the mountains.

They'd been lucky to find shelter in an abandoned barn the first night in the foothills but now they would be making camp with nothing more than a few pine trees as their shelter. Still Kiara knew it would be more comfortable than when they moved completely into the mountains.

Since they were staying outside anyway, they stopped their travels early and Kiara did a bit of hunting. She was able to get three rabbits for their dinner, which would supplement the bread they had from the inn the previous night.

As Kiara skinned the dead rabbits, her mind went back to Caedmon's killing of the Hunter in the inn. Was what he had done really so much worse than what she, herself, had done to these creatures? And she was going to eat the flesh of these – Caedmon hadn't done that.

Kiara couldn't say what it was about that night that had shaken her so much. She remembered the blank, brutal look on Caedmon's face as he broke the Hunter's neck. She knew the Hunter would have killed them without a second thought. Caedmon was only protecting them.

They had not spoken of the killing since that night. Caedmon behaved almost as if nothing had happened. Kiara knew that she would not be able to act with such coldness if she'd taken the life of a human, no matter how evil. At times it made her wonder how Caedmon had become so cold in killing. How many men had he murdered while in the army? Kiara wasn't sure she wanted to know the answer to that question.

By the time Kiara returned to camp, Teague had built a fire. Thia took the skinned rabbits and prepared them in a stew pot with some roots she'd found. Thia, always the cook, had also packed a small bundle of herbs for seasoning the stew and later as Kiara took her first spoonful of the tasty dish, she was once again grateful that her sister was so gifted. Kiara was sure that, had the cooking been left to her, dinner would have been a far less appealing affair.

Despite the warm stew in their bellies, it was a cold and uncomfortable night for all of them. Caedmon and her took turns with the watch. Teague had volunteered to also take a watch shift but both she and Caedmon had insisted that they wanted to keep watch. So Teague shrugged, rolled himself into his bedding, and was soon snoring.

The next day they began to climb into the mountains. Kiara could tell the climbing was hard for her sister. Thia didn't complain but climbing uphill in the snow while she was so much smaller than the others was not an easy task. As the day wore on, they had to slow their speed so Thia didn't get left behind. Teague began to walk with her. Although they didn't speak, he seemed to be silently encouraging her.

In the mid-afternoon the sky darkened.

"A storm is moving in," Caedmon announced. Kiara look at the darkening sky and her heart sank. "We need to find shelter and soon."

She agreed with him. A mountain storm was not something to be caught in. Survival in the mountains relied as much on the ability to locate shelter as it did on anything else.

Luckily, the mountainside where they now found themselves had multiple caves. Kiara and Caedmon began inspecting them, hoping to find one big enough for all of them to shelter in together.

After searching through caves that were either too small or too unstable, Caedmon called from a hundred meters or so ahead of them.

Kiara quickly climbed up to where he was, leaving Teague and Thia to follow more slowly in case what he'd found was not a practical shelter.

But he'd located a cave that was both large enough to shelter all of them and deep enough to keep them safe from the storm.

"Perfect!" Kiara said with a smile.

"Get them in there and I'll start looking for fuel – with luck maybe we can even have a fire," he said then looked skyward and dropped his voice. "I would guess this storm will last several days. I'll try to collect as much fuel as possible."

Kiara went into the cave with Thia and Teague. They would be warm and dry in the cave for the duration of the storm but she couldn't help thinking that they would be hungry. They only had a few dried apples and nuts in their packs. She looked out the mouth of the cave. The storm had yet to hit, she estimated she had a about a quarter of an hour to do some quick hunting and perhaps find more fuel. The hunting wasn't as plentiful in the mountain passes but they were going to need some food especially if the storm lasted more than a day or so as Caedmon suggested.

"Why don't you set up our bedding over there?" she suggested to Thia, pointing to the far end of the cave away from the entrance.

Thia looked at where she was pointing and nodded. Kiara put her pack in the back of the cave and took her bow and sheath of arrows from the pile.

Thia frowned. "Caedmon's stuff is not here," she pointed out.

Kiara looked around. "I think he didn't bother putting down his gear before he went to find fuel. Just set up the others. It will be easier to do while we have light."

"Hey did you see this, Kiara?" Teague was calling from the back of the cave.

Kiara walked over to where he was standing. Behind him was an opening.

"What is it?" she asked.

"It looks like it could be a route through the mountain," he said, his silver eyes flashing with excitement.

Kiara looked at the opening doubtfully. "You mean some kind of passageway?"

Teague nodded, barely containing his excitement. "If we could go through the mountain instead of over it, do you know what that could mean?"

Warmth, shelter and darkness. Or. "It could mean that we scout through to a dead end."

Teague shrugged, not to be deterred by her negativity.

"I think it could mean that we've found an easier route." He paused. "Look when Caedmon gets back and we're settled here, I'm going to do a bit of looking around."

Kiara shook her head and then marched to the entrance of the cave.

Thia straightened from where she was laying out their bedding. "Hold it! Where do you think you're going?" she asked.

"I'm just going to be 15 minutes. I have time to quickly scout for some food – if we're going to be holed up here for a while it won't hurt to have some game. Don't worry I won't go far and I'll keep an eye on the weather."

Neither her sister nor Teague looked too happy about her plan but Kiara left the cave before either of them could voice their protests. Outside the storm clouds were building but she estimated that she still had a bit of time. She looked around but there was no sign of Caedmon.

Kiara found hunting to be an act of frustration that afternoon. She didn't see a single living thing. It was as though all the animals were also taking cover from the storm. Finally, admitting defeat, she turned back to the cave. She arrived at the entrance to find Caedmon waiting for her, his expression murderous.

"Where have you been?" he shouted at her.

Kiara pushed her hair out of her face, annoyed that it had grown so shaggy on the journey. "Looking for game to keep us fed while we are stuck here."

He glared at her empty hands.

"Look," she shouted around the building wind. "I'm back alright. There was no game."

"Maybe I was wrong about your prowess as a hunter," Caedmon said darkly.

Just then there was an enormous cracking sound above them. Kiara looked at Caedmon before they both launched toward the entrance of the cave at the same time. Just as Kiara was about to step through Caedmon grabbed her by the arm and pulled her back.

"No, let me go!" She struggled against him as the entrance to the cave disappeared in a pile of rubble, snow and dust.

"Thia!" she screamed, breaking free of Caedmon and rushing at the now buried entrance, trying not to cough from the dust that was in the air.

Frantically Kiara began moving the rocks and debris from the entrance. Caedmon was heaving boulders to the side as if they weighed nothing. But after half an hour they'd made little progress and he sat back on his heels.

"Why are you stopping?" Kiara shouted above the driving wind and pelting snow, her voice frantic.

"This is hopeless, Kiara," he shouted back.

"What are you talking about?" she asked as she continued to claw at the rubble.

Caedmon grabbed her arms and turned her toward him. "There's nothing more we can do," He shouted above the storm. "We need to take shelter or we'd be dead."

Kiara shook her head. "I'm not leaving my sister."

"Kiara, you're being ridiculous. There's nothing we can do for them now."

She hit Caedmon in the chest but he didn't budge. 'You don't understand. It's my sister in there!"

He grabbed her shoulders suddenly, anger and grief on his face. "I do understand. It's my brother as well, remember?"

Kiara stopped anguish suddenly weighing heavily on her.

142

"I don't think your mother and Mina would like for us to perish here. We need to find shelter now."

Admitting defeat, Kiara followed Caedmon up the mountain through the driving snow, trying to see in front of her but failing miserably as tears clouded her eyes and froze on her cheeks.

Suddenly Caedmon stopped and grabbed her arm. "There's a shelter over here." He led her to a small cave.

"It is safe?" she asked doubtfully, remembering how the mountain had come down on Thia and Teague, trying to fight off the waves of shivers that were racking her body.

Caedmon shrugged. "It's safer than staying out in the storm," he said grimly and pulled her into the cave.

They sat in the dark, shoulder to shoulder, listening to the wind howling outside the cave and not speaking. Despite her heavy gloves Kiara couldn't feel her fingers. And she could not stop shivering. She'd never been so cold in her life. Her pack with her supplies and her sleeping roll was in the cave with Thia and Teague, buried under half the mountain or so it seemed.

Caedmon suddenly shifted next to her and awkwardly put his arm around her.

"You're frozen," he said gruffly.

Kiara shrugged in the darkness. "I-I'll b-b-be f-f-f-fine," she chattered, her teeth banging together.

Caedmon suddenly released her and she could hear him rummaging through his pack.

"Here." He pulled his sleeping roll out of the bag. "Get inside."

"W-w-w hat about y-y-you?" Kiara chattered.

He opened the roll, climbed in and then pulled her into it with him, his arms going around her. Kiara sighed into his warmness.

After a few minutes the shivering ceased. Caedmon was gloriously warm; Kiara had never felt anything so wonderful. Her fingers started to unthaw in painful bursts. As her body warmed her thoughts went to her sister, buried under those piles of rocks. Tears began to slide down her cheeks, soaking Caedmon's shirt.

Caedmon tightened his arms around her and she felt his body wracked with sobs. She wrapped her arms around him and, as the storm raged outside, the two of them offered each other what warmth and comfort they could in their grief.

CHAPTER FIFTEEN

Thia woke slowly. Pain knifed through her skull with a throbbing rhythm making her long to return to the nothingness of unconsciousness. But she was awake and there was no escaping that something was very wrong.

Panic engulfed her as she tried to remember what had happened. Was it a seizure? The throbbing in her head was familiar but, no, this felt different somehow. Pushing the lure of unconsciousness aside, she forced her heavy eyelids open only to be confronted with darkness. The black was so thick she didn't think she'd be able to see her hand in front of her own face.

She tried to lift her hand to her face to test that observation but she found couldn't. Fear washed over her. What was wrong with her arm? Thia wriggled, confused at first and then she realized that it was wedged to the ground beneath a very heavy weight. She tried to shift herself but she found she was pinned from shoulder to hip by that warm weight. She focused for a minute, feeling the cold, hard rock floor beneath her and the heavy lifeless but warm weight on top of her.

Thia took a deep breath, trying to calm her racing heart and immediately began coughing. Dust was thick in the air. She tried to focus. What had happened?

She shifted again and felt something warm and sticky on the side of her face.

Closing her eyes she tried to make sense of what her body was telling her. She was on a stone floor. And suddenly the memories came flooding back. The cave! Rocks falling.

Her vision came back to her. She had seen this before it happened. She tried to sit up but the weight on top of her was unyielding. Thia wriggled a bit more and got her hand free from where it was pinned beneath her. She reached up. Warmth muscle. It was a person on top of her. Her fingers explored some more and she encountered soft curls. Teague!

"Teague," she moaned. "Get off me."

But there was no response.

Thia pushed again but Teague was a dead weight. Suddenly her heart lurched to her throat. Was he actually dead?

Panic made her shift hard to the left. His body tipped to the right and Thia was able to squeeze out from under him.

"Teague," she said again more firmly. But still there was no response. She remembered the blood in her vision. Fear suddenly gripped her heart.

Reaching blindly in the dark, Thia felt the front of his shirt and could just barely feel his chest rising and falling. He was breathing.

Relief coursed through her making her dizzy. He was unconscious but alive. Obviously he was injured. She tried to see through the blackness in the cave to no avail. She needed light.

Crawling on her hands and knees, Thia slowly inched her way toward where she hoped she'd set up their sleeping area. It was hard to tell which direction she was going in the stark darkness. She remembered leaving their bags near the back wall of the cave. In her bag she had flint and steel along with a candle for light. She needed to see what was wrong with Teague in order to help him.

Her seeking fingers suddenly snagged on a piece of canvas – one of their travelling bags. Pulling it toward her she opened it in the dark and began to grope inside. Her fingers closed around an arrow tip and her heart sank. It was Kiara's bag.

A cry of despair escaped her lips. She'd forgotten about Kiara. Her sister was stuck outside in the storm without her supplies. Tears filled Thia's eyes again. She remembered all too well Caedmon's words about the danger of being caught outside in a storm. If Kiara hadn't found Caedmon, her sister had no chance of survival, especially with her pack trapped inside. Her throat tightened convulsively as images of Kiara lying frozen in the snow flashed before her eyes. Stop it! She told herself sternly. There was nothing she could do for her sister right now. She just had to believe that she was well.

Thia forced herself to continue feeling through the bag. She knew Kiara also had fire-starting equipment in her pack.

A few minutes later she had found a tinderbox and lit a small candle. It was difficult to see through the still settling dust but what she could see made her heart sink in horror. Teague was half buried in the rubble of the collapse. It turned out that only his torso had been pining her to the ground, that's why it had been relatively easy for her to wiggle from beneath him, despite his weight. From the way he was positioned she could only guess that he had tried to protect her from the falling rocks and in so doing had been buried himself.

Thia swallowed as she made her way back over to Teague. She knew she wasn't strong enough to pull him out of the rubble so she didn't even try. Dragging her eyes away from Teague she looked at the pile of rocks blocking the entrance to the cave. It looked as though half the mountain had come down there. She doubted that Caedmon and Kiara would be able to dig through the pile even if there hadn't been a dangerous storm raging outside.

Thia bit her lip as she wondered just how stable the rocks were. At the far end of the cave in, opposite from where Teague was buried, there was still the occasional rock tumbling down into the cave. It looked very unstable. She swallowed in sudden fear as she realized that if she tried to pull Teague from the rubble she might end up burying both of them.

Thia blinked suddenly as tears pricked her eyes. She hated to feel useless at any time but right now it was even worse. If she left Teague where he was, with his legs crushed in the rubble, he would eventually die. And while she had no idea just how severe his injuries were, she sensed they were very serious.

Teague. She sent out a silent call to see if he would respond to her subconsciously. They had been practicing using the silent communication a lot since she'd had her last seizure. She remembered when she'd regained consciousness from the seizure in the inn. Teague had been holding her head gently and sending soft reassurances to her as she surfaced from the vision.

Teague. She tried again but he didn't move. Thia moved the candle close to Teague face. He was extremely pale and had a faint sheen of sweat coating his features despite the frigid temperature. She blinked quickly, trying to not let fear overcome her.

Get it together, Thia, she told herself. She was a healer. She had dealt with serious injuries before. She knew what to do in emergencies and was often called upon with or without Brijit.

Pushing back her fears and taking a deep breath, Thia looked around the cave. That's when she noticed the passageway Teague had found earlier. It was still open. Her heart lightened suddenly as she remembered what Teague had said about a possible passage through the mountains. They might yet have a means of escape, if she could somehow ensure that Teague was well enough to move.

The three bags were piled in the back of the cave, far away from the rubble. Beside their belongings was the large pile of firewood that Caedmon had brought before he left to find Kiara.

Thia remembered how angry he'd been that Kiara had wandered off. She hoped he'd found her sister. Kiara was going to need to rely on the supplies Caedmon had in his bag if she hoped to survive in the brutal cold of the mountains.

Thia went back to the bags and began to take inventory. She had four candles. They wouldn't last long but the firewood was heaven sent. Sending silent thanks to Caedmon for his foresight, she quickly created a small fire pit and spent the next quarter of an hour coaxing the damp wood into a blaze. As the small flames weakly licked the wood, Thia nodded in satisfaction. A source of heat would be key to their survival.

Caedmon had collected enough firewood for three days. She knew this because Teague had teased his brother about being a bit excessive with the amount of wood he'd found. Caedmon had replied that it wasn't unusual for mountain storms to last for more than three days and his brother would be thankful for his preparations if they ended up being stranded for that long. Little did Caedmon know how true his words would prove to be.

In addition to the candles and the firewood, they had enough water to last them for a while since all of them had refilled their canteens at a stream they'd found on their midday break earlier that day. Thia felt a pang when she realized that they also had Kiara's water which mean her sister had none. But she knew the constant worrying for her sister was not going to help either of them. She needed to focus on things she could do something about.

Turning her attention back to Teague, Thia considered her options. She couldn't leave him where he was, he was too far away from the fire and the rocks were unstable. She needed to free his legs somehow and then try to move him. The easiest way to do that would be if he woke up but if she couldn't wake him then she would have to find a way move him.

She walked closer to where Teague was lying, holding the candle up to examine the rubble. How could she avoid a further cave in, she wondered then she shook her head and carried the candle close to where Teague's lower legs were buried. And what she saw had her heart sinking again.

Teague's right leg was buried beneath his knee; she couldn't see how badly it was injured without moving some of the rocks. His left foot was also buried in the rubble.

Thia furrowed her brow in concentration. Perhaps if she started moving the rocks herself rather than trying to pull him from the rubble she'd have more success and less chance of causing the rocks to crush them both.

It was time consuming work. Thia would move one rock, pause and listen to make sure the heap seemed stable and then move onto the next rock.

After what seemed like several hours she was exhausted. She'd made some progress but Teague's left foot was wedged beneath a massive boulder and she didn't know how she could remove that. His right leg was mostly freed now and it was definitely broken, in several places by her estimate. This was very, very bad.

Thia didn't even want to think about how they would be able to leave the cave if Teague did regain consciousness. He was not going to be able to walk any time soon. She felt tears of frustration and fatigue rise up in her eyes.

Shaking her head she went back to her bags and found her medical supplies. Now that she could get at some of his injuries, she would do the best she could to treat them. She also pulled Teague's sleeping roll from his bag along with a sweater he had buried in the bottom of his bag. She slipped the sweater under his head and wrapped the roll around him as best as she could. She would have liked to have put the roll beneath him, as he must be freezing on the hard cold rock floor but there was no way she could lift him to do so.

Thia then turned her attention to his broken leg. She had no supplies to set it and if it started to heal, it would have to be rebroken. That was assuming he lived long enough for his leg to mend.

Thia pushed that dark thought away. Instead she focused on finding her supplies to clean the nasty gash. She did so, flinching at the white bone that was clearly visible through his torn flesh. For once she was relieved that Teague hadn't regained consciousness. She could only imagine how much pain he'd be in if he woke. And she had nothing for pain relief.

Finally admitting that there was little else she could do for the moment, Thia reached up and pushed her hair out her face and encountered a crusty, sticky mess. She remembered the sensation of warm sticky liquid dripping on her forehead when she's first regained consciousness. She explored her forehead a bit with her fingers and winced. Clearly she'd cut her forehead in the cave in. From what she could feel it was not too deep but she couldn't really tell the extent of the injury without a mirror. Honestly infection was the biggest worry she faced at present – for both Teague and herself. Taking a small amount of water, she cleaned the wound the best she could without seeing it.

Thia then found her own sleeping roll and for good measure took Kiara's as well since her sister couldn't use it. She had a cold dinner of bread and dried fruit and stoked up the fire. She went back to where Teague was lying and made her own bed right beside him. It might not be as warm or as safe as further back in the cave but she needed to be near him for reasons she couldn't explain even to herself. Deep down she wondered what she would do if he died in the night.

Teague. She tried to get a response from him one more time but to no avail. Closing her eyes, Thia finally gave in to her tears and cried herself asleep.

****

When she awoke, the fire had burned down to embers. Cursing under her breath, Thia gathered the driest, smallest branches she could find in Caedmon's pile and coaxed the fire back to life.

To her surprise she had not dreamt at all during the night, if it was night. Technically it could be any time of the day or night but with the darkness in the cave, she could only assume that her body was on its usual day/night cycle. Usually her dreams were vivid and at times she would dreamwalk but fatigue had pulled her into a deep dark sleep of nothingness.

Her head ached and she reached up to where the gash was on her forehead and felt that a large lump had formed.

She continued to tend to the fire and Teague most of the day, trying to keep herself awake despite the fatigue that was pulling at her. She remembered that Brijit had always wanted to keep those that had suffered a head injury awake.

Teague's freed leg looked much worse than it had before she fell asleep but it was his buried foot that worried her the most. Several times that day, Thia checked his leg for any telltale red streaks on the skin of his leg, signs that would indicate the tissue was dying and he was succumbing to blood poisoning. But the skin above his foot retained its normal hue. Thia felt a sense of relief but she also wondered how long it would be before the tissue in his foot died. The boulder that trapped his foot was enormous and she had her doubts as to whether any blood would be circulating in his foot.

In desperation she continued to try to contact Teague. She decided that if he hadn't regained consciousness by that night, she would dreamwalk and see if she could contact him that way. She had never dreamwalked and not been able to find him before.

When finally she stoked the fire for the night and settled into her sleeping roll next to Teague, Thia felt his forehead and was alarmed to feel how hot it was. Desperation washed over her in a sickening wave as she stared at his unresponsive face. *Please, Teague, please wake up. I can't do this alone*, she pleaded. But his face remained relaxed in deep sleep and Thia fought to hold back the tears that threatened yet again.

The firewood pile had diminished by more than half and she didn't want to think about what she would do if he died or worse if she ran out of supplies and was forced to leave him by taking the tunnel.

Tears still wet on her cheeks, Thia fell into sleep, intent to dreamwalk to Teague but when she awoke later, she hadn't been able to contact him and his whole body was burning with fever.

With a sense of foreboding, Thia lit the candle and checked the skin above his leg only to see the red streaks like fingers snaking up his leg.

"No!" she cried, dropping her head onto his chest. "Teague you can't leave me. I need you," she sobbed.

Desperation engulfed her. Brijit always said that recovery from blood poisoning was almost impossible and that was with the best medicines available. Here Thia truly had nothing that could realistically save Teague's life. No medicine, no Brijit … and she was starting to believe no hope. The thought of life without Teague crippled her. She put her head down on his chest and wept.

After Thia had soaked Teague's shirt with her tears, she became aware of a sound beyond his breathing. Thia froze then slowly turned so she was facing the tunnel. A kind of rustling sound was coming from the darkness.

The rustling was coming nearer and nearer. Something was in the tunnel!

CHAPTER SIXTEEN

Mina became aware of herself gradually. She heard bird song in the distance, as if it were spring, but for some reason that felt wrong. Her limbs were heavy, as if they were pleasantly weighed down. She opened her eyes a crack to the brightness of daylight. Above her was an unfamiliar ceiling of warm knotted wood. Where was she?

She opened her eyes wider and tried to turn her head but a stab of pain flashed through her skull. Her head instantly began to pound and she felt as if it were going to split in two. A low moan filled the room and she realized it came from her own lips.

"Hush, darling." Brijit's gentle voice was soft and soothing. A moment later she felt her mother's cool fingers on her forehead, stroking away some of the pain. It felt so good, that soft, patient touch, just what she remembered from being ill and in bed as a little girl. Mina began to relax. "You're safe," Brijit whispered.

Mina's thoughts focused for a moment. Safe? What strange thing to say. Safe from what? She tried to open her eyes again and was assaulted by a bright light.

"Don't try to move just yet, Mina, you've been through a lot."

Her eyes drifted closed. It was too hard to stay awake. With Brijit's gentle touch soothing her, she closed her eyes and drifted back into soft sleep.

****

The next time Mina surfaced, she found she was able to open her eyes without the stabbing pain assaulting her. Now it was very dark in the room. She turned her head slightly and could just make out Brijit's shadow as she sat near the bed, her chin on her chest. Her deep breathing and soft snores filled the room.

It was night then. But where was she? Mina strained her eyes to examine the room in the dim light. After a few moments her eyes adjusted to the darkness and as she squinted she saw that the bed she was lying in was huge. This was very different than her humble corner at home in the Inn. She shifted on the bed, noticing for the first time the linen sheets that were cool and crisp on her skin.

Curious to learn precisely where she was, Mina tried to sit up. Immediately the room began spinning and bile rose in her throat. Hastily she lowered herself to her pillows, breathing hard.

What had happened to her? Why was she feeling so ill? She tried to remember but the last memory she had was of spending the afternoon with Thia in the storeroom before she went to collect herbs in the forest. She remembered opening the garden gate as she left the Inn's yard and heading to the welcome freshness of her forest. And then there was nothing.

Her head began to throb slightly as she willed the memories to resurface, but the harder she tried the more insistent the throbbing became. Finally exhausted and discouraged she closed her eyes for a moment. And sleep once again claimed her.

****

The sun was shining into the bedchamber when Mina woke and Brijit was sitting in her chair reading a book at the foot of the bed.

"Where are we?" Mina asked, her voice cracking and hoarse, rough from lack of use.

Brijit looked up at her, a wide smile of relief on her face. "You're awake," she exclaimed. "We are in Séreméla, the great valley of the Elders. The Elders have been using their most skilled healers to treat you." She stood and came to the edge of the bed. Mina felt her mother's cool and soothing fingers on her forehead again. "How are you feeling, darling?"

Mina paused and considered the question. She was surprised to discover that she was hungry. The ache in her head had subsided but was still thumping out a rhythm in the background. "I'm hungry. And my head hurts," she said softly.

Brijit nodded "I'll get you some food. Do you want to sit up?" But Mina shook her head. She was scared to sit up after the dizzy spell of the previous evening.

Brijit stood. "Alright, let me find you some breakfast and then we can talk."

While Brijit was gone, Mina studied the room in more detail. It was a lovely room. The sunlight spilled in through open windows that, to Mina's surprise, had no glass in them. The bed she lay in was as large as she had imagined the night before and the headboard was made of carved oak. Tipping her head backward slightly, Mina saw that there were leaves and vines carved into its surface. It was a piece of art. She smiled.

But she frowned when she saw the chair Brijit had been sleeping in. While it was a lovely wooden rocker, it did not look at all comfortable to sit in for hours on end. She felt a pang of guilt for worrying her mother so much that she'd resorted to sleeping in a chair by her bedside. That would have to end, Mina thought firmly. Surely the Elders would provide Brijit with her own bed now that Mina was awake.

Her mother returned with a tray that contained oatmeal, fresh fruit, water and weak tea. Brijit insisted on feeding her as if she were a tiny child. Mina was so hungry that she didn't want to argue.

"What happened to me?" she asked Brijit, between bites.

As she continued to spoon food into her mouth, Brijit told Mina all that had happened to her. Mina listened in stunned amazement as Brijit told of her encounter in the forest with the Hunter and how Teague had saved her along with the decision to separate her from her sisters for the journey.

Mina stared at her mother in shock. The story was so fantastical. She almost didn't believe it.

"So you're saying that Thia and Kiara have not arrived here yet?"

Brijit shook her head. "But they are not expected yet," she reassured Mina. "To ensure your safety we took separate routes. They are taking a very lengthy journey through the mountains."

Mina frowned. The sun streaming through the windows was the warm sun of summer but it was early winter when she'd gone gathering. "How long have I been asleep?" she asked.

"Almost two months. But you are in Séreméla, my dear. Winter doesn't touch this Valley. In the Five Corners it is the very depths of winter right now."

****

The next morning, while she was sitting up for the first time, there was a mild knock on the door. Without waiting for an answer the oak door swung open and a starkly beautiful Elder swept into the room. She introduced herself as Mina's healer.

Mina studied the woman for a few moments. Bellasiel was the image of an Elder. She was tall and graceful with the blond beauty that all Elders seemed to possess. But there was harshness around her mouth and a weariness to her pale blue eyes that Mina had never seen before in an Elder.

"You've had us very worried," Bellasiel told Mina softly, her voice drenched with relief. "For a while there, we weren't sure you'd be coming back to us." Mina was puzzled. The Elder was clearly thankful for Mina's recovery – far more thankful than a healer typically would be on the recovery of a patient. It was almost as if Mina's demise would have affected Bellasiel personally.

The Elder continued to examine her and then finally remarked with satisfaction on her progress. Eagerly Mina asked if she might be able to go to the gardens. She's glimpsed them through the windows and was longing to be outdoors again.

Bellasiel studied her for a moment, her eyes serious and assessing. "You are not strong enough to go out of doors," she said firmly. Mina opened her mouth to argue. But her mother shook her head.

"You've been through a lot, darling. Take this time to rest and recover fully," Brijit advised.

Disappointment rolled over Mina and she felt tears burning in her eyes. She was so frustrated with this room when she knew there was a whole world outside waiting for her.

Bellasiel was watching her. "You are eager, aren't you?" She seemed pleased with this fact. For a moment the Elder paused and seemed to be considering. "I have a compromise. Let me speak to Brigit."

Later that morning, Brijit told her that she could leave her chambers. "Don't get too excited," her mother said cautiously. "We must still stay indoors."

Disappointment was surging through her when Brijit held up her hand and smiled. "But Bellasiel has given us permission to explore the Sanctuary."

This did not overly excite Mina and it must have shown on her face. "Don't be too disappointed, Mina, this building itself is vast and unlike anything you have ever seen before. And Bellasiel has granted permission for you to explore the library. That is rarely given to visitors to Séreméla."

Intrigued, Mina followed her mother out of her room. She saw at once that the Sanctuary was an ancient building, with floors of polished old wood and walls of grey stone, interlaced with intricate carvings. And everywhere there were plants. Ivy grew over the stonewalls throughout the hallways. When they entered into what appeared to be a common area, there were small trees growing along the far walls, while a fountain bubbled in the centre. The cheerful song of unseen birds, hidden high in the branches of the trees filled the space. Mina felt an overwhelming sense of joy pass through her.

And everywhere tall, beautiful Elder people dressed in flowing light robes passed quietly by, smiling joyfully in her direction. Mina looked at Brijit in surprise.

"They are happy you are recovering," Brijit told her. "The Elders take the health of their guests very seriously."

Bemused Mina gave tentative smiles back to the people who drifted past them.

"Would you like to see the library now?" Brijit asked her.

Mina nodded.

The library was wonder onto itself. The ceiling of the circular room was so high that Mina wondered where it ended. A walkway spiraled up close to the walls, with ivy growing around endless shelves of books. In the very centre of the room was the largest tree Mina had ever seen. Its trunk was so wide she thought the room surely must have been built around it.

Brijit led her up the curving walkway until they came to a hidden alcove, two stories above the floor.

"Would you like to look at some of the books?" she asked.

Mina was speechless. There were more books in this room than she had ever seen in her life.

She soon found that while they were written in Elder language, she could understand many of them perfectly. She was suddenly very thankful for the hours Brijit had spent tutoring her in Elder language. There were books of Elder stories, Elder history, Elder philosophy and Elder geography. And they were all new to her. There was so much to learn. Mina let out a little laugh. Where was she going to begin?

Just as she was starting to feel overwhelmed, an Elder man with white hair and brilliant blue eyes approached her.

He bent his head in greeting. "May I be of assistance, Banphrionsa? I am Eöl Ar-Feiniel, the head archivist in Séreméla," he said kindly.

He called her by the Elder word for princess. She couldn't help smiling at the thought of this ancient Elder using a term of endearment with her. He certainly didn't look the type. He was the first truly old Elder she had ever met. She wondered fleetingly at his age but then realized she was staring at him rudely.

"Thank you," she said and then a thought took hold. "I would like to read about the history of Séreméla." Yes. That seemed to be the place to start.

He tilted his head and nodded. "There is much to read as we are an ancient people." Then he gestured toward the table in the alcove. "If you make yourself comfortable here, Banphrionsa, I will bring some materials to you."

Soon Eöl Ar-Feiniel had piles of scrolls and leather bound tomes piled on the table. Before Mina could feel too overwhelmed, the archivist sat down with her.

"Let's begin here," he said decisively, his lined hands grasping a bound scroll. "With the first known history of the Elder people."

****

Mina's routine soon revolved around her time in the library with Eöl Ar-Feiniel. The table in the small alcove became her domain and she couldn't get enough of the history of Séreméla.

Mina found that with her growing knowledge of the Valley, her desire to see the gardens beyond her rooms grew. But Bellasiel still was reluctant to let her go out of doors. She preferred to keep her in the Sanctuary and after some time Mina began to question why. She suspected there were other reasons the Healer wanted her indoors but she didn't know what they could be.

Mina discovered that Brijit had been given her own living quarters down the hall from Mina's room. Living quarters that she was supposed to be sharing with her husband, Weylon.

Mina hadn't seen Weylon since she'd awoken but she soon insisted that Brijit move out of her room.

"It's ridiculous that you sleep in a chair in my room when you have a perfectly fine bed just down the hall from me," Mina told her.

Brijit looked like she would argue but Mina was adamant.

"I do appreciate that you watched over me when I was unwell, Brijit, but I'm much better now. I don't need you jeopardizing your own health by sleeping in a chair instead of in a bed. Go."

Brijit. That was new. Mina had always called her Mama or Mother but upon waking in Séreméla, Mina found that those names felt odd on her tongue. Brijit was the only name that seemed to fit the woman who raised her. There was a growing distance between them and Mina couldn't explain why.

So reluctantly, Brijit moved to her own rooms and Mina was left on her own.

It worried Mina that there was little talk of her sisters. As the days passed, her worry grew and Mina asked Brijit more and more about Thia and Kiara. It soon became apparent to Mina that Brijit was making excuses for avoiding the topic. One day she would say that was that it was a long story and she wanted Mina to be well before she could share news of Kiara and Thia with her. The next day she would make an excuse about it being complicated.

Mina had a feeling there was something else behind her mother's refusal to talk about her sisters. And she was determined to find out what it was.

****

One morning as Mina was waiting for Brijit to come and take her to the library, a knock sounded at her door. Mina opened it expecting to see her mother but instead she found herself looking into green eyes that strangely mirrored her own. They belonged to a handsome young man she'd never seen before.

Surprised Mina just stared at him for a moment. He was taller than she was and was clearly an Elder. But there was something about his face that was hauntingly familiar. She couldn't put her finger on what it was that seemed so familiar about him. It was almost as though she'd seen him before.

"May I come in?" he asked after she stood studying him for a few minutes.

Mina started suddenly realizing that she was keeping him standing in the hall while she stared at him dumbly. "Forgive me. I just ... do I know you?" she asked.

He shook his head solemnly. "My name is Meldiron but I don't believe you know me." His deep voice had a musical quality to it and immediately Mina wondered if he sang. A harp had been brought to her room the previous week and she'd taken to playing it again. She noted that many of the Elders were musicians, often clusters of them would gather together in song as she made her way to the library.

"I'm very happy that you are doing better now," he told her earnestly.

Mina was surprised. How had he known she'd been ill?

He smiled apologetically when he saw the confusion on her face. "I'm sorry. I forgot that you were unconscious when we arrived. I was one of the party who escorted you back to Séreméla."

That explained it. She must have had some kind of subconscious recollection of him. Mina wondered if Meldiron knew more than Brijit about what had happened to her. "Can you tell me more about what happened to me? Do you know where my sisters are?"

"Your sisters are well," he said softly. "Put your mind at ease. They travelled a different route than you to Séreméla and we expect them at any day now."

Mina felt the worry that had been weighing on her heart lighten slightly.

"Minathrial, you must be very careful," he said seriously. "We know that your attacker could not be acting alone and we could only assume that there may be others hunting you."

Mina interrupted, "But why me?"

Meldiron shook his head. "We do not know if it is just you or all the Marked Ones. We could only assume that you were all in danger," he paused. "

Her heart sank. "So these Hunters could have found my sisters by now?"

Meldiron reached over and covered one of her hands with one of his own. "I can't say for sure, Minathrial, but I hope that what we've done has worked and that they are safe."

Mina nodded. "But you can't be certain of it, can you?"

Meldiron shook his head. Her heart clenched with grief and worry but she appreciated his honesty in telling her this.

"How long has it been since my sisters left the Inn?"

Meldiron hesitated. "Some time," he answered vaguely.

"They should have been here by now, shouldn't they?" Mina asked bluntly.

He nodded reluctantly.

"How overdue are they?" she pressed, determined to understand just how bad it could be.

"Seven weeks," he admitted quietly. "But I don't want you to worry about this. The weather has been very bad. We are protected in Séreméla by wards and summer is never far from us. But beyond our borders the Five Corners is

165

experiencing one of the worst winters in history. That alone could have delayed your sisters."

Mina looked at him closely. "Is that what you believe?"

Meldiron nodded firmly. "It is what I choose to believe for present. Our decoy parties are also delayed."

Mina nodded, suddenly feeling extremely tired. Meldiron noticed right away.

"I've kept you talking too long. I will take my leave now." He stood up.

Mina started to stand but he waved her into her chair. "Rest now. You are tired. I will come to see you tomorrow and we will talk more."

Mina nodded vaguely, her thoughts on all he had told her.

Meldiron paused at the door just as Brijit came bustling into the room, apologizing for being late. She halted when she caught sight of the Elder.

"Prince Meldiron!" Brijit gave a small curtsy. "I didn't realize you were here," she said apologetically.

He smiled down at her. "I was just leaving. I must apologize, I fear I've overtaxed your daughter."

Brijit hurried over to Mina as Meldiron left.

"Prince?" Mina asked weakly.

Brijit looked surprised. "He didn't tell you?"

Mina shook her head, "I suppose it slipped his mind to mention the fact that he was a prince."

Brijit raised her eyebrows. "Not just a prince, Mina. But the only living heir to the Elder dynasty. Prince Meldiron is the hope of the next generation."

CHAPTER SEVENTEEN

Thia saw an eerie glowing light beginning to emerge from the tunnel. She barely had time to move closer to Teague before the source of the glowing entered the chamber.

Strangely enough, it was a person, a woman. And it was her hair that was glowing. For a moment, the figure in front of her was so unnatural, so unreal that Thia wondered if she'd hit her head harder than she'd originally thought and was now hallucinating.

The woman was small, close to Thia's size. Her strange hair hung in waves down her back and lit up the cave. As she glided closer to where Thia and Teague were, Thia saw that her eyes were dark flat ovals. She was dressed in black robes and carried a small iridescent sphere. With a start, Thia realized that it was actually the sphere more than her strange hair that sent off the light that was illuminating the entire cave. Behind the woman were four more beings dressed in black, with the strange iridescent hair, following her into the cave.

Don't be afraid. The words in a female voice echoed in Thia's head as the woman continued to glide towards her.

Thia instinctively shrank away but the voice continued, *we are here to help you, Little One.* Soon the cave was overflowing with more of the glowing robe-clad humans.

The woman continued to approach Thia and Teague but her attention was focused on Teague. She was silent but seemed to be communicating without speaking with the others. Two of them came forward and gently took Thia by her arms, moving her away from Teague.

What were they doing? Didn't they realize how unstable the rocks were? They could crush Teague. And the boulder on his foot was impossible to move. Besides couldn't they see how sick Teague was? Moving him would just traumatize him further. She had to stop them! Thia began to struggle against the hands that were gently restraining her.

"Leave him alone," she said desperately, her words catching in her throat.

The woman ignored her and soon five more men moved forward and to Thia's amazement, they removed the massive stone from Teague's buried foot.

Thia was relieved to see that Teague did not move. She choked back a sob as she saw the black and yellow color of his foot. She knew from the frostbite cases that Brijit sometimes treated that the color indicated tissue death. Teague's foot was beginning to rot and if the resulting infection didn't kill him, it would be a miracle.

The woman seemed wholly absorbed in what she was doing. She began to run her hands over Teague, much in the same way Brijit and herself used their energy fields to sooth their own patients.

After what seemed like a very long time, Thia started to see something that she knew was not medically possible. As the woman ran her hands over Teague's injured legs his wounds appeared to be healing. Everything she had learned over the years from working Brijit told her this could not be true. But before her eyes she saw the color returning to his foot and his fractured leg beginning to knit.

The woman continued her work, her focus entirely on Teague. She looked up and two of larger men moved forward and lifted Teague. Then they began moving towards the tunnel from where they'd appeared.

"Where are you going?" Thia cried in panic, struggling against the arms that held her.

Suddenly the woman turned to her and held up her hand. Before Thia could process what was happening, darkness fell over her eyes and she lost consciousness.

****

When Thia awoke again she lying on a surface that was warm and gelatinous. She shifted slightly and felt the surface move with her, hugging her body. It was oddly comforting.

Turning her head she stared at her surroundings. She was in a strange chamber. Its walls glowed with iridescence and the walls and the ceiling were smooth and rounded. She had the sense that she was very deep in the earth. Warmth filled her and she felt herself drifting back towards sleep but then the thought of Teague crept into her mind and woke her completely.

Thia tried to sit up on the odd bed and after a few unsuccessful attempts, was able to push herself to a sitting position. She looked frantically around the chamber but she was alone. Neither the woman who had spoken to her in the cave nor Teague were in sight. Dread suddenly filled her. What if something had happened to Teague while she slept? She sent out a wordless message: Teague. But he did not reply. Tears flooded her eyes. She couldn't shake the feeling that she'd failed him.

Suddenly a rich female voice filled her head. *Be still, Little One. We will be with you shortly. Your friend is safe. I will come and take you to him soon.*

Thia was stunned that there were others who communicated in the same way as Teague.

Who are you? Thia asked in her mind. But there was no reply. She wondered if she'd imagined the voice.

A short time later the woman with the iridescent hair drifted into the room. There was no other way to describe the way she moved. While her feet were on the ground, she seemed to glide rather than walk. Thia stared at her. She was shockingly beautiful in a strange way. All of her seemed to glow except for her black, flat eyes.

She'd removed the robe she'd been wearing earlier and was clad in a long flowing material that seemed to reflect an inner glow. She appeared to belong in the chamber. She drifted toward Thia, her flat black eyes should have been cold but instead they were kind. Although she couldn't say how she did so, Thia recognized her at once as the owner of the voice that had spoken in her head.

An unexpected sense of deep love suddenly washed over Thia. She caught her breath, as she was held suspended in the most intense moment of love and caring that she had experienced in her entire life.

"Thia, I am happy to see you conscious," the woman said, her voice thick and strange as if she were not used to speaking aloud. The heavy words echoed through the chamber. Thia wondered how she knew her name. Fear pricked at her. The sensation of love returned tinged with an underlying soothing feeling. Thia's eyes narrowed. Were these feelings being sent to her from the woman in front of her? Was she being manipulated?

170

"Where is Teague?" Thia asked sharply, fighting against the calming sensations that were washing over her. The feelings suddenly ceased.

"He is safe. I will take you to him shortly. But first I must ask you to tell me how you and Teague came to be in our domain?"

Thia thought back to the storm and taking refuge in the cave and then the horrible slide of rock and mountain that had trapped them. She shook her head. "We did not intend to be here," she admitted. "The mountain came down and trapped us. We were merely taking shelter from the storm."

The woman floated backward, considering her words. "Interesting," she said thickly. *The mountain does nothing without a reason.*

Thia looked at her sharply. *What do you mean?*

She didn't answer Thia's question but instead asked another of her own. *Your friend is very special.* She was watching Thia closely. *Ah, you know this. Do others on the outside know what he is?*

Thia shook her head, uncertain what the woman was asking. "I don't know what you mean," Thia admitted. "He has been identified as a *Draíodóir.*"

The woman straightened, her face troubled. "Fools! They have no idea what they are dealing with," she growled. She studied Thia for a few moments. "Do you know what you are, my child?"

Thia was taken aback by that question. "I am Thia. I'm a girl and a healer." She paused. "I don't know what you mean," she admitted in a whisper as confusion clouded her thoughts.

"You may call me Celeste," the woman told Thia suddenly, "Your kind likes names, don't you? We forget the ways of the upper world."

"You don't have names?" Thia asked.

"We don't have need for names. We communicate without the archaic use of verbal speech. Less lost meaning," she sighed. "It is difficult to explain.

But you know how to communicate slightly in this way, although you are not fluent in our way of sharing. Still you are more proficient than most of the Above Grounders."

"Teague can do it," Thia said suddenly, "He communicates with me like that sometimes."

Celeste looked at her closely. "There are other ways you communicate with your friend as well, aren't there?"

The dreamwalks. Thia met her flat dark eyes in alarm. She had told no one of those, not even her sisters or Brijit.

"Don't worry, I can't read your mind, Little One," Celeste assured her. "You and Teague have a special bond. It is clearly visible to us." She gestured towards her flat black eyes. "We see differently from you Upper Worlders as well."

Celeste sighed. "There is much to explain and I don't want to overwhelm you," she paused. "Are you well?"

Thia considered that question for a moment. Despite the sensations having stopped, she still had an underlying feeling of contentment. In fact she thought she could have easily fallen back to sleep she was so relaxed. Then she realized the implication of that. She was not in pain anymore. Her hand went to her forehead.

"It is healed," Celeste assured her.

Thia shook her head in wonder. "How?"

"I will explain our ways in time. For now I sense your only reason for unease is the fact that you would like to see your friend?"

Thia nodded and leapt to her feet.

Celeste laughed softly, the sound musical in the small chamber. "Such haste. So unnecessary. But come we will set you at ease and then maybe you can help us."

172

Celeste led Thia through a complicated maze of iridescent tunnels with multiple branching points. It was impossible to tell if these were naturally occurring chambers or if the people who lived here had dug the tunnels. And Thia had never seen material such as that of which these walls were made. It was almost as if they were alive, for they seemed to be lit from within. She was tempted to stop and study them closer but Celeste was hurrying onward.

They soon arrived at a chamber that was similar to the one Thia had been in except this one housed multiple beds.

This is where we tend the ill, Celeste explained.

Thia looked around the room in wonder, noting that all the beds were empty. All except one.

Teague was lying in a bed on the far side of the chamber. She hurried across the room and automatically reached out to touch his forehead then pulled her hand back, remembering what happened when she touched his bare skin.

Are you afraid to touch him, Little One?

Without explaining herself, Thia nodded. And studied Teague. His color had returned to almost normal and he had the appearance of being in a deep but peaceful sleep.

Thia turned to Celeste, "Why is he not waking?" she asked. "Are his wounds are healed?"

Celeste nodded. "Yes. His body is healed but his mind seems to be trapped in a maze. We have not been able to bring him back to us."

Thia moved closer to Teague. His eyelashes curled in dark crescents on his cheeks. She noticed for the first time the light dappling of freckles over his nose and cheeks. His face was smooth and clean-shaven despite the fact that he'd been without a razor for at least a week. She tried to remember if she'd ever seen Teague with stubble and frowned as she realized she had not.

Do you know what he is? Celeste's question came back to her. Was Teague something more than a *Draíodóir?* If so, what?

When Teague was awake, his incredible eyes and overpowering personality took away from his other features. For a few moments, Thia just sat and studied his familiar face, her heart aching with worry and fear.

Teague. She reached out but there was still nothing from him.

"We have also tried to communicate with him, to no avail." Celeste paused. "I wonder if you could connect with him, Thia?"

Thia looked up at her, confused. "I just tried. There was nothing."

Celeste tipped her head to the side. "There is not nothing. He is there. Try again and you will see what I mean."

Thia shook her head but sent out the message once more, *Teague.* She waited but there was no response. It was as if his body was there but there was no presence that she recognized as Teague.

"You feel it?" Celeste asked.

Thia looked at her in confusion. "I feel nothing." She felt tears filling her eyes. "I don't understand that form of communication, Celeste. It only ever worked with Teague and he always initiated it. I think I'm doing it wrong."

Celeste considered her for a moment. "You can do it. You and I can communicate that way. But it is new for you." She sighed. "Let me explain what I sense when I try to communicate with Teague. He is there but it is as though he is behind a film. I can feel him and speak to him but I don't know if he understands me or not. And I have no idea if he is trying to communicate with me."

Thia looked up at Celeste in misery. "So what can we do?"

Celeste considered her for a moment. "I will teach you how to communicate as we do but I don't think even you will be able to get to Teague that way." She paused and looked at Thia. "The other way you communicate with him ... you initiate it, yes?"

Thia looked at her wide eyes. How did she know? In all the years Teague and she had dreamwalked together it was almost always Thia who found Teague rather than him finding her.

"At this stage, I think the dream communication would be best," Celeste said.

Thia spoke, "I tried it when we were in the cave but he did not respond."

Celeste nodded. "But you were both injured and fatigued. Now you are rested and well." She gestured towards a nearby bed. "I would like you to try again, if you would."

Thia considered. Maybe she could find Teague in her dreams. It had worked before she had known him, perhaps it would work now when it was impossible to reach him in any other way. She nodded at Celeste and sank down onto the strangely warm bed. Immediately Thia felt a soothing relaxation flood through her. She wondered what these beds were made of and then she suddenly didn't care as sleep pulled at her. She closed her eyes and let it tug her under.

****

As the dream world opened before her, Thia began to seek Teague. Their Dreamscapes were always the same but they did have a few reoccurring themes. Their favorite was the river path where they had first met in their dreams. When she arrived at the river path it was the same as it always was but Teague was nowhere to be found.

Thia concentrated and shifted to a forest grove where they sometimes found one another but again Teague was not there.

Quickly Thia shifted between every Dreamscape she could remember. In rapid succession she found herself in a great hall, followed by a wide and lengthy sandy beach, to a small schoolroom, a cliff edge, an open field full of wild flowers. All were empty and missing the one thing she was looking for: Teague.

Gritting her teeth Thia went to a place she'd only ever been once with Teague. It was a grey shrouded, frozen land that scared her. When she'd been ten years old Teague had taken her there and she'd been so frightened she'd begged him never to do so again. He'd agreed.

It appeared that he was keeping his word, as he wasn't anywhere to be found in the sinister Dreamscape. For a brief moment, Thia wondered what that Dreamscape represented for Teague and why he had taken her there that one time. She'd never thought to ask. Now she wondered if she would ever get the chance.

Defeated Thia returned to the riverbed, despair overcoming her. She didn't know where else to look for Teague. She'd tried all their usual haunts to no avail. She didn't think he'd keep away from her if he were able to come to her.

Thia put her head down on her knees. Was Teague truly lost forever? What if he was permanently injured? His body might be fine but his mind appeared to be missing. He showed no sign of life other than the breathing and the heartbeat. Despite what Celeste had sensed, deep down Thia feared that he might be gone forever.

Suddenly she knew that she wasn't ready for him to disappear from her life. She wanted and needed him to be there with her. She'd lost Kiara and Mina. Brijit was far away. If Teague was gone as well … it was too much to bear. Thia put her head down on her arms and gave in to her sorrow. Great retching sobs shook her body.

176

Then she felt a warm hand on her shoulder.

Thia, why are you crying?

She was so stunned to hear his voice just when she'd convinced herself he was gone forever that Thia could only look into Teague's silver eyes in confusion.

Teague! She exclaimed and leapt to her feet before throwing her arms around his neck.

He laughed at her. *Why are you so excited to see me? I guess I truly am forgiven now?*

Thia looked at him in concern. Did he not realize that time had passed?

Teague, we're in big trouble, she said a sob catching her words.

Teague draped his arm around her shoulders and sat down beside her on the grassy bank.

Shhh, now Thia, it can't be that bad can it?

She looked up at him bleary eyed. *You really have no idea, do you?*

A puzzled expression crossed his face as worry filled his eyes. Tell me, he said softly.

Thia told Teague everything that had happened. The mountain coming down on them. His legs and infection. Her certainty that he would die. Celeste and her people finding them and bringing them to their dwelling underground. And finally the fact that they couldn't wake him.

When she finished, Teague looked at her in amazement. *And I'm still unresponsive?* he asked, his voice edged with panic.

Thia nodded.

It worked, he mused almost to himself.

What worked? she asked in confusion.

Teague looked at her. *As part of my training as a Draíodóir I under went a spell that would be enacted if a life threatening injury were to occur.*

177

When he saw the confusion on Thia's face, he explained. *If a Draíodóir is seriously injured he or she could be susceptible to having his or her mind tapped and the secrets of the clan could be revealed.*

Thia nodded, understanding dawning on her. *So you are in this state as a way of protecting your knowledge?*

Teague nodded. *Even someone with as limited training as I, has enough knowledge that could be dangerous in some hands.*

Thia sighed. *So how can we wake you up?*

Teague looked thoughtful. *Is this Celeste a threat?*

Thia shook her head helplessly. *I don't think so. She seems concerned about you. She healed both our injuries and has been kind. And while her ways are different than ours, I do trust her. She seems to know more about what we are than any one else does. She said you are special.*

Teague nodded thoughtfully. *I would like to meet her. You say she speaks in this way always.*

Thia paused. *She said they don't speak with words. But her people don't seem to dreamwalk. This form of communication intrigues her. She does communicate like you do. It seems to be her preferred form of language.*

Teague dropped his head into his hands.

What's wrong? Thia asked in concern.

He looked up at her, his expression miserable. *I don't know how to break the spell,* he admitted.

What? Thia asked, fear gripping her. *Are you saying you can't just wake up now?*

Teague shook his head sadly. *The spell is only enacted if death is imminent, to protect the knowledge. But typically the person does not revive from death.* He stopped abruptly as if another thought had just occurred to him. *Was I dead, Thia?*

She shook her head. *I was with you through it all. You were never dead but you were close to dying and I think you would have eventually succumbed to your injuries if we had not been found but you were always very much alive.*

Then the spell should have broken when I was healed. I wonder why it hasn't been broken.

Thia suddenly thought of something else. *What were you doing here? Before I arrived I mean?*

He looked around in confusion. *I don't remember.* He paused searching for words. *I wasn't exactly here.* He gestured to the riverbank. *It was like I was floating in timeless space. I had no concept of time passing. When I heard you crying it seemed to almost wake me from a trance-like state.*

Well, there must be something we can do? she said in frustration. *Think, Teague. Is there anything can we try to break the spell?*

He frowned. *I'm not sure. It sounds as though the most obvious things have not worked. Does Celeste have any ideas?*

Thia shook her head. *She didn't seem to when I tried to contact you this way. But she may have more when I get back and she hears it is a spell causing this.*

Teague nodded. *Okay, see what she comes up with. The Draíodóir would know but it sounds like we don't have access to them at present. I'll try to think of other things we might be able to do.*

Thia watched him in concern. She wondered if Teague would go back to that place of unknowingness when she left. And more importantly would he be here if she returned?

CHAPTER EIGHTEEN

Kiara stood at the entrance of the cave and looked over the mounds of snow at the transformed world before her. Caedmon's prediction of a three-day storm had been wrong, thankfully. The storm had lasted only until midday. While it continued to rage, Kiara and Caedmon waited it out in the cave.

The cave was cold and they had no wood for a fire. So while Kiara had exited the bedroll she shared with Caedmon as soon as dawn came, she had spent the remainder of the morning sitting huddled miserably in a corner of the cave, fighting not to succumb to another round of shivers.

Kiara's face heated when she remembered sleeping in the bedroll with Caedmon. She had never slept with a boy and Caedmon was more of a man than a boy. But she had been grateful for his warmth through the night. It had been innocent enough, she rationalized to herself. After all they both had stayed fully clothed. And it was necessary to sleep together to avoid freezing to death.

She sobered as she remembered Caedmon's body shaking with sobs. Looking at his harsh features now, one would never imagine that he would give in to his emotions like that. But Teague was his brother. She felt as though her own heart had been ripped out whenever she thought of Thia trapped in that cold cave. She was sure Caedmon felt the same way. But she suspected it was not something he would want to speak about. And his silence through the last few hours of the storm assured her that he didn't like the fact that she had witnessed his grief.

He finally joined her and stood surveying the mountainside. The landscape beyond the entrance to the cave was brilliant. The sun reflected off the white world, creating a bright landscape that seemed to go on forever. It was a sharp contrast to the blowing snow that had extinguished all visibility only hours earlier.

Looking at the deep snow, Kiara swallowed hard as she imagined how they would have to climb through the fresh snow up the mountain. This route Weylon had planned for them had never been easy but now it was looking almost impossible. She wondered if Caedmon felt the same way.

But Caedmon had been through these mountain passes before, she reminded herself. And he'd done so in winter. Kiara turned to him now, hoping he had some magical way of easing their journey. But first they had to at least try to get Thia and Teague. They would be able to clearly see what they were doing now. Perhaps there was a weakness in the pile of rocks and debris that they'd missed in the storm yesterday. Surely Caedmon would agree with her.

"What do we do now?" she asked him, "Do you think we can climb down, through the snow?"

"There is no point in going back down, Kiara," Caedmon said firmly. "You know we can't get them." His dark eyes were shuttered, revealing no emotion. But Kiara wasn't fooled. She knew he was capable of feeling.

She stared at him; their eyes locking as she silently challenged him. They couldn't just leave Thia and Teague buried. She remembered Caedmon's grief in the night. She hadn't imagined his sobs. How could he just forget his brother so easily? She certainly was not going to forget about her sister. She opened her mouth to argue and he held up his hand.

"They could very well be alive, I agree, but we can't possibly shift half a mountain out of the entrance to get to them," he said exhaustion and sorrow mixed in his tone. "I wish we could," he added, sadness suddenly filling his dark eyes.

Kiara felt an instant stab of guilt. She was always the one who was quick to argue and slow to let something go. Was she arguing now just for the sake of arguing? She remembered the piles of rock that were blocking the entrance the previous evening. Now that rock would be buried in snow. Caedmon was right it was an impossible task for two people, even two people as strong as them. And attempting to move the mountain would only fatigue and chill them, putting them both at risk again. Kiara had not forgotten how cold she'd been the previous night when Caedmon had stuffed her into his sleeping roll.

"I'm sorry, Caedmon." She paused and considered. "Do you really think they may have survived the cave in?"

Caedmon nodded. "It's likely that they are trapped." He stopped, his voice rough with emotion when he continued, "Not that that's a better thing. It's worse to die a slow death of suffocation or starvation trapped underground."

Suddenly Kiara remembered Teague's comments before she left the cave. He had been excited because he thought he'd found another way through the mountain. Kiara hadn't taken him very seriously as she'd been in a hurry to find them food but now she tried to remember what he'd said exactly. He's been talking about going to explore the tunnel he'd found. He could be exploring it even now. There was a chance.

"They might not be trapped," she said slowly, her heart leaping with hope.

Caedmon looked at her blankly. "What do you mean?"

Kiara told him what Teague had discovered. The tunnel that Teague had thought could lead through the mountain. Kiara felt her lips lifting in a smile as a wave of hope passed through her. Then she became aware of Caedmon standing in front of her with a menacing look on his face.

He glared at her. "You just thought of telling me this now?" he bellowed, his deep voice echoing through the snow-blanketed mountains.

Kiara felt a stab of guilt. "I'm sorry," she said wryly. "I'd forgotten all about it until you described the trapped scenario."

Caedmon's scowl eased and for a moment he looked hopeful.

"At the very least there is a possibility that they will be able to go somewhere," she said with a smile. But then her smile slipped as she remembered thinking that the passage was probably a dead end. She looked at Caedmon glumly. "Where that way leads, if anywhere at all, is another question altogether. For some reason Teague seemed to think the tunnel might lead through the mountains to Séreméla." She paused and then shook her head. "Do you think that's at all possible, Caedmon?"

He silently studied the winter scene outside the cave for a moment, considering her words. "There are legends of such a passage but no one believes it's real. Except for Teague, of course," he added wryly.

Her heart lifted again. Caedmon was the most cynical person she'd ever met. If he thought there might be a chance the route was real, then she could allow herself to hope. "It would be ironic if the cave forced them to discover the lost road out of the mountains, wouldn't it?" Kiara said wistfully.

Caedmon nodded but he looked troubled.

"What's wrong, Caedmon?"

"The legend of the passage is not all good news, Kiara. While it tells the tale of the lost route, that road is not free from danger."

Kiara raised her eyebrows.

"The legend also tells of creatures in the dark who dwell in the mountain. They are the reason it has not been found and they will not be kind to those who try to invade their territory."

Fear pierced her heart. But then she looked sharply at Caedmon.

"You don't believe such stories, do you?" she couldn't help asking.

Caedmon grimaced and shook his head as he turned back to the cave. "But that isn't necessarily good news."

Kiara followed him, looking at him questioningly.

He glanced back at her over his shoulder. "Remember Kiara, I don't believe in secret passages, either."

CHAPTER NINETEEN

Hope of the next generation or not, Meldiron kept his promise and began to visit with Mina each day. The more time she spent with him, the more Mina liked the young Elder.

One day, in the second week after they had met, Meldiron suggested that he take her to the library.

"I know I've been disrupting your routine by tiring you out every morning. Why don't you let me take you to the library?"

Mina nodded eagerly. While she was enjoying her visits with Meldiron immensely, he was right about it tiring her out. By the time he left each morning, she found she didn't have energy left to go to the library. And she was missing her studies not to mention the fact that she worried that Eöl Ar-Feiniel would be concerned by her disappearance. She'd developed an instant fondness for the old Elder.

"What have you been reading about?" Meldiron asked her the first day he led her into the small alcove in the library. Mina was pleased to see that

Eöl Ar-Feiniel had left all her papers and books piled neatly on the desk, as if waiting for her. But she was disappointed that the elderly archivist did not make an appearance while Meldiron was present. She wondered where he was.

Quickly she told Meldiron of the scrolls that she had been studying. She picked up one that the archivist had called The Prophecy. "Eöl Ar-Feiniel has helped translate the ancient dialect somewhat," she admitted. "But even he doesn't know what the more intricate words might mean."

Meldiron nodded. Then picked up one of the older tomes, leafing through it. "I remember reading this one," he confided with a grin.

"Really?" Mina asked. "How old were you?"

He looked up from the book and wrinkled his straight nose in a comical way. "Six or seven."

Mina's mouth fell open. The tome he was holding had been difficult for her to get through without Eöl Ar-Feiniel's help. She couldn't imagine a small child reading it. "You must have a had a very strange childhood."

He laughed, a musical sound that echoed through the silent library. "Yes, it was an unconventional childhood, I suppose. I was Crown Prince after all."

Mina studied him for a moment, tried to picture him as a small blond haired, green-eyed boy with the responsibility of the Elder people on his shoulders. She failed miserably. Meldiron was too self-contained and composed to imagine as a child. It was hard to believe he'd ever been a child.

"What was it like? Being a child with so much responsibility?"

Something unreadable flashed in his green eyes, reminding Mina of a cold green sea. Then Meldiron stood up.

"Would you like to see the gardens?"

Mina's heart leapt and she looked at him closely to make sure he wasn't teasing. "Yes!" she said eagerly when she saw how serious his face was, "Yes, please."

He laughed again at her excitement. But then Mina remembered Bellasiel's refusal to let her go out of doors.

"But I don't think Bellasiel will approve," she said sadly.

Meldiron surprised her by winking. "Let me take care of Bellasiel. There are some advantages to being friends with the Crown Prince you know."

****

Mina was enchanted by the gardens. She had never seen such lush vegetation in her life. The forest next to the Inn paled in comparison to the overgrown throng of the Elder gardens.

Meldiron led her down one of the many groomed paths that led from the Sanctuary. He laughed at her exclamations over the odd flowery shrubs that lined the path.

"Do you know what this is?" he asked as the path they were on opened onto the bank of a calm flowing river. The river was wide and the banks were high, but the blue-green waters were calm and gentle.

Mina's heart gave a lurch. She looked up a Meldiron. "It's not ... the Aranel Pallanén?" she whispered in awe. The great river that she had heard countless stories about as a child and had been reading about in the History of Séreméla. She stared at the calm waters in front of her, remembering the great battles and travels that had taken place on the river in the early years of the Elder people's history.

Meldiron smiled at her indulgently. "You, Mina, remind me of the treasures of our land. Yes, this is indeed the Aranel Pallanén. What do you think of her?"

Mina paused, gazing out over the river. "It's calmer than I expected," she admitted.

Meldiron laughed. "Right now it is." When she looked up at him puzzled he explained, "This is our dry season, when the river is calm. When the rains come to the northern part of the valley the river swells and can be quite treacherous. Then it appears more like the Aranel Pallanén of legend and story."

Mina nodded and turned back to the river. She felt a great sense of peace and calm come over her. Suddenly she recognized what she was feeling. She felt like she was at home.

****

One afternoon, as they explored a small flower garden not far from the Sanctuary, Mina suddenly asked, "How can you stand all this beauty and not become completely overwhelmed?"

Meldiron smiled softly at her. "I am used to it. I forget that this is all new to you. Do you find it overwhelming?" he asked.

Mina shook her head. "I find it enchanting," she breathed, feeling that same sense of peace and contentment that she first felt on the riverbank.

"I don't know why but somehow I feel that I've finally come home," she sighed as she bent to smell a particularly beautiful teal colored lily.

Meldiron was silent and Mina looked up at him, a smile on her lips. It faded when she saw how serious his expression was.

"Have you ever wondered how you, clearly an Elder, came to be fostered with Brijit?" he asked.

She nodded briefly. "Brijit did tell us the story of herself and Weylon. I know they are *coimirceoirí.*"

He cocked his head, considering. "Yes. But did you ever wonder why you were sent so far from Séreméla?"

"Of course I did. But Brijit does not seem to know herself." She looked up at him curiously. "Do you know why?"

Meldiron shrugged. "I know some of the story." He looked sheepish. "I am not so much older than you that I clearly remember you leaving," he admitted. "I was a small child when they decided to remove you from Séreméla."

Mina stared at him. Did he mean that he remembered her leaving, if vaguely? "Who decided?" Mina asked suddenly feeling that it was very important.

"The Council of Elders," he explained, "I've come to know some details but not much." He paused. "I do know that your parents were both murdered. You also would have been killed had your grandmother not taken you to the gardens that afternoon."

"These gardens?" Mina couldn't help asking. Then she focused on the rest of his words. "My grandmother!" she exclaimed. "Can I meet her?"

Meldiron shook his head sadly. "No, she is dead. She was also murdered just after you were removed from Séreméla. You were only a few days old."

Mina felt tears rising for the family she never had the chance to know. "It has something to do with the Prophecy," she said softly, feeling in her heart it was true but uncertain as to why this was so. She suddenly wished that she could read that old scroll Eöl Ar-Feiniel had brought to her. But even Meldiron could make nothing of it; the dialect was so ancient.

"Yes," Meldiron agreed. "But I don't know what. Only that you were one of the Marked Ones and so were hidden deep in the realm. And after the murders Séreméla was protected by the wards."

"What kind of wards?" Mina asked carefully.

Meldiron shook his head. "Complex magik that was put in place by the *Draíodóir*. Even I do not understand it completely but I know that it protects all those within Séreméla. No one can be harmed while they are within the boundaries of Séreméla. Not animal nor human."

Mina nodded, feeling reassured that she was, for present, safe. Then another thought occurred to her. "Are there more of us? More Marked Ones."

Meldiron watched her for a few moments and then seemed to make up his mind about something. Suddenly he unlaced his tunic.

"What are you doing?" Mina asked in surprise.

He didn't answer but pulled the fabric over his head in a smooth motion. And then stood and turned to display the small mark on his right shoulder.

"You, too!" Mina gasped, stunned.

Looking grim, Meldiron pulled his tunic back on and nodded. "I don't know what it means. I don't think even the most experienced advisors know the meaning of the Marks. Nor do they know how many of us are in the realm. They have found dead children with the Mark. We are the only living ones they have found."

Mina shuddered, thinking of the poor children who were killed because of the Mark. Why had she been protected?

"They don't know who is killing the Marked Ones only that there is a force that doesn't want us to survive." Meldiron looked grim. "For that reason I have vowed to discovered the meaning behind this mystery."

After Meldiron had walked her back to her chambers, Mina thought about the Prophecy and the Mark. It was hard to believe that a prince was also

190

one of the Marked Ones. It seemed so random. But there must be some reason for the Mark, she felt sure of it. And she had a gut feeling that the answer lay buried in the Prophecy. If only they could find someone who could read it.

****

A few days later Meldiron came to tell her that he was leaving.

Mina stared at him in surprise. She had been looking forward to their visit that afternoon, as she wanted to ask him about the second monarchy of the Elders that had been destroyed by an internal war two thousand years before. She had been reading about it in the library with Eöl Ar-Feiniel but had questions she felt Meldiron would be better at answering.

She was also disappointed because she had come to enjoy their afternoon visits very much. With her sisters absent, Meldiron had become a close friend. Wandering in the gardens without him seemed a rather dull way of passing her time.

On the other hand, she had to admit that it was unlikely that the prince would be able to spend time with her on a daily basis indefinitely. Surely he had duties and tasks that would claim his time. She shouldn't be surprised that he needed to attend to other things.

"Where are you going?" she asked trying to hide her disappointment from him.

"I'm concerned that none of the parties we sent out have returned. I'm taking a small scouting party outside Séreméla to see what we can learn." He smiled at her. "I'll only be gone a week or so. And Bellasiel has informed me that you are now well enough to explore the gardens on your own."

Despite the good news from her healer, Mina felt a stab of alarm. What if whatever was hunting them found Meldiron? The wards protected him while he was within Séreméla but leaving it was dangerous.

"I'm the best guarded Elder in Séreméla," he assured Mina when she shared her concerns with him. "If anyone should be able to go abroad safely, it is I. There will be a party of guards with me. I will be fine."

Still she watched him leave that afternoon with a sense of heavy foreboding.

CHAPTER TWENTY

Kiara and Caedmon prepared to leave the cave late in the morning. Caedmon reasoned that they should make a start on the journey before another winter storm had the chance to move in and strand them indefinitely.

As she exited, Kiara stood on the lip of the cave and gazed at the bright, clean landscape. Now that the storm had lifted she could see the pile of snow three hundred meters below them where the mountain had buried the entrance to the other cave. Where her sister was trapped.

With a sinking heart, Kiara had to admit that Caedmon was right. It would be impossible to dig their siblings out from under that mess.

"We'd be best to assume that they made it to the tunnel and are on their way to Séreméla through the mountain, rather than over it," Caedmon noted. "Try to focus on them having an easier time than we are going to face. We'd better start on our own journey."

He turned back to their cave and grabbed the pack, putting it onto his back. The loss of Kiara's supplies meant they had to share the little food and water that was in Caedmon's pack and the sleeping roll was the only source of warmth they possessed. Kiara was grateful that she'd been out in the storm at least. It ensured that she'd been wearing her winter traveling clothes when her supplies were buried. Without the fur-lined coat, hat and gloves, she would already be dead.

Caedmon handed her a chunk of cheese and a dry roll. "Eat now. We'll find more food on the way." Kiara nodded glumly and began to eat even though she doubted there would be any sources of cheese and bread on this journey. She knew she could hunt but she wondered how many creatures they would come upon when they were so far up in the mountains in the dead of winter.

Caedmon saw her expression. "Let's look on the bright side," he said encouragingly. "We'll be able to make better time now. Both you and I are strong and can move faster than either Teague or Thia. I had my doubts as to how much of the mountain climbing your little sister would have been able to handle anyway."

Kiara nodded. He was right. With just the two of them they should be able to make good time. It was not much, but it was something.

They set off shortly after that and began climbing at a brisk pace. It was hard work, uphill and through the deep new snow but Kiara was enjoying the flush it brought to her cheeks and the pounding to her heart. It made it easier to ignore the bitter cold and her worry over Thia.

They agreed not to stop for a mid-day break, as they had nothing to eat anyway but to use that time to continue climbing.

Towards late afternoon, Caedmon began looking for shelter but they weren't as lucky as the previous night. This high up the mountain there weren't the caves that were found on the lower slopes. It was just snow and ice as far as the eye could see.

"Can we climb through the night?" Kiara asked, looking up at the sky. "It's a full moon tonight."

But Caedmon shook his head. "Even with the full moon, we'll be coming to the crevices soon. Those are too dangerous to navigate after dark." He paused. "Besides we are going to need our strength. Even at this pace, it will take us ten days to get through the mountains provided we don't run into any more problems."

Kiara nodded. He was right again. She was reminded that Caedmon was an expert when it came to these mountains. It was better they rest while they could.

Caedmon was more gifted than she was at finding shelter in places where it appeared that there wasn't any to be found. "One of the rewards of training as a soldier," he said when Kiara commented on it.

"One of them?" she couldn't help asking.

"The other is learning to sleep anywhere."

They laughed and then Caedmon went to find wood for a fire while Kiara started hunting.

She was lucky and caught a winter hare. She brought it back and they cooked it over the fire Caedmon had started. It wasn't much food, the meat stringy and tough, but it sated their hunger for the night.

Without talking about it, they automatically shared the sleeping roll that night. The air was bitterly cold this high on the mountain and Kiara was grateful for Caedmon's strong arms wrapped around her, chasing the worse of the cold away. She slept soundly despite the sleeping arrangements.

Three days later, they reached the summit of the mountain. Kiara was hoping the mountain would begin to slope downward after that but instead they were facing a huge glacier field. Kiara stared at it in dismay.

Caedmon came to stand beside her and survey their next day's path.

"This field is treacherous," he told her quietly.

Kiara looked at him quickly in surprise. "You've been here before?"

He nodded. "Several times. We came here for training. We lost eighteen careless trainees in the two weeks we were here."

Kiara held her tongue but she was shocked. What kind of army took its trainees to ice fields where they were sure to lose the inexperienced in their ranks? She wondered, not for the first time, about Caedmon's upbringing. He'd joined the army as a child, how old had he been when he'd come to the ice fields and watched his fellow soldiers die?

She remembered once again how easily he'd killed the invader at the inn that night. She studied the harsh, handsome features of the man at her side. He was a puzzle of sorts. The type of man who cried over the loss of his brother, who wrapped her gently in his arms each night and who could snap a man's neck without a second thought.

Something told Kiara not to ask too many questions about Caedmon's childhood. So she just nodded and followed him back to their makeshift camp.

"Tomorrow will be the start of a very difficult crossing," he told her. "Crossing the glacier field is always fraught with danger but this time of year it has the added element of the weather."

Kiara looked at him questioningly.

"We did training in the spring long after the winter storms had left." He pointed to the field below them. "If a storm blows up while we are on the field, it will be a miracle if we survive."

Kiara looked at the wide field of ice and shivered.

"What is the likelihood of a storm?" she couldn't stop herself from asking.

Caedmon looked at her grimly. "Almost certain."

Kiara turned to the small fire, irritation pricking at her nerves. "So do you have any suggestions for getting across the field safely then?"

Caedmon nodded. "We go as fast as we safely can."

****

Despite the need for haste, Caedmon warned Kiara that the ice field was dangerous for another reason. It was interconnected with thousands of crevices. One misstep and one could find oneself at the bottom of a three hundred meter drop. Very dead.

With that in mind, Caedmon insisted on tying them together with his rope.

"Well, that works in theory if I stumbled into a crevice," she noted drily. "But what happens if you fall in?"

"Then we're both dead," he stated grimly, tightening the rope at his waist. Then he surprised her by smiling. "But don't worry, Kiara, I won't fall." And he winked as he turned to start the climb down to the ice field.

Kiara moodily followed him down the slope. She hoped Caedmon was as gifted at avoiding crevices as he was at finding shelter.

As they started across the field, Caedmon taught her how to sense the crevices before she stepped in them. It was exhausting work, not just because of the physical endurance it took to walk into the howling icy wind all day but because one couldn't let one's concentration wander. One misstep and she'd find herself dead.

They were halfway across the first third of the field, when they came to a huge crevice. At least 5 meters across, there was no way to gauge its depth. They stopped and looked down.

"Ideas?" Kiara asked him grimly.

Caedmon looked first left and then right. There was no clear end in sight in either direction. There was no point in exploring either way; this crevice seemed to have cut the glacier in half. And to add to the worry, the sky was darkening with the threat of their first winter storm on the field.

"Can you jump it?" Caedmon asked suddenly.

Kiara laughed, thinking he was kidding. Then she saw the blank expression on his face. "You can't be serious," she said flatly, a sinking sensation in her stomach telling her that he definitely was.

He didn't smile. He looked at her steadily, his dark eyes grim. "So you can't?"

"You are serious?" She gauged the distance to the far side. Then answered bluntly, "No. Can you?"

He considered. "I think I might be able to"

She glared at him. Of course, he thought he might be able to. Her old competitive nature kicked in. "Do you want me to try?" she asked, her pride smarting.

Without waiting for an answer from him, she took a running leap and then she was falling, falling, falling down through jagged ice until the rope around her waist jerked her to halt, slicing into her skin. She grunted in pain, she didn't even want imagine the damage she'd just done to her middle.

"Kiara?" Caedmon called down, his voice raw with worry.

She took a deep breath, pushing the burning pain around her waist away. "I'm fine." She forced herself to call up to him. "Just hanging around," she added bitterly groaning at the raw ache that was radiating from where the rope was secured.

Caedmon's relieved laughter echoed down the crevice.

"Stop laughing and pull me up, you stupid oaf," she said grumpily, and then looked down.

The icy drop seemed to go on forever. Kiara gulped, not wanting to think about what would have happened to her had the rope not been securely tied around her middle. Despite the pain, she gave a silent word of thanks for Caedmon's ability to tie knots as well as his other skills.

She was about to look back up when a strange flickering light lower in the crevice caught her eye. It was about 3 meters below her on the opposite ice wall. What was it? She had a sudden urgent desire to see where the light was coming from.

She felt the rope begin to tighten around her waist as Caedmon prepared to pull her up.

"Caedmon wait!" she called in panic. She had to see where that light was coming from.

"What?" he called down, concern clear in the voice.

"There's something down here," she called to him. "Can you lower me a couple of meters?"

"Kiara, those clouds don't look too welcoming. We need to get moving," he said impatiently.

"Please Caedmon. Trust me."

She heard him grumbling above her but then she began to be lowered.

As she came closer to the light, Kiara looked ahead of her in stunned silence.

Unbelievably, there was an underground road visible through an opening in the ice. Was it possible that she, like Teague, had found an alternate route through the mountain?

CHAPTER TWENTY-ONE

Celeste was not in the room when Thia awoke from her dreamwalk with Teague. She sat up and looked over at Teague hoping he would magically open his eyes but he was as still and quiet as when she'd first fallen asleep.

Thia watched him for a few minutes, taking in his profile and the way the soft brown curls fell over his forehead. In sleep he looked young but she missed the animation that came with his waking state. It would be ironic indeed if the only way she would see his waking state would be in the dream world. Her oldest friend outside of her sisters and they might be trapped in their dream friendship forever, so soon after they'd found one another in the waking world. Sadness washed over Thia as she considered it.

You found him. Celeste's voice entered her consciousness.

Thia turned automatically but Celeste wasn't in the room yet. A few moments later she glided in.

Thia nodded to her. "He found me," she admitted.

Celeste shook her head at Thia. *No, more of that communication. You are new to this kind and you need to learn to be proficient at it. We will only communicate this way from now on. Do you understand?*

Thia nodded.

Good. Part of our communication is not just unspoken words but feelings and senses. You felt that when you first woke, didn't you?

Thia remembered the feelings that had threatened to overcome her when she had awoken in the cave.

Once you learn this language, you will find the old way of communication limiting.

Thia wasn't sure about that. She didn't know how she felt about someone being able to change her mood. It felt too much like an invasion of her mind.

"It feels manipulative," she said aloud.

Celeste shook her head. "No, it's not like that – we can't alter one another's moods or feelings. We can only emphasize the emotions that accompany our own words."

Let me demonstrate, Celeste said.

Suddenly Thia was bathed in a sensation of joy and happiness. *You made contact*. Celeste smiled. *That is more than we expected on the first attempt.*

Thia nodded. She could see how this could be a superior form of communication but it still felt too controlling to her. Then she focused on what Celeste had said.

"You mean -" Thia stopped at the look of reproof on Celeste's face.

You mean you didn't think we'd even make contact?

Celeste tilted her head. We had our doubts. *You are clearly closer linked that we originally anticipated. Did Teague have any idea as to why he is in the state he is in?*

Thia nodded. *Yes, he said it's a spell.* She explained the theory behind the spell as Teague had described it to her.

Dark emotions oozed from Celeste. *The fools. They do not understand what they are facing at all?*

Seeing the confusion and fear on Thia's face she softened her expression and sent out soothing thoughts.

Teague will return to consciousness, she assured Thia. *It will just take time. And while we wait for him, you can learn our ways.*

Thia was worried. *What about my sister in Séreméla?* she asked.

I'm sorry, Thia, I have no way of knowing how she is but the Elders are gifted healers and Séreméla is a special place. She will have the best chance of healing there.

I just wonder if I will ever see my family again. I feel like I've lost everything.

I sense you will get there but while you are here let us teach you as much as we can.

****

Thia continued the dreamwalks with Teague. She'd moved into the sickroom and slept there at night so she could be near him. She always hoped that when she woke Teague would as well but he continued in his comatose state. The more they met the more frustrated he became.

I just want to wake up. I feel completely powerless knowing that I'm lying in a bed somewhere while so much is happening, he admitted to her one night.

Try to be patient, Thia soothed him, sending out the calming feeling as Celeste had often done with her, experimenting to see if it would work in the Dreamscape.

202

Teague face changed. *What are you doing?* he asked, his expression intrigued.

Thia smiled. *Celeste is teaching me this form of communication,* she admitted shyly. *In addition to sending verbal messages, they use it as a way to express feelings and thoughts. They can even send visual messages back and forth.*

Teague stood up and began pacing impatiently. *Another thing you'll be more advanced at than I,* he said with a grimace as he turned back to where she was sitting on the riverbank. *I've never had the chance to actually practice with anyone. Caedmon never responded when I used it on him. You were the only one who ever did. It's just killing me knowing that I'm lying here missing out on a complete dialogue. And from what you're saying a more advanced way of using this form of communication.*

Thia reached up, grabbing his hand and tugging him until he sat down beside her. *Relax, Teague, Celeste believes that you will wake soon.*

They were silent for a few moments, just sitting together.

Have they made any progress at all? he finally asked in irritation.

No visible progress but she thinks these meetings can only help, Thia admitted truthfully.

He nodded but didn't look convinced.

****

I am curious as to why you never touch Teague? Celeste asked her one day. *It is clear that you long to do so, yet you always pull back as though you will be burnt. Why is that, Thia?*

Thia sighed. She explained to Celeste what happened when she touched Teague.

Celeste listened intently. *Does this happen in your dreamwalks as well?*

No, the first time it happened, I didn't realize what it was.

Celeste watched her closely. *And do you have an idea as to what it is now?*

Thia shook her head. *But it isn't just with me. Teague says no one has ever been able to touch him.*

Celeste looked thoughtful but then changed the topic to the harvesting techniques of The People, as they called themselves. Thia had been spending most of her days, the times when she wasn't dreamwalking with Teague, learning about The People's way of life below ground.

She was amazing by what she discovered. They had adapted their entire life to their existence below ground. There were underground gardens with the most interesting vegetation grown in them. Iridescent fungi and mushrooms, grasses that grew in the underground pools, and small plants that were edible and needed no sunlight to grow. Thia never imagined such a place could exist.

How deep are we? she asked Celeste one afternoon when they were discussing the bathing pools she had introduced Thia to.

Very deep, Celeste told her calmly. *It would take at least a week of your time to reach the surface.*

Thia was shocked. She realized that she must have been unconscious for a very long time when they transported her from the cave.

We stay separate from the above ground world. It is better that way. Celeste told her, with a smile. *One day you may understand.*

****

Several days later Celeste summoned Thia to Teague's chamber. *Has something happened?* Thia asked with hope. Perhaps Teague had woken.

I would like you to try to touch him for me, Celeste told her.

Thia immediately shook her head.

Please, Thia, I think it might help us bring him back. I have a theory as to what happens when you touch. But I need to see it for myself.

Thia swallowed. The last thing she wanted to do was to induce one of her seizures but that seemed to be exactly what Celeste wanted her to do. It was then that Thia realized that she hadn't had any seizures since she'd gone underground. She hesitated for a moment, trying to make sense of what that might mean.

Please trust me, Celeste assured her.

Thia nodded. She reached out and stroked Teague's forehead as she'd been longing to do for ages. Immediately the tingling sensation started moving up her arm. Her vision filled with indigo swirls and the darkness claimed her.

Brijit lying in a pool of blood. Dead children lying in a circle, their necks cut and the Marks on their shoulders clear. Monsters chasing Kiara and Caedmon. Her hands joined with Teague as his eyes opened. And then blackness.

When Thia woke she was lying on her bed with Celeste leaning over her. *You are well, my child.*

Thia assessed how she felt. Her head did not ache and she did feel relatively well. That was odd – usually she was ill after a seizure. She turned her head and looked hopefully at Teague but he was still asleep. She felt fatigue pulling at her as always after one of her episodes.

Sleep, Little One, we will speak when you are rested.

The next time Thia woke, the crushing fatigue had gone. She sat up but Celeste was not in the room

She sent out a thought message, Celeste?

I will come, child.

I now understand what happens when you and Teague touch, Celeste told her when she had arrived in her room.

Thia was puzzled.

I'm sorry if the experiment caused you any distress. Let me explain what I discovered and perhaps that will make you feel better.

Thia nodded, eager to hear what Celeste had to say.

You both produce energy. The energy you produce is directed inward when it becomes overbearing. Teague's is directed outward. When you touch, the energies combine, channel into you and overcome you.

She paused and looked at Thia.

Have you ever been able to control the energy surges?

Thia shook her head. *My adoptive mother said I've had the spells since I was days old.*

Celeste nodded. Yes, it is very common in our children but as they mature we are able to teach them to control it. I think it is time you learned to take control of your energy.

You can teach me to do that? Thia asked with wonder. She was scared to believe it could be possible.

Our children learn to do so from a very young age. And, of course, unlike you they've had the benefit of their parents. As a people, we have a sensitive lifeforce. If we don't learn to control it, we would all succumb to the episodes that you've experienced, Thia. If you'd been with your underground parent, the seizures would have been controlled for you until you'd learned how to control them yourself.

206

Thia stared at her. Was Celeste suggesting that she was a child of The People?

Celeste smiled at her sadly as if reading her thoughts. *You are partly one of us but partly of the above ground race as well.*

She looked at Teague. *He is, as well*, Celeste said

How can this be? Thia asked.

There are a few children like you who have grown up on the surface, Celeste explained. *A generation ago, some of our people decided to re-explore uniting with the surface dwellers. The experiment was a failure but some children, such as yourself and Teague were the result. We have been tracking them down one by one but it is a difficult task.*

How many? Thia demanded.

Celeste did not answer.

Thia pushed her anger and hurt at Celeste.

Celeste shook her head. *I do not know how many. We have found seven to date.*

Thia sensed there was something she was not telling her.

One by one we brought them below ground and taught them our ways.

There were others like her. Thia felt a stirring of excitement. *I want to see them.*

A wave of sadness came from Celeste. *You can't.*

Why not?

Celeste turned to her, her flat black eyes filled with sorrow. *They are all dead.*

CHAPTER TWENTY-TWO

It was almost three weeks before Prince Meldiron returned to Séreméla. Mina was in the garden closest to the Sanctuary with Bellasiel and Brijit when suddenly there was a commotion at the entrance.

"Prince Meldiron is injured," a young Elder called, fear ringing in his voice.

Mina stood up in sudden alarm, her heart clenching with fear.

"Take her from the gardens, Brijit," Bellasiel said in a commanding voice, but they had not left the gardens when a party of four Elders carried a broken and bloody Meldiron into the courtyard. Blood oozed from his body and at least one of his legs was viciously broken. He looked near death. Mina let out a cry.

"Remove her!" Bellasiel commanded as she hurried toward the prince.

Before Mina could protest she found herself back in her rooms.

"Brijit, why make me leave?" she raged, worry making her frantic. "I must know if he will live."

"Hush, darling." Brijit tried to calm her. "Prince Meldiron is the future of Séreméla. The best healers will be working on him. He will survive."

Brijit was right about that. Within an hour Bellasiel arrived in Mina's room and said something to Brijit in Elder language. While Mina was beginning to learn the written language she was far from fluent in the spoken tongue. Brijit looked grim but nodded.

"Mina, they need to take what is called a transfusion of your blood for Meldiron."

Mina shook her head. "I don't understand."

Brijit nodded. "I know darling but it is the only way we can be sure he will live." She paused. "You are still very weak from the attack on you and we would not ask except that you are the only hope."

Bellasiel spoke up. "Without your blood the prince will die."

Mina gasped in shock. "Take it then," she said quickly. "I'll do whatever it takes." How could she lose Meldiron after her sisters were both missing? It was too much.

Bellasiel brought in complex equipment of tubes and needles and performed the procedure, while Mina lay still and grief struck. As the healer hurried from the room with several vials of her blood, Mina sagged on her bed, both drowsy and weak.

"Sleep now, darling," Brijit urged her.

It was only as she was drifting towards sleep that Mina suddenly wondered, why did they need her blood specifically? Couldn't any of the Elder's blood do? It was her last thought before sleep overtook her.

****

Hours later Bellasiel came to check on her.

"This has over drained your energy," she told Mina with a worried look in her eye.

"But is Meldiron?" Mina could not finish the sentence.

Bellasiel gave her a draught of medicine. "He will live." Her face softened. "Prince Meldiron is a strong Elder. He will survive and be well, faster than you will recover from this, I fear," she said quietly. "Now sleep."

The next day Mina learned that Meldiron and his companions had been ambushed. He was the only survivor, arriving within Séreméla limits the day before, hanging close to death on his Elder horse. As soon as he crossed the wards, an alarm was raised and a rescue party went to retrieve him.

Soon Mina and Meldiron were visiting in the gardens again, this time both as invalids. Bellasiel was correct. Meldiron healed much faster than Mina was recovering. His leg was knit and he was looking much like his old self within a short week's time. It hardly seemed possible.

"I'm relieved that you are well, Meldiron," she admitted when they were finally left alone in the garden.

He looked at her. "I believe I have you to thank for my life, Minathrial," he said softly. "Thank you."

She shook her head. "It wasn't so much to give," she said. "I don't know what I would have done had you died." She paused for a moment, searching for the words to address the issue that had been bothering her for several days now.

"Meldiron?" she said slowly.

"Yes."

"Why me?" she asked. "Why did they need my blood to save you? Bellasiel said taking the blood put me at risk but that I was the only one who could help you. Why?"

Meldiron sighed then closed his eyes.

"Minathrial, we are in far more danger than I suspected," he said softly. "There are things that the Elder Council wanted kept from you but now I don't know who to trust."

Mina looked at him sharply. His handsome face was pinched and drawn. Worry lines creased his forehead. "What do you mean?" she asked.

Meldiron swallowed. "You are not just a Marked Elder, Minathrial. You are my sister."

Mina gasped then looked closely at Meldiron. Although she hadn't guessed the truth she found that she was not entirely shocked. There was something in the shape of his nose and the fall of his fair hair that reminded her of the reflection she saw in the mirror. She realized with a start that she had subconsciously begun to recognize the resemblance weeks ago. And this also explained why he had always seemed so familiar to her.

"You're my brother?" she asked softly, trying out the new word on her tongue.

He smiled. "Yes. And you are Princess Minathrial, the lost one."

She gasped. "Banphrionsa?"

Meldiron looked at her sharply. "What did you say?"

"Eöl Ar-Feiniel always calls me Banphrionsa." The Eldest word for princess. "I thought it was a form of endearment," she admitted ruefully.

Meldiron laughed. "Eöl Ar-Feiniel is the last Elder I would expect endearments from," he said with a twinkle in his eyes.

Mina nodded in agreement. Then she looked at him in confusion. "What did you mean by the lost one?"

"I'm afraid you are a bit of legend in Séreméla. That's why Bellasiel has not let you wander far and never on your own. She couldn't risk having others discover that you were here."

Mina stared at him.

Meldiron sighed and ran his hand through is hair making it stick up in blond spikes over his head. "When our parents and grandmother were all murdered, those who hid you with Brijit spread the rumor that you had gone missing. They couldn't tell the Elder population that the king, queen, old queen and princess had all been murdered. They weren't permitted to tell lies within Séreméla limits," he grimaced, "so they improvised."

"Did you know this?" she asked.

He shook his head. "I never knew precisely what happened to my sister until I came of age and took the throne. Then I was told that you were hidden for safety."

Mina thought about it for a few minutes, not sure how she felt.

"There's more, Minathrial," Meldiron said carefully.

"What?" The tone of his voice alerted her that what he was going to tell her was very important and not at all pleasant.

"My group was not ambushed," he admitted, watching her keenly to gauge her reaction.

Mina gasped. "What do you mean?"

"There was no enemy lying in wait for us." He looked down at the green grass at his feet. When he looked up at her again, there was pain reflected in the depths of his green eyes. "My own men attacked me."

Mina gasped.

"I am beginning to think that there are far more sinister forces at work here." He paused. "I don't think we can trust anyone, Minathrial."

She nodded thoughtfully, her brow furrowed. "What do you mean anyone?" she asked cautiously.

Meldiron grasped her shoulder tightly until she met his eyes. "Minathrial, it's very important that you understand this. We can't trust anyone, and I mean anyone, within Séreméla. This includes your mother and Bellasiel. You and I, as Marked Ones, can only trust one another."

"My sisters?" she asked faintly.

He swallowed; the fear and pain she was feeling were reflected in his eyes. "We can only pray that your sisters along with Teague and Caedmon had as much luck as I did escaping because I believe we've all been given a death sentence. None of this is by chance." He closed his eyes. "And the others ..."

"Others?" Mina asked confused.

Meldiron stood and began to pace, his head bowed. "You know that Marked Ones have been showing up dead, so we are not the only ones in the Five Corners." He lowered his voice. "What I am going to tell you is something that I have guarded with my life. Can you keep it to yourself?" He looked at her hard.

Mina nodded, wondering what could be so important.

He watched her for a few more minutes and then seemed to make up his mind. "You remember that I told you we'd sent decoy teams south?"

Mina nodded.

"One of those parties was led by one of my most trusted confidants and a good friend. His name is Arion." Meldiron paused. "Unbeknownst to anyone in Séreméla, he is also a Marked One."

Mina shook her head. "How could he hide it?" she asked, thinking of the prominence of the marks on their shoulders. She knew from experience it would be difficult to hide. She couldn't imagine how anyone could hide the Mark for his whole life.

Meldiron grimaced. "You are familiar with the Prophecy?" he asked.

Mina nodded. "Somewhat."

"Not everyone thinks the Marked Ones will bring good. Some think they are evil and must be destroyed." He paused and seemed to be reflecting on something. "Many parents are horrified to find a Marked child in their cradle. A fair number of the dead Marked Ones we've recovered have been newborns."

Mina gasped in shock. She couldn't fathom anyone killing an innocent baby.

Meldiron nodded grimly. "Arion's own mother, a senior Elder who lived in the Sanctuary, was horrified to find the Mark on her newborn son. However as an Elder living in Séreméla, she could not kill the child. And by the time he was old enough to travel from our borders, his existence was too well known for her to kill him. So she began to travel outside the borders and do everything in her power to eradicate the Mark from his skin."

Mina listened cautiously; afraid to ask what measures Arion's mother might have taken.

"Nothing worked. You know the Mark is not something that can be easily erased. It is a part of our skin." He looked at her. "When Arion was three his mother began taking more extreme measures to remove the Mark. But nothing she did worked. Finally one day she took him from Séreméla far into the Outlands. There she procured some acid and attempted to burn the Mark from his shoulder."

Mina gasped in horror. "Did it work?"

Meldiron's face was grim. "Yes, but it also severely mutilated his back and chest. When she returned to Séreméla with Arion near death, she had invented a story of a horrible accident in a far away land. Many believed her. Because of her position in the Sanctuary, Bellasiel was the healer who treated Arion and was able to save his life but his body would forever be scarred. I

214

believe Bellasiel suspected the reasons behind his mother's actions but, as far as I know, she never spoke to anyone about it."

"Arion and I grew up almost as brothers. When my family was murdered, I was a lonely boy. Arion, with his disfigurement was an outcast from the other children. We became very close. He is the closest thing to family that I've known. And now I fear I've sent him to his death." Pain was etched on Meldiron's features.

"But you don't know that, Meldiron," Mina insisted.

He sat down beside her again, fatigue lines on his forehead. "I don't. You're right but these Hunters seem to be able to almost sniff us out. I don't know how else to explain it. They seem to be able to sense where we are. I suspect they do not need to see a Mark to find a Marked One."

"I have to believe they are all safe and will make their way here," she told Meldiron softly. "We are safe while we are in Séreméla, right?"

Meldiron nodded. "But we can't stay here forever. Our enemies know this and will try to attack as soon as we leave Séreméla. I'm convinced of it."

Mina felt tears filling her eyes. "You mean Kiara and Thia could already be dead."

He nodded. "And Arion, as well. I hope not and I don't want to give you unnecessary worry but I fear it is a very real possibility."

They sat for some time afterward in silence. Mina tried to process all she'd learned from him and tried not to think of her sisters lying dead in the cold snow.

CHAPTER TWENTY-THREE

It took Kiara a ridiculous amount of time to talk Caedmon into exploring the road beneath the ice field. He insisted on pulling her up to the surface again before he would even discuss it.

He shook his head. "Kiara, what are you talking about? How could there be a passage halfway down a fissure in the glacier? Think about it - it doesn't make sense."

Kiara looked at him in frustration. It was like he didn't even want to find an easier way to Séreméla. Did he enjoy the cold and snow and constant storms?

"Will you at least stop being stubborn for a moment and have a look?" she asked in exacerbation.

Finally, he only conceded to the investigation because the storm was bearing down on them. But first he insisted on securing the rope at the top of the ice field, in case they had to come back.

216

"That's not going to happen," Kiara said confidently as he lowered her for a second time.

Caedmon didn't reply.

Once Kiara was in the tunnel, Caedmon climbed down the rope himself and swung into the passageway, looking at the strange eerie glow that seemed to come from the walls.

"This place doesn't feel ... natural," he said suspiciously.

Kiara had to agree with that. There was an unnatural feel to the entire tunnel. But she was still confident that this marked a safe way across the glacier and maybe even out of the mountains.

"Who do you think created it?" she asked Caedmon. "What do the legends say?"

He shook his head and looked back at the drop into the ravine behind them. "The legends mention no place like this," he said as he reached out and touched the glowing wall. He jerked his hand back. "Feel this, Kiara."

What was he on about now? Caedmon was far too suspicious, she thought but she humored him by feeling the wall of the tunnel. Her fingers immediately sank into the wall. It was unnaturally warm and moist. Kiara pulled her hand back and looked at Caedmon in concern. A sliver of doubt worked its way into her mind.

"It feels like it's ..." She paused searching for the right words.

"Alive," Caedmon answered for her and backed toward the entrance, more nervous than she'd ever seen him before. But he was being ridiculous. Did he not want to find a safer route across the ice fields? Kiara looked down the tunnel, the path disappeared around a corner and she had a sudden compulsion to follow where it was leading.

"Come on," Kiara said to him, irritably. "We might as well see where it ends."

Caedmon held up his hand. And she paced back and forth impatiently as he drove a spike into the wall to secure the rope. A loud shrieking suddenly ripped through the tunnel as thick red liquid began to ooze from where the spike was impaled.

Kiara stared at it, her mind cloudy and confused. "Caedmon?" she asked uncertainly, as raw fear began to replace her confusion. Then the floor began to tip. Kiara watched as Caedmon used his unbelievable speed to grab the rope in one hand while reaching for her with the other. Without thinking she grasped his hand just as the floor disappeared completely and her feet fell out from beneath her.

"Caedmon!" she cried in terror as they dangled from the rope.

He pulled her toward the entrance and for once Kiara was glad that he was so strong. He tugged her upward until she was able to scramble onto his back. As they dangled from the rope the entrance to the cave seemed to be closing above them. Kiara stared, positive her eyes must be playing tricks on her as fear immobilized her.

"Can you reach the pack?" Caedmon shouted.

"What?" she asked, her voice a sob.

Caedmon shifted. "My pack, can you reach into it?" He groaned with effort as she clung to him and he held onto the rope with both hands.

Kiara looked at the pack, which was pressed against her belly. "I think so."

"There are two knives in the side pocket. Can you get them?" he asked, strain clear in his voice.

In reply Kiara, reached in the pack and dug for the knives. Her fingers closed around the handle of one. She pulled it out and then the other. She handed them to Caedmon but both his hands were occupied.

218

"Whatever you do keep holding on," Caedmon instructed as he bit down on the knife handles. Then he began to swing them on the rope toward the entrance, which was now barely large enough for them to fit through. Using their combined weight, he swung the two of them until they cleared the entrance. Then before Kiara could ask what was next, he let go of the rope and jumped into the chasm. Kiara screamed.

With a knife in each hand Caedmon slammed first one then the other knife into the ice walls. As they found purchase he began scaling the ice wall. A loud howling sound was now echoing through the entrance they had just vacated. Caedmon climbed faster. And Kiara was happy for his unnatural speed. She wrapped her arms around his neck and shut her eyes tightly, fear coursing through her body. Finally, Caedmon pulled them out of the chasm on the other side of the ice field.

Caedmon dropped her unceremoniously on the ground and then collapsed on the ice, huffing and trying to catch his breath. "Well, you got us to the other side," he puffed with a grin.

Kiara stared at him in horror. He was joking after what had just happened. This man was insane.

She lay beside him shivering on the ice. After a moment, it occurred to her that it was bright daylight again. Kiara stared in confusion. When they had lowered themselves into the chasm there had been a storm approaching.

"What happened to the storm?" she gasped.

Caedmon swallowed as he caught his breath and sat up looking around. "I think we were in the chasm longer than it seemed," he said hoarsely.

Kiara stared at him. Then she shuddered as she remembered the howls that were only now fading. "What was that?" Kiara asked him, her fear raw in her voice.

Caedmon shrugged off his pack and began putting his knives away. "The legends of the ice field speak of ancient monsters. Monsters who have an intelligence of sorts and set mental traps to lure their prey." He paused.

Kiara remembered how she was drawn to the tunnel; sure it was a safe way through an ice field when realistically it didn't make any sense that such a thing could exist. She sat up and swallowed in horror. Had some hungry ice monster tricked her?

"Do you mean I was ... brainwashed or something?" she asked.

"Lured by the beast, would be a more appropriate description," Caedmon said. "Kiara your waist."

She looked down and saw the blood seeping through her tunic where the rope must have dug into her skin. He gently lifted her top to reveal deep gouges in her flesh. She didn't feel a thing. "But why weren't you affected?" she asked as Caedmon began digging through his pack for medical supplies.

Caedmon shrugged. "You fell into the chasm, remember? Perhaps the creature affected you while you were hanging around." His lips twitched with humor. "I was on the field so it couldn't touch me."

Kiara shivered as she remembered the floor falling out beneath her feet. She closed her eyes, her body beginning to shake, with cold or residual reaction to what had happened she didn't know.

"Hey," Caedmon called and she opened her eyes. He stood up and held his hand out to her.

She swallowed and put her hand in his. He pulled her to her feet and into his arms.

"You're okay," he whispered into her hair and hugged her hard.

Kiara sunk into his embrace. Feeding off his strength until she felt the horror of the crevice retreat.

"Thank you," she whispered as she pulled away.

He smiled. "No, I think I should thank you."

Kiara looked at him, puzzled.

"I think my feelings about the accuracy of legends may be shifting thanks to you," he said with a grin. Caedmon looked up at something in the distance. "On more than one count."

Kiara turned to see what had caught his attention. Approaching them were two small figures, shuffling across the ice purposefully. It looked as though they weren't alone any more.

****

The small figures approached with remarkable speed for their size. They were tiny, no more than child-sized, but had wizen features that suggested great age. Their appearance on the ice field was completely surreal. Kiara couldn't stop herself from staring.

In addition to their odd appearance, the newcomers were dressed in nothing but brown robes that hung off their small frames. Hoods covered their hairless heads and their feet were bare.

Kiara rubbed her eyes, wondering if her injuries were worse than she thought and if she was hallucinating. But Caedmon was watching them as well.

"Caedmon?" she asked softly. "Are they real?"

He closed his eyes briefly and nodded before turning to her. "They are the manach."

The manach were a mythical group of holy folk who lived in seclusion from the rest of the world. They were believed to have strange powers. Some said they were real but many believed they were just a legend of the northern realm.

"You've encountered them before?"

Caedmon shook his head. "No, I didn't think they were real."

"Of course you didn't," she murmured under her breath as the creatures approached.

"Caedmon Forborrow and Kiara Carnesîr." The first wizen creature halted as it said their names. "We have anticipated your visit for many moons."

Kiara glanced at Caedmon, uncertainly.

"Come," they beckoned. "You need warmth and food. And we can care for your wounds. Come. Come."

Caedmon looked at her and shrugged then began to follow the creatures across the snow. "You heard him, Kiara. Food and shelter. It's a better offer than the last creature we encountered here," he said when she hesitated. "And besides your wounds do need treatment. I have no medical supplies in my bag."

Unable to argue with his logic, Kiara followed Caedmon and the strange creatures across the ice.

The manach lived in an enormous tower made entirely of ice. Kiara rubbed her eyes when she saw it, certain that they were playing tricks on her. The tower hardly looked strong enough to bear the weight of even one person and yet the manach indicated it was their home.

The tower was also larger than it appeared from the outside. Kiara didn't know how it was possible. It seemed to be an optical illusion of some kind. Inside the building was vast and they found many more manach all of whom greeted them by name.

Despite the building's structure of ice, it was comfortably warm within it. Kiara and Caedmon were led in different directions. When Kiara hesitated at being separated from Caedmon, the small wizen creature accompanying Kiara halted.

"He will be fine," she assured Kiara.

"What?" Kiara asked in confusion.

"Caedmon will be fine. You are worried about him. You should not worry. We are here to help you. You would not survive the ice fields without our help."

"What about that thing that almost killed us." Kiara shuddered remembering the creature in the ice.

"Yes, you woke an ancient one." The wizen creature smiled, her face creasing. "He was very hungry. It was his cries that alerted us to your presence."

"What was it?" Kiara asked.

The manach looked thoughtful. "There are many old beings that live in the ice. They are dormant until awoken. They have lived for many years by doing what that one tried to do to you."

"It tried to eat us!"

"Yes, it was hungry. Such creatures do not mean harm. They are only trying to survive. There are others that you must fear more than the ancient ones."

Kiara stared as the creature led her into a small chamber and nodded toward the bed. "Rest while I find you food and a healer. Then we will talk."

Kiara sat down on the bed, determined not to rest. But she found herself almost instantly becoming weary. And her waist was now aching with a throb that she was certain would prevent any kind of sleep. But the bed was so inviting with a soft mattress and warm blankets. And it had been so very long since she'd known the comfort of a bed. Sighing, she sunk into it and before she could think about what she was doing, she drifted into a deep slumber.

****

"Kiara. It is time to wake."

Kiara opened her eyes uncertain where she was. She sat up quickly reaching for her dagger and finding that her injuries didn't ache. She looked down. She was clad in a loosely fitted white robe. Her fingers probed her waist only to find smooth skin.

"The Healer came while you slept. You are well now."

Instantly she wondered if she had been drugged. She remembered falling to sleep so easily. But how could her wounds have been healed without her knowing.

"Be calm, Kiara. Be calm. You don't need to know the answers to everything, you know. I've brought you food."

The wizen one handed Kiara a tray laden with potatoes, vegetables and bread. And against her will her stomach rumbled loudly. Unable to help herself, Kiara began eating hungrily.

"Caedmon?" she asked, when her frenzy for food had abated.

"He is well. He also slept and is now eating. Do not worry. You will see him soon but men and women do not share chambers while here. I know that will be hard for you."

Kiara stared at the small figure wondering how she knew about her longing to be with Caedmon.

"You are safe while with us. But we can't protect you forever," she added. "We will help you get to Séreméla but you must be careful when you arrive there."

"What do you mean? How do you know what is going on in Séreméla?"

"We know more than you can imagine. You, all you Marked Ones, are all in great danger. Do not trust the Elders."

"What?"

"They wish to harm the Marked Ones. You must band together. You are the only hope for the future."

Kiara stared at her.

"Find the other Marked Ones before they kill them all. It is your destiny."

Afterward Kiara could never say how long they'd been with the manach. At times it seemed like hours and other times it seemed like weeks. But finally they were told they must continue with their journey.

The manach led them to the very edge of the ice fields.

"Go and be well, Marked Ones. Remember your destiny."

And with that they left.

****

It took them five more days to leave the mountains.

As they starting hiking downward, the landscape slowly changed. Finally pine trees began to appear. Kiara let out a yelp of joy when she saw the first real tree and ran over to hug it. Caedmon stood laughing at her.

"What?" she cried. "I could care less if I see snow and ice ever again."

"Well, you're likely to see snow until we reach the outskirts of Séreméla," he told her as he sobered. "It is winter after all."

Kiara nodded. "Yes, that's true but the snow we'll see is real snow not the insanely evil ice snow of the last month." She shuddered.

Caedmon smiled in understanding. They had both had more than enough of the mountain weather.

That night they made camp under a copse of trees, built a large fire and ate their fill of the rabbits that Kiara had caught and cooked over the fire. Even though they were still outdoors, as Kiara snuggled up to Caedmon in his sleeping roll, she felt for the first time in a long time that they were going to be successful in their journey. She could almost feel the end in sight.

She tried to imagine what it would be like to be in Séreméla with her mother and sisters again. She frowned as she shifted in the sleeping roll. It was going to be different. She had become used to sleeping with Caedmon. That would surely end once they reached Séreméla. She knew Brijit would not have approved of their sleeping arrangements. But even though they shared the bedroll out of necessity, Kiara was surprised to feel a pang of disappointment at the thought of going to bed alone again.

She frowned trying to make sense of her thoughts. Despite their unconventional sleeping arrangements, Caedmon had behaved as a gentleman throughout the journey. The sharing of a bed had been necessary but had also been a comfort to Kiara. She didn't want to think about it ending. But she knew that too soon it would.

The next day they arrived at the outskirts of Revuover, the largest city in the Five Corners and the closest one to Séreméla. As they broke camp that morning, Caedmon dug his ring out of his bag.

"I suppose your ring was lost in the cave in?" he noted when he saw her watching him. Then added a touch sardonically, "I thought at least one of us should have a symbol of our wedded bliss."

Kiara rolled her eyes at him. They'd agreed that they should revert back to the story Weylon had given them with the minor edit that now they would be going to meet Caedmon's mother in the Outlands.

Kiara raised her eyebrows at him and pulled her silver chain from around her neck, the gold ring still hanging from it.

Caedmon whistled. "Ah, me lass, my ring was so important to ye that ye had to wear it near your heart," he teased, taking on a strong Outland accent.

"Oh, stop it." She hit him playfully on the shoulder. "I figured that since it was gold, it must be worth something so it wouldn't be wise to stuff it in a bag that could be looted at any point." She took it from the chain and put it on her the middle finger of her right hand.

As they weaved through the semi-crowded streets of Revuover, Caedmon narrowed his eyes at Kiara.

"What's wrong?" she asked finally.

"You don't look much like a new bride," he noted gesturing toward her dirty leggings, tunic and jacket. He wrinkled his nose at her short hair. Kiara glared at him. She knew it had grown to a shaggy mess over the two months on the road but there was no need to make faces. "You look more like a boy playing at being a man."

Kiara's temper flared but then she saw some of the other women in the streets. Even the most rustic peasant in this part of the country seemed to dress in skirts and frills. And she couldn't see a single woman with close shorn hair.

Kiara grimaced. "Well there's not much I can do about it now, is there?" she asked Caedmon angrily. "I lost the one dress I owned in the cave in. And I like my hair this way."

"You only owned one dress?" he asked incredulously. Then seeing her angry expression, he held up his hand in mock defense.

"I know. I'm not blaming you, Kiara, it's just that if we don't want to draw attention to ourselves, we should be putting some thought into how to acquire a proper dress for you." He grimaced as he looked down. "And some clean clothes for me," he added gesturing at his stained and ripped clothing.

Kiara frowned but she knew Caedmon was right.

"We can get away with it at this end of Revuover but as we go further into the heart of the city, your current state of dress will draw notice." He paused and then grimaced at his own dirty appearance. "As will my own. But don't worry, I have an idea."

Caedmon took them to an inn where he'd stayed often when he was in the Army. He told Kiara that the middle-aged woman who ran the Inn had been very fond of him. It turned out Mistress Clare was rotund motherly woman with a perpetual laugh in her voice and smile on her face. She was delighted to see Caedmon and he soon showed that he was almost as adept at weaving a tale as his brother Teague was.

"We've had nothing but bad luck," Caedmon told the happy Innkeeper as he ordered them a room and a two hot baths. "First the carriage broke down, then when I went to find some help, the two horses ran off. We were forced to walk across country, sleeping in the woods last night."

The Mistress Clare tutted and shook her head.

"My new wife is not too pleased with me," he confided. "You see she didn't want to go on this trip to begin with as she's going to have to meet my mother for the first time. My mum is a bit difficult at the best of times," he acknowledged wryly. "And to be honest, I expect her to be even worse this time as she's none too pleased about me marrying outside the Outlands."

He turned and pretended to study Kiara. "Now tell me, as an unbiased judge, Mistress Clare, what is your first impression of my wife? I confide I find her too fetching to be able to judge."

Mistress Clare seemed flustered for a moment. "I don't think it's my place to make any such judgment on your lady's appearance, sir."

Kiara could tell the woman didn't want to make trouble with her guests but it was clear what she thought of Kiara's appearance. She instantly liked Mistress Clare for her tact and politeness.

"Oh, don't worry, she won't take it to heart. I just want to know what another motherly woman might think of her looks. She's a beauty, yes?" Caedmon asked, really getting into the role of moonstruck lover.

"Well," the Innkeeper paused as she studied Kiara's filthy appearance. Then she licked her lips and answered carefully, "She is very pretty, anyone can see that but her style of dress is not precisely what a mother might want in a daughter-in-law." She lowered her voice a bit. "A woman wearing trousers, you know."

Caedmon narrowed his eyes and then smacked his forehead. "Of course. I was so accustomed to seeing her in such clothing that I didn't think twice about it but you're quite right. I knew something was off."

Suddenly he looked very glum. "But how can we fix that problem? We're due to meet Mum the day after tomorrow."

The Innkeeper brightened up. "Why my sister's a great seamstress. I could put in a word to her. And a little bath and clean up, after your horrific experience in the woods, mistress," she said kindly to Kiara, "Well, that would put it all to right. We'd be happy to give it a try."

Caedmon looked thrilled as a boy in a candy shop. Kiara refrained from rolling her eyes at him.

After they'd gone up to their room, Kiara shook her head at him.

"I think you missed your calling as a play actor, Caedmon."

He shrugged, "You think so?"

She laughed. "Well, I'm not sure but I do know I'm taking first turn at that bath you've ordered." The maid had filled a brass tub behind a screen in the corner of the room.

Caedmon laughed good-naturedly. "Fine, you go ahead. I'm going to scout around and see if I can't find a place to purchase some new clothing for myself."

After they'd both bathed and eaten a full supper of roasted mutton, vegetables and tiny delicate cherry tarts Mistress Clare had insisted on bringing to their room. Kiara patted her stomach in appreciation.

"I don't think I've felt so warm and full in years," she moaned softly.

"Or so tired?" Caedmon asked with a smile as her eyes began to droop more.

Kiara nodded in agreement and looked longingly at the big bed.

"Too bad it's your turn to take the floor," Caedmon jibed.

Kiara sat bolt upright "Caedmon, that's not fair!" she protested.

"I believe it was you who set that deal," he reminded her.

"Oh but we've been sharing the sleeping roll for weeks now," she pointed out. "Besides the bed is surely big enough."

Caedmon relented. But before Kiara drifted off to sleep that night, with Caedmon's big body lying next to her in the sheets, she couldn't help but question her reason for wanting to share the bed. She was afraid that the truth was she had become so accustomed to sleeping with Caedmon's arms around her that she didn't want to back to sleeping on her own. And a little sick feeling started in her stomach as she wondered what would happen when they reached Séreméla.

CHAPTER TWENTY-FOUR

Despite her worry about Teague and the mysterious illness that had claimed the lives of the other Halfling children, Thia was excited at the possibility that she might learn to control her seizures.

Celeste had warned her that it could take some time until she'd perfected the knowledge. There was also the problem with Thia's age. She was much older than The People's children were when they were taught to control their lifeforce. But Thia was determined to learn how to do so.

Celeste introduced her to a woman who could have been Celeste's clone. *This is my daughter, Delphine. She will act as your guide.*

Delphine sent soft encouraging emotions to Thia and Celeste left them.

Do you really think it's possible for me to learn to control my seizures and visions? Thia asked the woman in front of her.

A soft smile came to Delphine's face. *It doesn't matter what I think, Thia. You must believe that you can do it. If you don't, then control will not be possible.*

Thia nodded. She had seen incredible things in the Underground. She remembered how Celeste had healed Teague's injuries. What was considered a miracle aboveground was simply the way of life in the Underground.

How do we start?

****

Thia was mildly disappointed when they started the training with what Delphine called meditation.

The key to learning how to control your lifeforce is to become aware of it. And that starts with clearing your mind.

Thia had expected something more challenging than merely sitting quietly in her room. But when she tried it, she found it amazingly difficult to clear her mind of all thoughts and worries. Delphine had her focus on her breathing.

They started with very short sessions several times a day. By the end of the first week, Thia was able to sit quietly and free her mind for more than an hour at a time.

When she told Teague about his lessons he wasn't surprised. *We did similar exercises with the Draíodóir*, he explained.

Do you think that's why the Underground way of communicating is so easy for you? Thia asked suddenly.

Teague shrugged. *Maybe. But I know learning to sit quietly was never easy for me. It took me several years to master the practice. The fact that you're already able to sit for long periods is amazing, Thia.*

She smiled, pride filling her up.

After the first week, Delphine said it was time to introduce the energy work into their sessions.

Energy work? Thia asked, intrigued by the name of it.

Delphine nodded. *First, you must become aware of your lifeforce. Only after you can sense it, can you control it. But you have used energy before, Thia.*

Thia looked at Delphine wondering what she meant.

I can sense it. Have you used it in healing?

Thia thought of how she would try to ease the discomfort of her patients by soothing the energy she felt flowing through their bodies. She nodded. I think I have. She explained to Delphine what she'd felt with the injured she cared for. *But it was instinctive. Brijit said it was an ancient art, she also would practice it at times but she always said I was better at it than her.*

Then learning to control your lifeforce will be easier for you. What happens when you have an attack?

Thia thought of how she felt when a seizure was coming on. The loss of control she experienced and how she almost felt as if she left her body. *I feel unwell usually. Then I see strange things, usually purple swirls in my eyes. It's hard to explain. And then I lose consciousness and fall into a vision.*

Delphine leaned forward. *What do you mean a vision?*

I see things that are going to happen. But they never make sense at the time.

Delphine was quiet, considering Thia's words. *If you gain control of your lifeforce, I believe the loss of control will cease completely. But it is possible that you will still have visions. They will probably come to you in your mediations instead of in the attacks.* She smiled suddenly. *Don't you see, Thia? The attacks may have been how the visions forced themselves upon you.*

Thia thought about it. It did make some sense. To be able to control her visions as well as avoid the seizures seemed impossible. Her heart leapt. This was more than she had ever hoped could be possible.

****

Thia, now sense the light.

Thia let Delphine's calm thoughts intrude on her meditation. She opened her eyes and saw the purple swirls that indicated a seizure was coming.

Don't let it take control, Delphine urged, you are controlling it. See it. Hold it. Embrace it as part of you.

Thia's heart sped up as the purple light encompassed her entire field of vision.

Breathe.

Thia took a deep breath, calming her panic, pushing those thoughts back. Then for the first time she embraced the energy. She noticed the beauty in the swirls.

Delphine held out her hand, and Thia lifted her own hand and let the purple light intermingle with the pale pink glow that was coming from Delphine's skin. It was as if a loved one was embracing her.

Happiness engulfed Thia and she didn't know if she was sending out the emotion or Delphine was.

Slowly Thia let the energy ebb and calm until it was just a faint glow from her fingertips. She smiled at Delphine.

I did it!

Delphine nodded and returned her smile but then horror suddenly engulfed her face. *Thia!*

Thia looked at her surprise. What was wrong?

Your nose.

Thia reached and touched her face. Her fingers encountered something warm and sticky. She pulled them away and stared at them. Blood.

Delphine was looking at her in her alarm.

Thia tried to smile. *It's just a nosebleed*, she assured her with a weak smile. *We have these Above Ground occasionally.*

We don't get nosebleeds Underground.

Thia felt fingers of fear closing over her heart.

The others did, didn't they? she asked thinking of the seven Halflings who had died Underground.

Sadness emanated from Delphine and she nodded.

Fear chased the euphoria of the session away.

****

Celeste found her by Teague's bedside later that day. *It is time for you to return to the surface, my child.*

Thia shook her head. *Not without Teague*, she insisted.

Celeste looked at the immobile Teague. *He is not responsive, Thia, we have to assume that he won't wake. You may have a chance at life on the surface. Here you will die.*

I'm fine, Thia insisted and suddenly Celeste bombarded her with a series of images that clearly illustrated what had happened to the Halflings who had died.

We have all come to love you. We have decided that a return to the surface is worth a chance. It could save your life.

Did any of the others – the seven like us – return to the surface?

Celeste shook her head. *They deteriorated faster than you have. For most of them death came within hours of the bleeding but you have shown no sign of getting weaker. We've decided that it is at least worth the effort to try to return you Above Ground.*

And Teague? Thia asked, sensing that they would not let him go.

We feel we should keep him here.

Thia shook her head. No! She was not going to abandon Teague to certain death.

Teague has no symptoms. Perhaps his condition is protecting him. Moving him would be an onerous task and one we will not undertake unless he is showing signs of illness.

Celeste was calm. *I will give you tonight.* They both knew it was a gift – a final dreamwalk in which Thia could say her goodbyes.

CHAPTER TWENTY-FIVE

Mistress Clare and her sister descended on Kiara. The seamstress had brought several of her dresses based on the description of Kiara. She ultimately decided, with the strong opinion of her sister, on a deep blue dress of velvet, trimmed with satin ribbon. Kiara refrained from making a face – it was not the type of clothing she would ever choose for herself. She just hoped she'd be able to get some new leggings and a tunic when they reached Séreméla.

As the older woman worked away measuring and pinning the dress, she explained to Kiara that usually she would make a new dress for a client but since time was so short they would just have to make do with the dresses she had in stock.

Kiara ignored the idle chatter from Mistress Clare and her sister. When they realized she wasn't going to gossip with them, the sisters took to catching up on the topics and people that were important to them. Kiara tuned them out and let her thoughts wander. She wondered how Caedmon was going to pay for such a fine gown. She had no money of her own since the little she'd had for the journey was lost with her pack in the mountains. Caedmon had been paying for their food and lodgings for the entire trip so Weylon must have given him some money or perhaps he had money of his own. She just hoped this fancy dress didn't deplete their resources completely.

Then it occurred to her that she didn't know how close they were to Séreméla. She never paid much heed to maps in her lessons. All she knew was that Revuover was the closest city to Séreméla. She'd have to remember to ask Caedmon how much further their journey would be.

After an abundant amount of time, wasted in Kiara's mind, spent on adjusting the dress, Mistress Clare and her sister finally laced Kiara into the gown. Kiara, who had never been in a laced gown in her life, and after this experience could not understand why any woman would want to wear such a garment, was impatient and irritable when they turned her toward the mirror. But her mouth fell open when she saw her reflection.

"Why you truly are a beauty," Mistress Clare said with awe. "That soldier boy has better taste than I first gave him credit for." Then catching herself she looked quickly at Kiara. "No offence meant, my dear, but you were quite bedraggled when you arrived."

Kiara smiled, still a bit stunned by her reflection. "I think you're being generous in your description," she said with a smile.

The Innkeeper suddenly looked a bit shy. "Would you mind, dear, if I perhaps took the time to tidy up your hair?"

"Oh, yes, do!" her sister exclaimed. "Before Maggie married old Mr. Clare, rest his soul, she worked as a maid in one of the great houses and used to do all the gentleladies' hair."

Kiara took a deep breath. She was not one to fuss with her hair. She liked to keep it sheared short and close to her head. But it had grown an incredible amount while they were travelling. And cutting it while making camp and hunting hadn't seemed a practical use of her time. Cleaning it up a bit couldn't hurt.

She nodded. "Alright. I usually shear it close."

Mistress Claire gasped. "What?" she asked in horror. "Oh, your hair is so short already. Just a little clean up will do I think," she said firmly.

Kiara resigned herself and sat still while the older woman began to snip and comb her hair. Again after what seemed like an immense amount of time spent on one's hair, Mistress Clare led her to the mirror once again.

Kiara stared at her reflection in surprise. With the ragged ends trimmed from her hair, it now fell to just below her ear lobes. Mistress Clare had tied an extra ribbon from the dress trimmings in her hair. The blue dress and ribbon brought out the color of her eyes. Kiara, for the first time, was mesmerized by the pretty reflection in the mirror. She was sure it couldn't be herself.

"See, my dear. You are lovely," Mistress Claire murmured.

After a day of primping and preparing her, Mistress Claire made a big production of showing Kiara off to Caedmon, who was waiting in the great room of the inn. Kiara stared at him for a moment. He'd found himself some clean clothes as well and this was the first time she'd seem him dressed in anything other than soldier's clothes. Kiara's mouth went dry as she took in his gentleman's clothes of a linen shirt, trousers and a fine dark coat. His long hair was pulled back to the nape of his neck and secured with a leather cord.

As if sensing her presence, Caedmon turned when she entered the room and froze, his gaze dropping to the hem of her skirts and then slowly traveling up to her face. He openly stared at her.

"You see, dear! I knew he'd be impressed," Mistress Clare gushed, her laugh filling the room.

Caedmon walked over to her, a stunned expression still on his face.

"Do I look okay?" she asked nervously.

He reached out and caught a black lock of her hair between his thumb and finger. "You look like a girl," he said in awe.

Kiara glared at him and was tempted to kick his shin. "I am a girl," she reminded him testily.

Caedmon laughed, "Ah, it is you under all the polish."

Kiara suddenly felt hot tears prick her eyes for no reason. She looked down to her feet and felt her face heat in embarrassment as she fought to control this sudden stupid wave of emotion.

Then she felt Caedmon's finger under her chin, lifting her face so she had to meet his eyes.

"You look beautiful, Kiara," he said solemnly.

Kiara suddenly couldn't look anywhere but into his dark eyes.

Caedmon stepped closer to her, lowered his mouth and gently brushed his lips against hers. Kiara's heart began to pound.

The Innkeeper clapped in delight, not realizing that it was their first kiss.

Kiara closed her eyes as his lips continued to gently press into her own. Then abruptly he stepped away. And Kiara felt a wave of panic sweep over her. She didn't know what all this meant. Suddenly she was afraid to meet Caedmon's eyes.

Mistress Clare, unaware of the tension between Kiara and Caedmon, led them to a table in the far corner of the room. She had arranged for them to have a dinner and this time she'd gone to great trouble with the menu preparing them an elaborate meal of fresh fish and greens with tiny potatoes, carrots and onions.

Dinner was an awkward affair. They didn't talk about the kiss but it hung in the air between them. Kiara tried not to think of it but, of course, her mind kept going back to it. As usual Caedmon was a master at hiding his emotions so there was no way for her to know how he was feeling.

After an hour and a half of stifled conversation, Caedmon pushed back his chair and suggested they get to bed early, as they needed to be back on the road the next morning. This was news to Kiara and it reminded her of her earlier questions.

"How long will we be on the road before we reach Séreméla?" she asked.

Caedmon told her he was hoping they could make it to Séreméla by the following evening.

"Oh. So soon?" she asked softly, hoping that he didn't detect the disappointment she could hear in her voice.

Caedmon nodded. "Séreméla is only a day's journey from here. We are almost at the end of this trip at long last," he said, relief tinting his words.

Kiara tried to hide the stab of pain she felt at his eagerness for their journey to be over. She pushed back her chair and after thanking Mistress Clare for the lovely meal and the dress, then she followed him upstairs.

As soon as they arrived in their room, Caedmon dug his sleeping roll out of his bag.

Kiara watched as he unrolled his sleeping mat and arranged it in front of the door, a lump rising in her throat. She hoped her face was as implacable as his was. But she felt a pain in her heart that she didn't want to think about. She bit her lip and started making her own preparations for bed. That's when she realized that she couldn't reach the lacing of her dress. Another reason why such attire was ridiculous, she thought darkly.

"Caedmon," she said hesitantly, her face burning with humiliation.

He looked over at her and raised his eyebrows.

"Um, can you," she faltered for a moment, gestured with her hand toward her back, "I, um, can't ..."

He didn't say a word but stepped across the room and deftly unlaced her gown with practiced ease. To Kiara felt it like a slap. It was obvious Caedmon was experienced in helping ladies out of their gowns. She didn't want to know how he'd come by such experience. It was clear he had no intention of using that experience on her. She knew she should be thankful that he was treating her with such respect but she couldn't help wondering if her kiss had been so horrible that he didn't want to be near her any more.

She whispered a quick thank you and then waited until he'd climbed into his sleeping roll and turned his back to her before she took off the dress, carefully laying it on the chair by the bed. She slipped between the sheets hoping sleep would come to her easily.

She listened as Caedmon's breathing slowed into the long slow breaths of sleep. She willed herself to also go to sleep but it eluded her. She spent most of the night tossing and turning, telling herself that her lack of sleep was due to her anticipation and worry about the trip tomorrow. But deep down she feared that her lack of sleep was due to the fact that she had become accustomed to sleeping with Caedmon's arms around her. And after that kiss she had no idea what that might mean.

****

The next day Kiara and Caedmon left the inn in a carriage. Caedmon had contracted the carriage driver to take them all the way to Séreméla. He reasoned that there was no sign of them being followed at this stage and they were overdue anyway so the sooner they could get to the end of the journey the better.

CATHI SHAW

"Plus, I wouldn't mind staying warm and dry for a change," Caedmon said with a grin. His attempt at levity however fell flat and they ebbed into silence.

Kiara wasn't completely convinced. She wondered if he'd decided to get the carriage after he saw her dolled up in her dress. Mistress Clare had returned Kiara's travelling clothes, clean and dry in a bundle when she came to help Kiara dress for the day. Kiara had been tempted to put them back on and leave the dress in the room of the Inn for good but then she remembered their story about trying to impress Caedmon's mother.

Séreméla was a seven-hour carriage drive. Caedmon suggested that they could stop for the night if Kiara didn't wanted to travel for such a long day. She looked at him wondering what had happened to change his behavior toward her. Suddenly he was treating her like she was a fragile doll. Had he completely forgotten who she was based on a dress and a bit of ribbon in her hair? She shook her head in disbelief.

"I'd rather make good time and get to Séreméla as soon as we can. If we can be there by tonight, why would we stop?"

Caedmon looked at her, hurt she didn't understand reflected in his dark eyes. What was his problem now? He was the one who had said the sooner they ended this journey the better. His face emotionless, he nodded. "I agree." He gave some instructions to the driver and they set off.

It was dark when they entered Séreméla. Kiara couldn't help but notice the change in the temperature as they approached the gates. It was significantly warmer and the snow that had been on the ground just a kilometer back was now gone, replaced with green. The coach rolled to a halt.

"This is as far as I go," the driver told them as he opened the door for Kiara.

Caedmon nodded and paid him. After he had rolled away, Kiara looked at Caedmon. "Now what?"

"Now we walk," he said and turned to the gate. She watched him for a moment in surprise. Although he had never mentioned it during their journey, it was clear that Caedmon had been to Séreméla before.

Kiara followed him slowly, expecting him to stop at the gate but to her surprise the gate swung open for him.

"Come on, Kiara!" he called to her impatiently and she hurried to where he was standing.

Despite the darkness, the scent of the air made it clear to Kiara that they had entered a very different climate. A pleasant flowery scent floated to them on the warm breeze.

They hadn't walked far when they were greeted by two tall figures on horseback. They introduced themselves as the Guardians of Séreméla. They told them they would take them to the Sanctuary where they were expected.

CHAPTER TWENTY-SIX

Mina couldn't believe that Kiara was standing in front of her. She had to fight the urge to rub her eyes. "I was so worried." She paused and then asked quietly, "Thia?"

Kiara shook her head, tears in her eyes.

Mina felt a stab of fear in her heart. "What happened?"

Kiara looked sick. She swallowed and started talking, her voice raw with emotion. "We were separated. We hoped maybe Teague and her had found their own way here?" She trailed off the hope clear in her voice.

Mina sighed. "No, they haven't arrived yet." She paused. "But there is still hope then – you didn't see any harm come to her?"

Kiara stared at her sister. "Did you expect that I had?" she asked.

Mina looked around nervously. She had to be careful of what she shared with Kiara. "I have a lot to tell you but not here." She looked into Kiara's confused blue eyes. "Kiara, we are in danger."

Suddenly Brijit rushed into the room and swept Kiara into an embrace. Mina saw Kiara watching her over their mother's shoulder. Mina shook her head slightly in warning and she was relieved to see understanding dawn in Kiara's eyes.

Weylon was right behind Brijit and seemed thrilled to see his son. Mina watched as he clamped Caedmon on the shoulder. Could it really be that they couldn't trust their own parents? She found it hard to believe that Brijit and Weylon knew what was happening to the Marked Ones? As she watched them embrace Kiara and Caedmon it didn't seem likely. And yet Meldiron was adamant that they couldn't discuss their suspicions with anyone – especially not Brijit or Weylon. He said their positions as *coimirceoirí* meant they would be bound to tell the enemy anything that was shared with them, even if it meant their own children would be harmed.

Meldiron stepped forward, interrupting the reunion.

"Caedmon and Kiara, there is much for us to catch up on," he said. "But you must be tired from your journey. Why don't we meet in the morning after you've had a night to rest and catch up with your families?"

Brijit came with Mina and Kiara back to Mina's bedchamber. Brijit sat holding Kiara's hand, seeming to be unable to take her eyes off her daughter's face. Mina felt tears gathering in her own eyes as Kiara spilled out the story of what had happened on the mountain.

"I tried to dig her out," she sobbed, "I tried."

"Of course, you did, darling," Brijit soothed. "But one woman against a mountain rarely wins."

They sat in silence for while. Then Brijit stood. "I'm going to leave you girls now. But don't stay up talking all night – you must be exhausted after your journey, Kiara, and Mina you are still recovering."

Kiara turned to her as soon as the door shut behind Brijit. "What does she mean recovering? How long were you sick for, Mina? Tell me what has happened to you?"

Mina sighed. "Where to start? I feel like I haven't seen you in a year, never mind a few months."

"Start at the beginning," Kiara said. "I want to know everything."

Kiara was surprisingly patient while she listened to Mina's recounting of her experiences in Séreméla. That was until Mina told her about Meldiron's attack and the revelation that he was her brother.

Kiara was stunned. "You're a princess?" she asked, her expression darkening to one of anger. "Brijit has some answering to do, doesn't she?"

Mina shook her head. "I was surprised as well, Kiara, but we can't blame Brijit for doing her job. Her duty as coimirceoirí is to do as the Elders instruct. She couldn't tell me where I was from. We don't even know how much she knew." Mina paused and bit her lip. "But Meldiron believes that we must be cautious now."

Kiara sat up from where she was lounging at the foot of the bed.

"His attack wasn't random, Kiara. His own men attacked him."

Her sister cursed.

"He's convinced that the Marked Ones are being targeted." She paused wondering if Kiara would think Meldiron was paranoid. "He says the only ones we can trust are each other."

Kiara looked troubled.

"What's wrong?" Mina asked when her sister was silent.

Kiara next words shocked her. "I think he's right, Mina. We can trust no one."

****

The next morning they met Caedmon and Meldiron in the gardens. As Meldiron led them deeper into the trees, Mina couldn't help noticing the silent byplay between her sister and Caedmon. She suddenly wondered what had happened on their journey. It was clear that Caedmon's feelings for Kiara had shifted. He kept looking in her direction but whenever Kiara met his eye he quickly looked away. Mina pressed her lips together. Something was going on between the two of them.

Meldiron finally stopped near the massive waterfalls that were located a fair distance from the Sanctuary. Mina smiled. He'd picked a perfect location if he thought there was any danger that they might be watched. It would be impossible to overhear any conversation this close to the thundering water.

He gestured for them to sit on the rocks surrounding the falls. "I won't waste your time or intellect with small talk," he said once they were settled. "It has become more and more apparent in recent months that all of us are in grave danger."

Kiara met Mina's eyes.

"What do you mean?" Caedmon asked, his dark eyes on Meldiron.

He told them of how he'd been ambushed by his own men.

"Are you certain it was your own men? You say you were close to death," Caedmon pointed out.

Meldiron looked at him steadily. "I know when I've been attacked and this time I knew who was doing the attacking. At least who was set up to do the attacking."

"Are you saying that you think someone may have put those men up to attacking you?" Kiara asked.

Meldiron nodded. "I'm certain of it," he said grimly. "But I don't know who."

"You're the crown prince of Séreméla," Caedmon noted. "It is possible that there are many who could want to harm you, is there not?"

Meldiron inclined his head. "In theory. But that is not the case this time."

"How do you know?" Caedmon demanded.

"Because of this." Meldiron pulled his tunic roughly over his head and turned his shoulder for them to see the Mark. He looked at Caedmon. "That is why they are trying to kill me and that is why they have and will continue to try to kill you."

Caedmon's face was suddenly guarded. "What are you saying?"

Meldiron pulled his shirt back over his head. "I know you are Marked, Caedmon. As is your brother and all three of the girls," he paused considering. "And we are not the only ones."

At that Caedmon looked surprised.

"He's right." Kiara spoke up. "Brijit and I saw dead children in the Lowlands. All of them murdered in the same way and all of them Marked."

Mina stared at her sister. "Kiara? Why didn't you tell us?"

Kiara looked at her. "Because our mother told me not to. In fact, she swore me to secrecy. I thought it was just because she didn't want to burden you with the knowledge that children were being killed. Now I'm not so sure."

Caedmon looked troubled. "Okay. So Marked children are showing up dead and your life has been threatened. Why does that make you think that someone is out to kill all of us?"

Meldiron shook his head. "You misunderstand me," he told them, "I think that there are many individuals both within Séreméla and beyond its borders that are behind this."

"In other words," Kiara said softly, "you are saying we can't trust anyone."

Meldiron nodded. "And I'm not convinced the mountain slide that separated you and the others was unintentional." He paused. "Something that is made to look like an accident is better than something that is not."

Caedmon looked puzzled. "Are you saying the mountain came down intentionally?"

"Perhaps," Meldiron said. Then he added quietly, "I believe the Draíodóir are involved."

Caedmon looked grim.

"But the storm could not have been planned," Kiara protested.

Meldiron nodded in agreement. "No, but winter storms in the mountains at that time are hardly unheard of." He paused. "Let me ask you this, Caedmon, who gave you your route."

Caedmon met his eyes, his own troubled and a touch angry. "I don't like what you're suggesting," he said darkly.

"Neither do I," Meldiron admitted. "But there are those who are not happy that you made it to Séreméla. I know this and your lives are in danger if you leave."

"Who did give you that route?" Mina asked curiously.

"Weylon." Kiara answered and the four of them looked at one another in stunned silence.

CHAPTER TWENTY-SOMETHING

Celeste's gift of a last dreamwalk was hardly generous. Thia couldn't bear the thought of leaving Teague behind while she returned to the surface. She was sure that they could come up with a plan that would insure they both safely return aboveground. But when she saw Teague in the dreamscape, her emotions overcame her. She ran directly into Teague's arms and wrapped her arms around his body. She couldn't bear the thought of losing him and not seeing him ever again. Tears filled her eyes and spilled over.

Thia? What is it? Teague asked her as he tried to pull away enough to see her face.

They want me to return to the surface, she told him between sobs. *I won't leave you.*

Teague stepped back. *Have you been ill?* he asked, concern filling his face. *Why didn't you tell me?*

Thia shook her head. *Not exactly. I think they're overreacting. I had a small nosebleed when I was meditating this afternoon. But they say that's how it started with the others and the end came quickly after the bleeding started.*

Teague pulled away. *And they believe that if you returned to the surface you will survive?*

Thia nodded reluctantly. *Well, yes, that's what Celeste and Delphine are hoping. But there is no guarantee.*

Teague grasped her arms tightly. *Thia, you must go. If there's even the slightest chance that your life will be spared, then you must go.*

Not without you. Please, Teague, don't make me leave you. I'd rather die here.

Teague paced away from her, his head down. Finally he turned and looked into her eyes deeply. *Thia, you can't do this to me.* The torment on his face was clear. *You can't leave me here not knowing if you've died underground when I know you could possibly live if you go to the surface.*

Thia felt tears spilling down her cheeks. *But Teague there is no guarantee that I will live. And here I can be with you when you wake up.*

He laughed bitterly and Thia stared at him. *Let's be realistic, Thia. I may never wake up. In fact, it seems likely I won't. I'm stuck in this trap and it's only a matter of time before I die anyway now. Thia, please, promise me you will leave.*

Thia looked at him, his eyes were filled with tears and anguish. She was certain that there was a way she could save Teague. But she needed to stay and perfect her control of her lifeforce. She needed more time.

Then Thia tried to imagine what it must be like for him to be stuck in this dreamland since she'd woken him to it. He never told her what he did in the long hours when she wasn't present but she knew he'd been growing more and more restless.

Alright, I will go, she whispered.

Tomorrow? he urged. *You'll leave tomorrow?*

She nodded as despair filled her. She might need more time but it didn't look like she was going to be getting it.

****

When she woke from the dreamwalk, she looked over to Teague. A thin trickle of blood was flowing from his nostril, painting a red line down his cheek. Celeste was sitting in a chair watching him silently.

When did this start? Thia demanded.

While you were both asleep, Celeste replied calmly.

Thia watched that blood pool on the bed by his cheek. Now it was clear that Teague would die if he stayed her. Celeste could not sentence him to that.

I will go to the surface, Thia said, *but you must let me take Teague with me.*

Celeste looked at her, her expression unreadable. Thia sent out her feelings of fear and sadness.

Please, he will just die here. You felt it and now you know it.

Celeste sighed. *Yes, he will die here but he may die on the surface as well.*

Thia nodded. *He may but he may not as well. Please, Celeste, let us try at least. You owe us that.*

Thia felt a gush of liquid run down from her nose, her hands going to her face and coming away with blood.

Celeste watched her. *We will prepare for you both to leave shortly.*

Celeste sent three of The People with them. Two to carry Teague on a stretcher they'd devised and the other to lead the way. Celeste had explained that it would not be a fast climb. They would only go short distances each day and then rest until her body adjusted to the lessening depth. A fast surfacing could be deadly in its own way.

Delphine took Thia aside before they left. *You must continue to practice your meditation, even while on the journey.*

Thia nodded. Truthfully she couldn't imagine not doing so. Her practice had been an essential part of her life.

You know that you have the ability to help him. Delphine glanced at Teague.

How? Thia asked.

The spell he's under has disrupted his energy force. You need to reactivate it. You are the only one underground who reacts to Teague so strongly. Use that to your advantage. I know you can do this, Thia.

As Thia bid farewell to both Celeste and Delphine she felt a flicker of hope start in her mind. Maybe she could save Teague.

****

It took nine days to reach the surface. Celeste had explained that their guides would only take them there and then they would return to the Underground. Thia, with or without Teague, would have to find her own way to Séreméla.

Celeste wanted to avoid having an encounter with the Elders. Apparently there were still some of the Elders who remembered her and she had no desire to renew their acquaintance. Thia wondered what kind of animosity existed between the two races but her instinct had told her not to ask Celeste about it.

Thia's nosebleeds had stopped after the first three days of climbing and Teague had no reoccurrence of the bleeding. As they got closer to the surface, Thia felt her energy returning.

The People who had led them onto the surface and looked around distastefully.

I don't like the smell of this place, one of them said, extreme distaste projecting from him.

Thia didn't agree. She was stunned at how long they'd been below ground. On the surface winter was fast disappearing and buds were appearing on the trees. The air smelled fresh, light with the scent of approaching spring. She couldn't see what was distasteful in the odor. She felt almost as though she were home again.

After settling them in a sheltered area beneath some trees, The People returned beneath ground as quickly as they could. Thia sent thanks and warm greetings to Celeste and Delphine through them.

Once she was sure they were gone, she sat beside Teague. He was lying still and motionless under the trees. She began to breathe slowly and deeply, clearing her mind of all her worries and fears. Once she achieved complete peace, she opened her eyes and studied Teague's sleeping form.

She then took both his hands into her own and concentrated. As the tingling warning began to snake up her arm she focused her mind on the energy. As it began to surge through her, she firmly held onto it and then focused on directing it back into Teague. She closed her eyes and focused hard. *Teague come back!*

Nothing happened for several moments but as Thia rode out the energy bursts, redirecting each one back to Teague she felt a shift in the energy flow. Suddenly his eyes flew open.

Thia?

"Teague!" she said aloud, laughing in relief, while her eyes clouded with tears.

"You're holding my hands," he said with wonder.

She laughed and nodded. "I am."

Teague shook his head "But no one has ever been able to touch me."

We're on the surface, she said unnecessarily, automatically shifting to the more complete form of communication.

You didn't leave me? he asked.

Thia shook her head. *I couldn't.*

Teague smiled at her and she helped him sit up. He closed his eyes for a minute. Celeste had warned her that when Teague first woke he would be exhausted from the weeks of inactivity below ground.

It's going to take a while for you to feel better, Thia told him. *We can rest, we have supplies.* She gestured toward the pile of supplies that The People had provided them with. *There is no rush to move onto Séreméla until you're stronger.*

And as she found some food for Teague, she felt a feeling of contentment wash over her. He was back with her. Optimism surged through her. She felt certain that good things were going to happen to them.

CHAPTER TWENTY-SEVEN

Kiara and Mina watched Caedmon stride across the lawn away from them.

"You two don't seem very close considering you spent the last two months together," Mina observed softly.

Kiara watched as Caedmon stopped to talk to two Elder girls, laughing and looking completely at ease and she felt a twinge in her heart. She turned to her sister. Mina was watching her with an expression of pity on her face. Kiara's anger at Caedmon surged. She didn't want anyone's pity, not even her sister's. He'd put her in this position.

"Tell me what happened, Kiara. I hate to see you in pain," Mina urged, when Kiara looked away.

Kiara swallowed. Would it help to talk about it? She wondered. She looked at Mina; her green eyes were full of worry. Well, she reasoned, if it didn't help her at least it would perhaps ease Mina's worry for her.

"I guess it started before we left the Inn," she admitted thinking back to how Caedmon had helped her with her training.

Mina raised her eyebrows. "I remember you being very distrustful of him."

Kiara nodded. "Yes, you're right. At first I didn't like him at all. But then you were hurt and he helped us get you back to the Inn. Once the Elders arrived, we were confined to the Inn and its grounds, forbidden to wander at all. It drove me mad," Kiara said remembering how frustrated she'd been.

"Caedmon felt the same and so we started training together." Kiara paused and smiled at her sister. "I guess that was when I realized I could actually learn a bit from him."

"Once we started on the journey, it was clear that Thia would not be able to keep up, so Teague found a cart for them to travel in. With Caedmon and I on horseback, we were thrown into one another's company even more. And then Weylon's idea for keeping suspicion off us while travelling emphasized the time we spent together."

Mina looked confused. "What was Weylon's plan?"

Kiara felt her face heat. "He insisted that we pose as married couples. He said it was the only explanation for our travelling with Outlanders."

Mina nodded thoughtfully. "It does make sense." Kiara was thankful that her sister didn't ask too many questions on that topic.

"After the cave in, I was without any supplies. My pack had been buried in the cave." She paused. "I was ... not myself at the thought of losing both Thia and you." She looked at Mina and her sister nodded, sympathy on her pretty face. "Caedmon found us shelter and forced me to stop trying to dig Thia out, which would have been futile anyway. Then he saved me from freezing to death by using his sleeping roll as shelter for both of us."

Mina didn't comment as Kiara told her of the long days and nights on the trip, how Caedmon and she had talked, shared their worries and concerns and how every night they had slept wrapped in one another's warmth.

"So why the distance now?" Mina asked after she heard Kiara's description of their relationship during the trip.

Kiara sat down and shook her head. "I don't know what happened. Everything was fine until we were arrived at Revuover." She fell silent remembering the kiss. It was her first real kiss and it really should be a happy memory but Caedmon's behavior since the incident ruined it for her.

"What happened?" Mina prodded gently.

Kiara shook her head.

"Did Caedmon behave inappropriately toward you?" Mina asked, concern clouding her voice.

Kiara looked up in surprise. She didn't think her sister would jump to that conclusion. "No!" she said quickly. "No, nothing like that."

"I don't understand, Kiara."

She sighed. "I know. Remember how I looked when I arrived here. Dressed in that ridiculous outfit?" The blue dress had quickly been replaced with her usual garb of tunic and leggings when she arrived in Séreméla.

Mina smiled. "You looked beautiful."

Kiara snorted in disgust. "Well, it was Caedmon's idea that we procure fancy clothes so that we would not stand out in our travelling clothes. I'd lost my dress and all my other clothes in the cave in so you can imagine the state of the clothing I'd been wearing."

Mina nodded.

Kiara added, "When he first saw me in the fancy dress, Caedmon started looking at me differently. He said I looked like a girl."

Mina laughed, "That's one way to put it."

Kiara bit her lip. "Then he kissed me," she whispered.

Mina's eyes widened. "And how was that?"

Kiara looked down at her hands remembering the sensation of Caedmon's warm lips on her own and how she'd felt in that moment. How her stomach had dropped away. "Wonderful," Kiara admitted, "except right after that he started pulling away from me."

She told her sister how Caedmon had slept on the floor that night. "Then he rented the carriage and we arrived in Séreméla the next day. There was no opportunity to talk about what had happened," Kiara said miserably. "And you know how he's been since we arrived here."

Mina nodded soberly.

Kiara looked up at Mina. To her horror she felt tears filling her eyes. "I just miss him," she whispered. "This seems so stupid."

"Then why don't you talk to him?" Mina suggested gently.

Kiara took a deep breath and looked out the window at the greenness that characterized Séreméla. "Do you think that would help?" she couldn't help asking, hopelessly tingeing her words.

She felt Mina's hand on her shoulder. "I think that's the wrong question to ask, Kiara," she said gently. "I think what you should be asking is how could talking to him make it worse?"

****

The next afternoon, Kiara took Mina's advice and worked up the courage to go looking for Caedmon. She found him in the archery grounds with the same Elder girl he'd been with the previous day. Kiara felt her heart sink but then she forced herself to stick to her plan.

Rather than interrupt his training, Kiara walked up to the Elder who was in charge of the equipment and asked for a bow.

He smiled and gave her a beautiful bow and quiver of arrows so light they felt as if they were made of air. Kiara began making her way through the training grounds and soon she was so lost in the flow of training that she'd almost forgotten about speaking to Caedmon. In Séreméla the training grounds were both beautiful and challenging.

Half an hour later she looked up and saw him putting his bow away and preparing to leave the training area. The Elder girl was nowhere to be seen.

Gathering up her own archery things, Kiara strode over to where Caedmon was.

"Caedmon," she called as he started to turn away.

He paused and turned to her, his expression unreadable.

She set her bow and the arrows on the stand.

"Do you have time to talk?" she asked, hating how her stomach was churning nervously.

He didn't look happy but he nodded reluctantly.

They exited the training grounds in silence. Then as if by unspoken consensus they headed towards the river where there would be few people this time of day.

As they continued to walk in silence, Kiara tried to think of an easy way to introduce the topic but she was coming up with blanks. Just as she was beginning to think that this was not such a good idea Caedmon stopped walking.

"Kiara, was there something in particular you wanted to talk to me about?" he asked carefully, his gaze somewhere over her left ear.

Stupidly she felt tears start to gather in her eyes. This was a disaster. How could one man reduce her to such an emotional response? This was a bad idea.

She turned her back and shook her head. "Never mind," she whispered.

Suddenly she felt Caedmon's hand on her arm as he tugged and softly coaxed her into turning back toward him.

"Kiara," he said gently, brushing the tears from her face, his voice echoing pain. "Has something happened?"

She looked down. "No, not really."

Caedmon sighed. "Look, you're clearly upset about something. Did I do something?"

She looked up at him then, suddenly realizing how ridiculous this was. She decided to find the courage she liked to brag that she had and just tell him.

"Why have you been so distant since we came here? I don't understand what I did to make you angry but I thought if we talked maybe you could explain and I could fix it."

He laughed darkly. "Fix it?" She was shocked by his bitter tone. "No. There's no way you can fix it."

Kiara stared at him stunned by his tone. "What did I do, Caedmon?" she asked not being able to keep the hurt from her voice.

He shook his head in frustration. "You didn't do anything in particular, Kiara." He sighed. "Look, I just realized things were changing between us and it would be better if we took control of it before we arrived here."

Kiara stared at him. "Changing how?"

Caedmon looked at her darkly. "That kiss was a long time coming. I didn't want to put you in an awkward position when we arrived here."

"Awkward how?" Kiara asked, confused.

He just looked at her silently.

"You didn't like the kiss?" she asked, anger building. "Did you just kiss me out of pity or something?"

Caedmon was the one who looked angry now. "I kissed you because I wanted to. I'd been thinking about it for days, weeks even." He stopped then added quietly, "and I still want to – that's the problem."

Hope lightened her heart. "You still want to?"

Caedmon shook his head. "Forget it," he said savagely. "It's my problem and I will get over it. But for now it's just easier for me if I stay away from you."

He brushed passed her heading back toward the lodgings.

"I liked it," Kiara called to his back and he froze. He stood there for a moment, then turned and looked at her, his expression guarded.

"What did you say?" he asked.

Kiara stood straighter, a smile on her lips. "I said I liked it." She looked down at her feet then back up at him. "I wish you'd do it again," she admitted softly.

Caedmon's expression was stunned, then he took two large steps back to her and pulled her into his arms before he lowered his lips to her own with such speed at Kiara's breath was taken away.

When Caedmon lifted his head and gazed down at her, Kiara couldn't stop herself from laughing up at him.

"I've missed you so much," he said softly.

"Oh, Caedmon, I've missed you too." She wrapped her arms around him and nestled her head on his chest. "Can we stop being so silly?"

He nodded and kissed the top of her head then straightened. "Come on, let's head back."

They were both unaware of the dark shadowy figure watching them from the copse of trees. It waited until they had disappeared from the path and then it turned and disappeared through the trees in the direction of Council headquarters.

263

FIVE CORNERS: THE MARKED ONES

CHAPTER TWENTY-EIGHT

When Teague was finally well enough to travel, Thia did as The People had asked of her. She erased all signs of their camp and destroyed the supplies they had left them with.

It's imperative that none of our technology is left on the surface, Celeste had told her when she gave Thia the deconstruction device.

Now Thia stood with Teague on the edge of the camp and watched as what remained of their supplies wilted into the ground. All trace of her time with The People seemed to have been erased.

They set off in the direction of Séreméla. Although Teague was feeling well enough to travel, they didn't rush. It took all his concentration to move so they focusing on putting miles beneath their feet and didn't talk much.

They'd gone half a day's journey when they saw two figures on the horizon.

Hunters? Thia wondered.

Teague squinted in the direction of the figures and then nodded.

Should we hide? Thia questioned but Teague didn't answer. He seemed fixated on the figures in the distance. Teague?

Suddenly he gave a yell and began running toward the figures. What was he doing?

The distant figures froze and then the larger one gave a returning yell and suddenly they were galloping toward them. Thia looked for cover but there was no place to hide and besides they'd already been spotted thanks to Teague.

As the distance closed between them, Thia blinked her eyes in disbelief and then began to move toward the riders herself. It was Caedmon and Kiara.

"Thia and Teague! You're alive?" Kiara was off her horse and had her sister in her arms within seconds.

"We thought you were dead," Kiara whispered and Thia was surprised to see how close to tears her sister was.

"We're not," Thia said assured her sister unnecessarily, happiness making her giddy.

"What happened?" Caedmon asked. "Did the tunnel actually lead to a way through the mountain?"

Teague nodded. "A roundabout one but it saved our lives," he said with a grin. Thia knew they would have to tell their siblings about the Underground but she was relieved Teague didn't blurt it out immediately. And Kiara and Caedmon were too happy to see them to ask too many questions. She had to think about how she would reveal the secrets of Celeste and her People.

****

Their arrival in Séreméla caused a lot of excitement. Brijit cried openly, admitting for the first time that she had believed that they were lost forever.

Mina and Thia embraced, both of them stunned and relieved that the other was alive and well.

Later when they were alone in Mina's bedchamber and Thia told her sisters what had happened since they'd been parted.

"So there's a whole other kind of people living below ground," Kiara said in disbelief after Thia finished her story.

"Yes, I know it sounds crazy but it's true."

"Trust me, I've seen enough outrageous things in the last few months to believe you." Kiara said.

Thia went on, "But they don't want their presence widely know. They are peaceful and retreated from this world so they could be left alone. I promised we would keep their existence a secret. You must promise, too."

"Of course," Mina agreed. "But, Thia, do you think the Elders know of their existence?" she asked carefully.

Thia nodded. "Yes, in ancient times they were of the same race. I'm sure they must know of them. Celeste suggested that some Elders still knew her." She paused and thought of Celeste with her flat dark eyes and white luminescent locks. "But they are very different now. They have lived underground for a long, long time."

"There is no need to speak of them to the Elders – at least not at present," Kiara said slowly. "It's odd that the Elders did not mention them to us though, isn't it?" she asked Mina with an edge in her voice.

Thia wondered what had happened to make her sister sound so distrustful.

"But what about you and Teague? You're Halflings of a kind, really?" Mina asked.

Thia nodded. "I know it's hard to believe at first but I do believe it now after spending so much time there." She paused searching for the right words. "In some ways, it was like finding my true home."

"But you became too ill to stay?"

"Yes, I have no doubt that both of us would have died if we had stayed. They have found other Halflings over the years but all died when they tried to live below ground. Teague and I survived the longest and in the end they were forced to send us above ground for fear we would also die."

"Did the other Halflings have the Mark?" Kiara asked suddenly.

Thia frowned. She hadn't thought to ask Celeste that question. "I don't know," she admitted.

Mina shrugged. "It's okay. But we do know that there are other Marked Ones. Many more than we'd ever imagined. Kiara, tell her about the child you and Brijit saw."

Kiara shared what she knew.

"And Meldiron and at least one of his kinsmen are Marked as well."

Thia shook her head. "Why would Brijit let us believe we were the only ones?" she asked in confusion.

Kiara and Mina exchanged a troubled look. Kiara finally answered grimly, "I don't know but we must be careful now. We don't know who our enemy is."

****

The next morning the five of them were exploring Séreméla when Meldiron found them.

"Teague, the Elder Council wishes to speak to you," he announced, his eyes troubled.

Teague paled visibly. But he nodded in agreement. Thia knew he was dreading going before the Elder Council. They had talked of it while he was recovering. Thia hadn't understood why he had to answer to the Elder council but Teague had explained that the *Draíodóir* were accountable to the Elders and other leaders of the Five Corners. He feared that when the *Draíodóir* clan learned of his time Underground, he would have much to answer for. The Elder council would inevitably summon the Heads of the *Draíodóir* clans. And based on the spell that had claimed Teague for so long, he surmised that at least some of them had wanted him dead.

Teague! Thia called silently.

I must go to them, Thia; we knew they would summon me. Too much has happened.

But what will they do to you? She sent the full tide of her worry to him with the words.

Teague looked grim. *I don't know.*

Caedmon moved to accompany his brother but Meldiron shook his head. "The council requested that he come alone."

Caedmon stood looking menacingly at Meldiron. "The council will change their minds or they won't speak to my brother."

Meldiron bowed his head in acquiescence, and motioned for Caedmon to follow.

Thia turned to her sisters, worry clear on her face. "This is not good."

Mina looked in the direction the three men had disappeared. "Meldiron will take care of him, don't worry," she reassured her sister, "He is the prince after all."

Mina was right, of course. Meldiron would make sure no harm came to Teague. And yet, Thia couldn't shake the feeling of dread that had fallen over her.

****

When they returned later in the afternoon, the news was not good. Meldiron's position didn't help Teague as much as Mina had suggested it would.

The council had ordered Teague to take them back to the underground entrance so they could find The People.

"You told them about The People?" Thia exclaimed. "Teague, how could you?"

"They didn't give him any room to keep it from them. The *Draíodóir* are connected on various mental levels, with that many in the room working on Teague he wasn't likely to resist them," Caedmon explained bitterly.

"It's becoming clear that even while in Séreméla we are in danger now," he added grimly.

Teague, you can't take them to The People! Thia protested.

"I know I can't," Teague said miserably for all to hear, "I just don't know how I can resist."

"We need to leave," Caedmon said seriously.

Mina shook her head. "It's impossible to leave Séreméla unobserved."

Meldiron nodded and explained the warding system to them.

Suddenly there was a shadow at their door. Kiara and Caedmon both jumped to their feet. But the shadow did not retreat; instead it stepped into the room. It was Bellasiel.

"I don't think I have to tell you that you are all in great danger. Staying here is not helping you it's only delaying the inevitable."

"And what do you mean by that?" Caedmon asked aggressively.

Bellasiel's face was grim. "There is much you don't know and it's time you were told." She bowed slightly to Meldiron. "I apologize, Prince Meldiron, for keeping this from you but I was under strict orders."

"Orders from whom?" Mina asked.

Bellasiel looked around nervously. She motioned with her head. "Come with me and I'll explain."

"How do we know we can trust her?" Kiara demanded.

Meldiron stood up. "I trust her," he said quietly, and led the way out of the room. They all followed.

Bellasiel took them to her private offices which were located underground. Once they were all there she said, "You need to know what is happening and in order for me to show you I need you to trust me."

She looked at each of them closely. When they had each nodded in agreement, she asked them to join hands. Linked in a circle she began to softly chant. At first nothing happened but slowly, Thia saw a strange fog begin to rise from the floor. It collected in the middle of the circle. Kiara looked at it suspiciously but Meldiron did not look surprised. Teague and Caedmon both looked miffed.

"This is what I wanted to show you," Bellasiel said as her chanting died away.

In the middle of the fog was the clear image of an Elder child, obviously dead. Her throat had been violently slashed.

Kiara gasped. "Like the children Brijit and I saw in the Lowlands."

In silence Bellasiel nodded. As they watched half a dozen similar images appeared in the fog. Elder children of various ages. All of them dead.

They stood in silence as the images disappeared and the fog slowly dissipated.

"Why?" Meldiron asked, his voice raw.

271

"They were all Marked." She paused and looked at the group.

"Hold it," Mina said slowly. "Are you saying that Marked Elder children are also being killed?"

Bellasiel nodded. "I first became aware of it when the Elder children's bodies were brought to me." She shook her head, pain flashing across her features. "Then they began taking me to view bodies of other children in the Five Corners."

"Why?" Thia asked in shock. "Why would they take a healer to see murdered children?"

Bellasiel raised her eyes. "They wanted me to ..." she swallowed painfully and then carried on, "Dissect their bodies to see if I could discover anything useful about them."

"Did you?" Meldiron asked.

Bellasiel shook her head. "No, upon examination all the children appeared normal. The only extraordinary thing about them was that they all had the Mark."

Just like the six of them. No one spoke the words aloud but the knowledge was thick in the air.

"Why?" Kiara asked savagely. "Why would they kill innocent children?"

Bellasiel closed her eyes. "You have to understand this is part of the Prophecy." She paused. "You have only seen the smallest fragment of the text. But the Prophecy is long and foretells the coming of a new age ruled by the Marked Ones. There are those who aren't keen for this kind of era to begin."

Mina spoke, "There is a longer copy of the Prophecy in the library here. Eöl Ar-Feiniel showed it to me but we left the studying of it until I was more proficient in the Ancient tongue."

Bellasiel nodded. "Eöl Ar-Feiniel is working with us. You are not alone. There are a number of us who wish to help the Marked Ones. We believe you are the saviors of the world, as we know it. Eöl Ar-Feiniel's job was to educate Princess Minathrial in the ways of the Elder people and to help her interpret the Prophecy."

"That's why you let me go to the library," Mina said suddenly.

"Yes and it is also why I forbade you to go out of doors. We knew time would be short and we wanted you to use what time you had collecting knowledge that would help you. Unfortunately, Eöl Ar-Feiniel's work has been interrupted multiple times."

"Why was I not shown this scroll or informed of the plans for Mina?" Meldiron asked.

"For several reasons," Bellasiel answered. "Forgive me, my prince, but we did not know if you could be trusted. You have been raised to lead us and the most influential Elders have molded the way you look at things in the Valley. We did not know if they had been successful in corrupting you. Now we know they have not. They realized the same thing and they tried to have you killed."

"Do you know where that scroll is now?" Meldiron asked Mina.

Mina nodded. "It's on my desk with the other readings Eöl Ar-Feiniel gave to me." She looked guilty. "It's kind of buried under a bunch of stuff."

"Hidden in plain sight." Meldiron hugged her. "Perfect, Mina!"

Bellasiel looked grim. "It may have been a brilliant plan but we need that scroll. It is one of the only copies of the complete Prophecy."

"I'll go get it," Mina offered. "I know exactly where it is."

"I'll come with you," Meldiron said.

They hurried through the Sanctuary to the library. But they hadn't made it to Mina's alcove before something stopped Meldiron.

"What's wrong?" Mina asked, turning to her brother.

Meldiron was standing still, listening. "The birds," he said, his face puzzled. Mina paused and realized that all the birds in the library were silent. It was something that had never happened – at least not since she'd arrived.

Suddenly there was a loud *Caw* and a coal black crow swooped from the upper branches of the tree, circled above their heads and flew through the window.

"Someone is dead," Meldiron said.

Mina looked at him, thinking he was kidding but his face was white. They stood still for another few seconds and then Meldiron began running toward Mina's alcove. Mina followed him. He came to a sudden halt as he reached her desk.

Mina looked past Meldiron and let out a cry. Slumped over her desk was Eöl Ar-Feiniel, his white head stained a gruesome mixture of red and black, blood and ink intermingled in a pool beneath his head. Mina reached out with trembling hands and set right an overturned inkbottle. The books and papers were scattered everywhere.

"But who would do this?" Anguish ripped through her. Eöl Ar-Feiniel was her friend and mentor. Why would anyone kill him?

"Obviously, someone who knew what he was doing," Meldiron said quietly. "Where is the scroll?"

Mina looked at the mess on top of the desk. She sifted through the remaining papers, trying not to touch Eöl Ar-Feiniel. She sniffled as tears burned her eyes.

"Meldiron," she whispered, "It's gone."

****

After they found the archivist dead and the scroll missing it was clear that their departure could not be delayed.

"How could he have been killed if the warding system is in place?" Kiara asked.

Bellasiel had looked grim. "The warding system must have been interrupted somehow." She paused. "And if Eöl Ar-Feiniel is dead then we must assume that our resistance has been discovered. I suggest you make preparations to leave immediately."

Kiara had returned to her chambers with Mina and Thia. She watched silently as Mina and Thia prepared their supplies for the journey. Despite the horror of Eöl Ar-Feiniel's death, her sisters were trying to stay positive. They had both changed over the last six months, she thought. They all had, she supposed, but both her sisters now knew a little bit about their beginnings. Of course, there were still gaps in that knowledge but Mina knew she was an Elder child and Thia had met The People and recognized a piece of herself in them. Kiara, on the other hand, still had no idea where she had come from.

It had never bothered her before but now that her sisters had a bit of knowledge, she couldn't help wondering about her origins. The *manach* had given her no hints. And she doubted that there would be any magical revealing of her birth parents. No one seemed to know where she'd come from.

Kiara paused. Except – a thought occurred to her. Brijit had known that Mina was an Elder child when she saw her. Could she possibly know where Kiara had come from? Kiara straightened from her preparations. If they were to leave the Valley, she might never see her adopted mother again. This was her one chance to ask Brijit about her origins. She had to see her one more time.

"I'll be back in a little while," she told her sisters vaguely.

Kiara hurried down the hall to Brijit's chambers. It was early evening and her mother typically retired to her room after the evening meal. Weylon didn't usually join her until late at night. This would be a good time to get Brijit alone.

Kiara knocked on the door, wondering what her mother would be able to tell her, if anything at all. When there was no answer to her knock she pushed the door open and called "Brijit?"

There was only silence in the chamber. Kiara's brow furrowed. She didn't like the feel of this. She looked up and down the hallway and saw no one. Then she slipped inside the room.

"Brijit?" she called again.

Her mother was not in the sitting room. Kiara wondered if she was ill – it was too early to retire for the night. She walked through to the bedchamber and then froze.

Brijit lay crumpled on the ground, blood oozing from a gash on her head.

Kiara let out a cry and hurried to her mother's side. "Brijit," she whispered as she lifted her mother's head into her lap.

Brijit opened her eyes and slowly focused on Kiara's face.

"Who did this?" Kiara asked.

Brijit swallowed. "You are in danger," she said, her voice thin and weak. "Take your sisters and run. They will kill you all."

"Brijit! Who did this to you?" she asked again sternly.

Brijit closed her eyes.

"Mama." Kiara called, a sob on her lips.

The corners of Brijit's lips turned up in a small smile. Then she sighed and breathed no more.

Kiara felt tears streaming down her cheeks. She couldn't stop staring at the blood that was still weeping from the back of Brijit's crushed skull, soaking her leggings. Then she heard the sound of the outer door opening and she froze, her eyes darting to the window. But she immediately discounted that as a route of escape. It was simply too far of a drop.

"Well, I see you found your mother."

She turned and met Weylon's hard gaze, the cruelty that had always lurked in his features now on full display.

"You?" she asked in disbelief.

"Why are you so surprised, Kiara? You recognized what I was from the beginning, didn't you?"

Kiara ignored his words. She thought fast. She was a strong fighter but she felt that she would have a challenge with Weylon.

"Why would you kill Brijit? She was your wife."

He laughed bitterly. "She had not been my wife in years. She'd forgotten her loyalties. Brijit had decided to warn you girls, that you were more important to her than was her duty. The council decided that she would have to be dealt with before she could do any damage. I was happy to volunteer to get rid of her."

Kiara stared at him in horror. How could he pretend to love Brijit and then turn on her like this?

"And now it's time to deal with you." Weylon reached into his belt and pulled out a dagger with a curved blade. "I'm actually happy I get to finish you –you after all are the most dangerous of them, aren't you?"

"What do you mean?" Kiara asked.

"You're the one who has mated. And a more dangerous mating I couldn't imagine." Disgust tinged with fear dripped from his words. "A child by you and Caedmon would be more deadly than anything we had feared."

Kiara stared at him. What was he talking about? Her and Caedmon had been careful to hide their relationship from others. How had Weylon discovered them?

"The others will have to die, too, of course. But you need to be dealt with sooner," Weylon said as he stepped toward her.

Kiara reached to her waist for her own dagger but found it was missing. She'd left it in her room with her travelling things. There was no need to carry weapons in Séreméla. Kiara glanced around the room looking for something she could use against Weylon but there was nothing.

He laughed at her. "Let's see what kind of warrior-girl you truly are." He lunged at her suddenly.

Kiara jerked to the side but not fast enough. The dagger bit into her shoulder and Weylon growled. He'd aimed for a more lethal spot. Ignoring the burning pain, Kiara knocked him onto the ground while he was off balance. Then she took a deep breath and pulled the dagger from her shoulder, ignoring the pain that knifed through her arm.

Weylon was on his feet again, advancing slowly. But Kiara had the advantage now – she was the one who was armed. She was thankful for the hours Caedmon had spent with her, training her. Would he have done so if he thought she'd be fighting his father in the end?

Pushing such thoughts aside, Kiara concentrated on Weylon. She could afford to wait for him to attack but suddenly she heard a movement behind him and as she turned to see Caedmon, Weylon lunged toward her and knocked her to the ground. Kiara's head connected with the edge of the armchair and stars danced in front of her eyes.

"I saw her kill Brijit," Weylon was telling Caedmon. "Then she attacked me."

Kiara couldn't believe her ears. Weylon was going to blame her for Brijit's death. Would Caedmon believe his father? She remembered how upset he'd been when Meldiron had suggested that Weylon had sent them on the dangerous path on purpose.

But Caedmon spoke and his tone was cold and devoid of emotion. "Kiara would never kill her mother. I know her better than that," he said. "But you are a killer, Weylon. You raised me to be a killer, too. You wouldn't hesitate to kill your wife if she was in your way."

And with that lightening quick speed, Caedmon had Weylon in a tight hold, his arm holding him to his chest.

"You created me. You did a good job," He whispered before he violently twisted Weylon's neck. Kiara cringed as she heard the loud crack of his neck breaking. Caedmon threw the body to the ground in disgust and was at her side in the next instant.

"Kiara. Are you alright?" She looked at him blearily. Beautiful, tragic Caedmon.

Then she lost consciousness.

****

Bellasiel bandaged Kiara's arm. "It's only a surface wound, you're lucky." She told her before straightening and looked at them all.

Caedmon had carried Kiara to Bellasiel's private offices and then gone to find the others. Now they were all together.

"This changes the urgency of your departure," Bellasiel told them. "We had thought that Eöl Ar-Feiniel's death meant there had been a breach in the warding system but this -" she nodded towards Kiara's arm. "Indicates that the warding systems has been dismantled. And that means we are all in great danger."

Meldiron nodded. "Bellasiel is right. Our lives are in danger now in Séreméla. We must leave immediately."

"Where are we going to go?" Mina asked, her eyes puffy from crying for Brijit. But they all knew that the time for grieving was not now.

"I'm not the only one who believes the Marked Ones are important to our future," Bellasiel told them. "Over the last five years a growing group of supporters has been making preparations and plans for when this time would come."

"You knew?" Teague asked.

"We knew that eventually we would have to shelter the Marked Ones, especially the young ones. A secret refuge has been prepared and has become home for the few Marked Ones we've been able to find before the enemy has. You will be safe there."

Kiara looked at her. "Where is this safe place?"

"It is hidden in the Eastern Mountains – in old mines."

Kiara remembered the miners who were out of work in Silver Vale.

Meldiron smiled suddenly. "You've been planning this for some time, Bellasiel."

She nodded.

"Alright then we will go there."

Caedmon stood up. "I agree that we must leave but how? If the warding system has been dismantled, as you've suggested, then the ways in and out of Séreméla will be watched. How are we to safely leave this land?"

Bellasiel spoke up, "I have a way. Gather your things and be back here within the hour. Don't let anyone see you."

****

Kiara was surprised at how quickly they were able to gather their belongings and assemble in Bellasiel's chambers.

"Now what?" Caedmon asked darkly.

Bellasiel beckoned for them to follow her into her lower chambers where she had originally shown them the pictures of the dead children. She continued passed the small room to the end of the hall, which was lined with a bookshelf. Pressing a cleverly disguised mechanism the shelf opened to reveal a dark opening.

"This passage was built before the wards were put up." She told them. "It does not lead to the Eastern Mountains, of course, but it will lead us beyond Séreméla's borders."

There was no sign of pursuit on their way through the tunnels. As they emerged into sunlight, a coolness on the wind indicated they were, indeed, beyond Séreméla's boundaries.

Kiara estimated the journey to the hidden refuge in the Eastern Mountains would take them several weeks. And they were sure to be followed shortly. She didn't like it. Their escape would only put the remaining Marked Children in the Five Corners in danger. There had to be something they could do to help those children.

As they started on their journey East, Kiara brought up her concerns with the others.

"What are you saying, Kiara?" Mina asked

"We have to help the children. Their lives are in danger now more than ever."

Bellasiel nodded. "You are right, of course. If they are not able to capture you, they will double the efforts to kill all Marked Ones."

"Why?" Thia asked in horror.

It was Meldiron who answered her. "Because the Prophecy also says that the Marked Ones will build an army of their kind."

"We will be passing through areas where Marked Children must live," Teague noted. "Can we collect the children we find on the way?"

"What kind of parent would give up their child to a group of strangers?" Thia asked.

"You'd be surprised," Meldiron said wryly.

Bellasiel added, "Many parents are horrified when they find a child with a Mark. But as well, if a parent loves a child and knows this is his or her only way to safety, they will give them up. The Prophecy isn't as secret as the Council would have you believe."

"So what should our strategy be?" Caedmon asked.

"Split up." Kiara said with a grin. "They would never think that we would chose to do what they originally had us do on the way to Séreméla."

Caedmon nodded. "Good plan."

Bellasiel looked at them. "I will continue directly to the Eastern Mountains," she told them. "I must give warning to the others so they can fortify the entrances."

Meldiron agreed. "I would like to take a Southern route and try to find Arion. He needs to be warned."

Mina spoke up, "I will go with Meldiron."

"It would be helpful if we could be in contact while we are separated."

They all looked at Thia and Teague. It was Thia who spoke first, "If Teague goes with Caedmon and Kiara and I go with Mina and Meldiron, we will be able to be in contact – via the dreamwalks."

Teague nodded in agreement. "That will give us an advantage."

"Teague is in great danger from the *Draíodóir*," Bellasiel noted. "We do have someone who I hope will be able to help you in the Refuge but I can't guarantee your safety until you arrive there. As you know the *Draíodóir* are connected mentally and Teague is only a novice in their ways. There is always the danger that the more powerful of the clan will be able to tap into his mind."

Teague looked nervous. "I can't guarantee that I won't give our location away," he admitted.

Caedmon spoke up. "Can we agree to a compromise, Kiara?" he asked. "You and I can accompany Teague and Bellasiel to the Eastern Mountains. We can collect any Marked Ones we find along the way, but our priority will have to be to get there as quickly as possible. Then Teague will be safe and we can leave again to find more."

Kiara thought about it. Caedmon was right. The sooner they arrived at the Eastern Mountains, the sooner they would be safe. She nodded her agreement.

****

Thia watched the small party of four disappeared into the distance. *Teague*, she called.

We'll be okay, Thia. We'll see one another soon.

She knew Teague was trying to make her feel better but she had a bad feeling about this separation. She had just got Teague back, they'd had hardly any time together and now they were being separated again. It wasn't fair. She tried to swallow the lump in her throat.

"Are you ready, little sister?" Mina asked at her side.

Thia blinked away her tears and turned. Excitement sparkled in Mina's eyes and Thia remembered that this was the first time her sister had gone on an adventure. All her life Mina had wanted to travel and now she was finally getting her chance. Despite the circumstances, Mina was radiating with the newness of it all.

Thia smiled sadly. She'd only ever wanted to be safe at home. She'd hoped that now that Teague had recovered and they'd been reunited with their families, that they'd be able to go back to a quiet little existence. Adventures were not something she had ever craved and if she could change her fate, she would. She would settle in a quiet dwelling in the woods with her loved ones safe and secure by her side.

Her eyes were drawn to where Teague and the others had disappeared over the horizon. *Be safe, Thia.* His words floated back to her thin and waverly. And she knew that they were passing beyond the distance of their non-verbal communication. All they would have until she reached the Eastern Mountains was their dream walks. So much was uncertain now. "Do you think we'll see them again?" she asked her sister softly.

Mina nodded with confidence. "I know we will."

Thia wasn't so sure. Mina was an innocent in the realities of the world. And in many ways Thia envied her.

CPSIA information can be obtained at www.ICGtesting.com
Printed in the USA
LVOW08s0530210514

386624LV00001B/9/P